FIGHTING FOR HOPE

Redemption Harbor Security, #7

Katie Reus

KR Press, LLC

DEDICATION

For all my wonderful readers, don't be afraid to start over. You never know what's waiting for you on the other side.

Prologue

Before

"Wooo! We just got married!"

Bradford had to pull Hope down from where she was standing up through the moonroof of the limo he'd sprung for after their quickie Vegas wedding. He'd never seen her this carefree before, but he loved it. She needed more joy in her life, something he'd realized about her right from the start.

She slid onto his lap, straddling him, her dark hair down and around her face in soft waves. "Why'd you ruin my fun?" she whispered before brushing her lips over his, her kiss sweet and gentle.

"Pretty sure I've got the fun part covered." He rolled his hips slightly, making her laugh as she came in contact with his very clear reaction to her.

It'd always been like that with her. When she was around, no one else existed. Just his Hope.

Their kiss deepened, but she pulled back far too soon for his liking. Hers too if her groan of frustration was any indication.

"This is not the fun I signed up for." She nipped his bottom lip, then yelped as the limo driver took a sharp turn.

"I'm not sharing you with anyone," he growled. "And I don't trust those privacy windows." He knew they weren't soundproof and that was enough for him. Her moans of pleasure would be solely for him. Not some pervy driver.

She snickered as she slid her hands through his short hair, cupped the back of his head. "Fine. But as soon as we get back to the hotel—"

The vehicle pulled to a stop and that was when they both realized they were already at the hotel. He'd completely lost track of everything from the moment he'd told her the only way he would get naked with her was if she married him—and she'd agreed.

It took a lot to shock or distract him, but she had. Before she'd changed her mind, he'd hustled them to one of those little all-night chapels with Elvis impersonators he couldn't believe even existed.

He didn't look at anyone else as they hurried through the lobby of their hotel and finally made it to the elevators. He might have growled at other patrons to ensure they were the only two on the elevator up to their room.

And he couldn't take his eyes off her. Overseas while working, she'd never worn her hair down, had always worn a protective helmet over her braid as she shadowed him and the others for the piece she'd been writing. Now her hair was down, she was in a dark blue dress that brought out her Mediterranean blue eyes, and somehow he'd convinced her to marry him.

He still wasn't even sure if this was real or he was imagining it all. If he was dreaming, he never wanted to wake up.

"I don't know what to think when you look at me like that," she murmured, stepping out of the elevator as it dinged.

Right beside her, he pressed her up against a wall, caging her in with his arms as he stared down at her. There was a lot he wanted to say, but he couldn't find the words. So he scooped her up, was glad when she wrapped her legs around him, and carried her to their room.

It didn't take long to get inside, and even less time for him to get Hope naked and underneath him.

After that they stayed naked for two days, ordering room service and only coming out of their little bubble to eat or shower. He'd never had so much sex in his life—and never with someone he loved. Not the way he loved her. An all-consuming sensation that made him feel like he was drowning and soaring at the same time.

She hadn't said the words and neither had he—he knew enough about her that he didn't want to scare her off. And yes, they were married now, but he wasn't stupid. This wouldn't last; it was a fun, drunken weekend in Vegas—for *her*. He would *never* divorce her, but he had a feeling that was coming soon enough. At least he'd had her for a moment in a way he'd never expected.

He was just pretending that this thing could last, that their bond and friendship could carry them beyond an alcohol, sex-fueled weekend in Vegas.

So when he woke up two days later to find her and her bag gone and a note telling him she'd had a good time and would be in touch, he tried so desperately not to take it personally. He knew who she was, knew she wouldn't settle down with a roughneck like him.

But it still hurt in ways he wasn't sure he would ever recover from. Because hope had dug its talons into his chest that this might be real, that once he won her trust they would have a future.

As he set the little note down on the bedside table, and buried his face in the pillow to capture her rose oil scent, the ringing of his phone pulled him back to the present, grounded him.

"Hey," he managed to rasp out as he answered.

"Where the hell are you?" Rowan demanded. His team leader was always in a mood, but it was even worse since they'd returned stateside for reasons Bradford understood.

"Vegas."

There was a long beat of silence. "Seriously?"

"Yep."

"Get on a plane as soon as you can... Actually, I know a guy who'll fly you back private. Owes me a favor. We're wheels up in two hours. I'll stall if you don't make it."

"Okay." He didn't ask where they were going because it didn't matter. The flight from Vegas to San Diego would take an hour and a half tops. And if he was flying private, he'd make it in time.

It was back to reality for him. He'd done more than enough time in the desert, and lately the powers that be had been sending them down to South America on covert missions.

He figured that was where he'd be going now. There was no dread at the thought of heading back into harm's way. No emotion at all. Just an empty sort of numbness to go along with the lead weight in his chest.

At least facing possible death would distract him from the fact that Hope had left.

CHAPTER 1

Present day

"I don't know if I want to go on the record." Mia Poulos sat across from Hope Berkley at the out-of-the-way diner Hope had picked for privacy.

It didn't hurt that they made chicken and waffles that reminded her of her mom's cooking.

"Then you don't have to." Hope kept her voice gentle. Mia had been through enough, from a powerful boss who'd been sexually harassing her for a year to everyone else who'd turned a blind eye to the creep.

"I keep telling myself to go on the record, to put him on blast..." She traced her finger down the condensation of the water glass in front of her.

The temperature outside was in the nineties, though it felt more like a hundred-plus with the humidity added in. Mississippi and all of the Gulf Coast were a beast in the summertime. Hope remained silent, waving off their waitress who approached with a pitcher of water.

Neither of them needed a refill and Mia simply wanted someone to talk to. Someone to listen, to believe her. Hope wasn't sure anything would come of this story, and while she hoped to be the one to break it, she wanted

Mia and the others her boss had hurt to find peace more than anything else.

And Mia was right to be hesitant at coming forward with her story. The world had a solid track record of not believing women. Of holding them to a higher standard than the men with all the power. Of asking inane questions like *What was she wearing?* Or *Why didn't she report it sooner?* And as soon as a woman became "too successful," even other women came for her.

It was a vicious world out there, and the more Hope tried to make a difference, the less it seemed to matter.

Was she spiraling right now? Kinda. But the world had been beating her down and she could feel the burnout coming.

Forcing those thoughts from her mind, she glanced at her buzzing cell phone.

"Take it," Mia murmured. "I've got to use the restroom anyway."

Hope nodded and pressed the green button. She didn't recognize the number but that didn't mean anything. This was her work cell, not her private one, so she answered more often than not. She never knew when someone might be calling with information about a story or wanted to tell their own story. "Yeah?"

"Hope? This is Sheriff Crow."

Her stomach immediately tightened. Even though she hadn't seen the man in years, she'd have recognized that raspy voice of Steve Crow even if he hadn't identified himself. There was no reason for him to be calling her...except one. "Sheriff. Is my dad..." Even though they were more or less estranged, she still couldn't say the word. She and her dad occasionally talked on the phone about absolutely nothing at all (the weather, what kinds of seeds to plant during the spring, the Saints football season), but it had been a while since he'd checked in.

"It's not looking good. I know you two don't talk much, but I still

***

The drive to her hometown hadn't taken long since she'd been across the state border in Mississippi. As she drove through King's Creek, Louisiana, she saw more shops than before and other clear signs of growth that told her this place wasn't suffering as much as some rural areas. Though this was more rural adjacent, since they were twenty minutes from a larger town.

She was glad to see so much activity, but didn't stop anywhere. Instead, she kept on driving to the neighboring town and its hospital where her dad was supposed to be.

After parking, she tried to steel herself to see her dad, but it was useless. Nerves had settled in her bones and she wasn't sure what she was going to say at this point. When she stepped outside her car, she was bathed in a wave of heat and humidity. Immediately she stripped off her cardigan as she made her way to the main entrance.

She started to approach the front desk but saw Sheriff Crow striding down the hallway toward her. She veered in his direction, but his expression of pity told her everything she needed to know.

"Hope," he said in that raspy voice, his mouth set in a grim line. "I'm sorry."

Her stomach grabbed tight, a strange numbness taking hold. "I'm too late?"

He nodded. "I told him you were on the way though. He knew you were coming home."

She wasn't sure if that was worse or better and blinked away the hot tears that stung her eyes. "I...don't know what to do now." She always knew what to do, but as she stood there in the sterile hospital, with this man she hadn't seen in years, surrounded by strangers... She felt blank almost.

"Come on, let's go get some coffee." He placed a gentle hand on her forearm and she followed him to the cafeteria that had seen a revamp sometime in the last few years.

Her head was all over the place and she was having a hard time getting a handle on her emotions.

"Your dad got his affairs in order a year or so ago," he said as he sat across from her, sliding a coffee in front of her.

She took it, thankful for the warmth since the hospital temperature was the opposite of outside. "I didn't realize," she murmured.

"He also got sober. Almost six years."

Hope blinked, unable to hide her surprise. "Wow. That's great." A little too late for their relationship, but she was glad he finally kicked the drinking. But she wished... She wished he'd loved her enough to do it while she was still part of his life.

The sheriff nodded. "Yeah. He went to AA at least twice a week, was mentoring someone... He has a will. Or trust, not sure. I'm sure his lawyer will contact you but it's my understanding that he has everything in order. He didn't want you to have to worry about anything."

Hope nodded, struggling to take it all in. This wasn't what she'd been expecting at all. Absolutely none of it, but definitely not that he'd gotten *sober*. Her father had called her a few times over the years and they'd made painful small talk. He'd never once told her that he'd stopped drinking.

To be fair, she wasn't sure she'd have believed him. He'd broken her mother's heart, and while Hope knew the reason her mom died wasn't actually his fault, she'd worked herself to death trying to keep the bills paid. For years Hope had wished her mom would be strong enough to leave, but at the end of the day, she'd loved Hope's dad.

Anger began to burn through the awful numbness. Stupid to love someone like that. Stupid to love anyone so much that you lost yourself. Sacrificed yourself. *Stupid, stupid, stupid.*

"I honestly don't know what to say to any of this," she finally managed.

"I know. And I know what your dad was like back then. Just...know that he really got his shit together. Was trying to be a better person at the end."

Those hot tears were back, but she dashed them away. "I guess I should talk to his lawyer and stop by the house." She hadn't been back since she was eighteen. There was no way she wanted to see his body. She didn't want to remember him like that.

The sheriff slid a business card across the table to her. "I figured. His lawyer is Chelsea Ortega."

Hope didn't recognize the name, but pocketed the card all the same. "I'll need to talk to the staff about...where to transfer him." Even saying the words were hard.

Nodding, he stood with her. "Come on, I'll take you."

Feeling as if her feet weighed a thousand pounds, she fell in step with him. For a brief moment she thought about calling Bradford.

Okay, lies—much longer than a moment. Right now the yearning was so strong she almost couldn't contain it.

She wanted to call him, but she'd ended things with him for a good reason. And she really needed to get around to divorcing him. For his sake.

But...she didn't want to. And he'd never filed either so... *Damn it.*

She couldn't call him. Couldn't lean on him. She didn't deserve kindness from him. She had no idea how to love anyone and was terrified of letting anyone in. She'd seen where that got her mom and she'd never wanted someone to have that kind of power over her.

So she'd kept people at a distance her entire life. And look where that had gotten her. Lonely, in a job that was killing her. Sighing, she fell in step with the sheriff and locked all those depressing thoughts up tight.

CHAPTER 2

*Every sunrise is a reminder that it's never
too late to start over.*

"Thank you for seeing me so quickly." Hope sat across from a woman who had to be close to her age—or maybe closer to forty than thirty, but it was hard to tell. She had flawless skin and a kind smile.

The lawyer's office was neat and tidy with a handful of pictures on the shelf behind her, as well as framed degrees, but it wasn't overly personal. Still, the seats were comfortable and the space itself was inviting.

Chelsea Ortega nodded as she pulled out a thick file and set it on the table. "First, I'm really sorry for your loss. Your dad was a good man."

"I wasn't really close with him," she murmured, feeling awkward.

"I know. And I know why, for the record," she added. "We met in AA so no judgment here that you didn't have a relationship with him. He was really honest about what kind of husband and dad he was."

Hope hadn't been expecting that kind of bluntness from this woman at all. "Oh."

"He said he was lucky you ever took his calls at all."

She blinked again, unsure how to respond. It was true, and she'd ignored some of them...but the link of family was a powerful thing.

Thankfully Chelsea didn't seem to need an answer. "Your father got sober six years ago and never stumbled."

Hope tried to shove down the bitterness that wanted to bubble up, tried to ignore the voice of the little girl who wanted to know why he couldn't have done that when she was a kid, back when she'd needed him. When her mom had needed him.

"A few years ago I convinced him to get his estate in order and he took it seriously. He put almost everything in a trust for you. And he created a Transfer on Death deed for you, so the house and property won't go into probate."

Hope listened as the no-nonsense lawyer went over everything, knowing she wasn't retaining all of it. Probably not even half of it. But the woman had a big binder for her to look at later.

"I don't want to step on your toes, but after the funeral we—our AA group—were hoping to handle the funeral reception," Chelsea said. "But only if it's okay with you."

She nodded, those damn tears back. "Yeah, that would be great, thank you."

"Anything you need, we're here. I know Hank was a shitty dad, but he still loved you and he was proud of you. We want to be there for you now in a way he never was. He'd want that."

Well, the tears were flowing now, no way to stop them. An absolute stranger was showing her so much kindness and she didn't know how to handle it.

Chelsea rounded her desk, all five foot nothing of her, and sat next to Hope, gently pressing a box of tissues into her hands.

"Thank you for being so kind," she whispered.

The woman gently rubbed her back. "You don't have to thank me for that. We'll talk more about the finances after the funeral, but if you'll let us, we'll handle *everything* if you want. Not just the reception."

Hope wanted to say no. This was her responsibility. Even if they hadn't had a good relationship, she couldn't let strangers handle this. Except...they were only strangers to her. Not to her father. They'd been his friends.

"He left explicit instructions for the funeral home," Chelsea added, her voice gentle.

"Seriously?"

The woman gave her a half smile. "Oh yeah. No church, what kind of music to play and what kind of food to serve. He said he spent most of his life letting other people take care of him and clean up his messes, so he wanted to handle this. He didn't want you to have to make any decisions once the time came."

More tears spilled over at that, but the lawyer didn't rush her or make her feel embarrassed. She just kept rubbing her back in the same way Hope's mom had done when she'd been too scared to go to sleep by herself.

Eventually she got herself together and headed out. Sunglasses on and binder in hand, she went back to her childhood home, a place she'd been avoiding for seventeen years.

***

Hope frowned as she heard the engine of a very loud vehicle rumbling down her dad's driveway. Technically the place was hers now, but she had no idea what to do with that.

The two-story farmhouse out in the country was cleaner than the last time she'd been here. And he'd done some clear updates in the last few years. He took care of the place now in a way he hadn't after her mom had died.

That knowledge had a lot of anger bubbling up and she hated that. She knew it wasn't healthy, but being here in a place she'd loved and hated at the same time... At least she had a lot of good memories too. Mostly with her mom. Some with her dad, if she was being brutally honest with herself. When she was young, he'd been fun and had loved doing things with her and her mom.

They'd gone camping as a family, he'd taught her to fish, and sometimes the two of them had snuck off for kayaking days. But slowly the drinking had taken over everything to the point where he was passed out by the time she got home from school. He'd started missing everything by the time she was in fifth grade, and her mom couldn't hide it from her anymore.

Meet-the-teacher nights, trick-or-treating, even the big holidays he was drunk. He might have been at some of those things physically, but he hadn't been there mentally.

Alcohol had become a poison to their family.

She glanced at her phone, realized it was almost nine, and wondered who the hell could be here that late. And without calling.

After turning on the front porch lights, she grabbed her dad's old rifle and set it by the front door. She didn't care for weapons as a rule, but she'd grown up out here and understood the need for them.

She glanced through one of the windows, saw it was a truck with huge tires pulling up to a stop. Not one she recognized. And when a guy with a trucker hat, jeans, and T-shirt stepped out, she eyed him, thankful for the plethora of sensor floodlights her dad must have installed, because they lit up the guy and his passenger like it was Friday night at the high school football field.

Instead of letting him get all the way onto the front porch, she opened the front door and took one step out onto the porch. "This is private property." Did she sound like a bitch? Yep. Did she care? Nope.

There was something about the way this guy walked, the aggression rolling off him, that had her hackles up. Back when she'd been young and fearless, she'd been in enough war zones to be able to read body language well. She'd had to in order to survive.

And her dad's place was almost a couple miles off the main road. This guy hadn't ended up here by accident.

The guy jerked to a halt, his eyebrows raised even as he held up an arm against the bright lights. "You must be Hank's daughter."

She simply eyed him, wondering what this was about.

"I heard about your daddy and I'm sorry."

She continued to watch him carefully, took a small step backward so she could grab the rifle if need be.

"Listen, your dad owed me some money."

Oh, *hell* no. "Uh huh." Her tone was dry. "I'm sure he did. I'll point you in the direction of his lawyer, and if he did indeed owe you anything, she can pay you from the estate." This was one of the oldest scams in the book, preying on grieving family members. Now it was done more online through phone or email cons, but in person was still a thing too. And she was here alone. This guy was an asshole for coming to intimidate her.

He took an aggressive step forward. "Now see here—"

She moved fast, had the weapon up before he could get out another word. Must be muscle memory, because it felt comfortable in her hands as she trained it on him. "No. You see here. My father just died. Today. Literal hours ago. Now you show up after dark looking for a payday. I know what you're about. Now get the hell out of here." She cocked the rifle for good measure.

"You're gonna pay for this," he snarled. But he was already moving backward.

She pulled out her phone and snapped a picture of him and his truck, making sure to get the license plate. She could tell he didn't like that, but boo freaking hoo.

Only a ghoul tried to scam people in mourning, and showed up to intimidate a single woman out here by herself.

As soon as the truck rumbled out of sight, she hurried back inside, locked up, then called the sheriff directly, hoping he'd know who that asshole had been.

"Hey, Hope."

"Hey, Sheriff." She quickly relayed what had happened. "You know who that guy is?"

"Sounds like Jed Tanner. He's usually with his brother."

The name wasn't familiar at all, but that didn't mean anything. She hadn't been back in a long time. "There was someone sitting in the passenger seat."

"Yep, sounds like him. I'll talk to him, see what the hell he was thinking."

"Thank you."

Once they got off the phone, she thought about going into town to get a few security cameras, but after a quick online search saw that the hardware store had shut hours ago. *Okay, then.*

At least her father had a security system—another update in the last decade-plus. And he'd left the code in his big binder of information. So she set it and kept the rifle at her bedside that night.

The guy—Jed Tanner—had been an asshole and maybe he would be back, but she'd faced off with worse people than some redneck who wanted a payday. She had her rifle and wasn't a sound sleeper. If he came back, she'd be ready.

CHAPTER 3

To love is to be vulnerable.

"Talk to me," Tiago murmured next to Bradford, drawing him out of his own stupid thoughts.

"What? You see something?" He shifted his long-range binoculars to the left, wondering if he'd missed an incoming boat. They were about a mile out on the water, using a fishing boat as cover to watch potential smuggling.

This was a relatively easy case for them. They'd been hired by a friend with the DEA to simply watch and report, something out of the ordinary for Redemption Harbor Security. But he was glad for the slower pace because his head was all over the place.

"Yeah, *you*, not paying attention."

"Shit, sorry." He scrubbed a hand over his face as he set his binoculars down on the console. They were in a forty-foot yacht they'd borrowed, so even with the waves lapping against them from nearby boaters and jet skiers, they didn't feel the impact of any wakes much.

"Not looking for an apology. Just want to talk." Tiago was back to looking out of his binos, and for that Bradford was grateful.

He didn't want to look at anyone while he talked. "Just thinking about Hope."

"I figured. You reach out to her again?"

"Not since the last conversation." If he could even call it that. He'd seen her on the news as someone of interest to the FBI, but it turned out it was all a misunderstanding. Or that was what she'd told him weeks later. He had a feeling something had gone down with a story she was writing, but whatever it was, she wasn't talking about it.

Not to him anyway.

She had responded to more texts at least, a big change from the last few years of mostly silence.

"Still can't believe you guys got married and didn't tell us," Tiago said into the stillness between them.

Didn't matter that there were boaters nearby, right now felt like it was just the two of them out on the water. "I didn't know how to tell you guys." A few months ago their friend Berlin had told all their friends at a party, so the cat was out of the bag so to speak. Though why anyone would want to put a cat in a bag was beyond him.

"I always knew you were into her."

"Didn't really make it a secret." Hope had been assigned to them when she'd been in Afghanistan, and he and his team had been overly protective of her. She'd been there to do a job, sure, but it had been clear that she gave a shit about what she was reporting on. She cared too much sometimes, it seemed.

Just not about him. At least not the way he cared about her. Or maybe she wasn't capable, he still wasn't sure.

Tiago snorted and set his binos down to look at him. "You really didn't. Still...could've invited us all to the wedding."

"It wasn't like that. It was just a drunken thing in Vegas." Not exactly true, but he didn't want to talk about this with one of his best friends. There was a reason he'd never told anyone—and then Berlin and her big mouth had decided to tell the whole crew.

"I'm gonna call bullshit on that, but...you should go see her. She's stateside now. Has been for a while."

He knew that. His Redemption Harbor hacker friends Berlin and Hailey had sent him a plethora of information on Hope in the last couple weeks. They were clearly trying to be helpful, but it hurt to read so much about her and know that he'd never have a future with her.

"You need to cut ties, to divorce her. Seriously." Tiago's voice was hard now, out of character for the laid-back man who'd had his six more times than he could count. "I know you were into her years ago, but you deserve a future, B. You deserve to find real happiness and you can't do it if you're hanging on to part of your past."

Bradford blinked at the vehemence in his friend's voice, then looked away, picked up his own binoculars. Of course there was a whole lot of nothing going on at the small port. Normally they didn't see anything until after sunset, but they were still watching this place in shifts round the clock because that was what they'd been paid to do. "Thank you for the advice," he finally said.

Deep down he knew he needed to cut ties like his friend said. Because yeah, he was hanging on to the past and he couldn't move forward the way he was. But this was Hope, and there would never be any way for him to move forward without her. She was in his blood, a part of him. "She's the first woman I ever loved," he added. To be fair, she was the only woman he'd ever loved.

"Shit," Tiago murmured. "I didn't realize that."

Yep. And that was what made it even harder. He'd fallen so hard and fast, had never seen her coming. She'd knocked him on his ass and he'd never really gotten back up from the impact of her.

When his phone buzzed in his pocket, he pulled it out, frowned at the incoming text from Berlin. He muttered a curse, went to show the screen to Tiago and got another one from Hailey with the same incoming alert so he read that one.

Then he got one from Skye, of all people, with similar information.

Hope's dad had just died and the funeral was this Saturday. Two days from now.

"Who the hell is texting you so much?" Tiago frowned over at him.

He held out his cell phone and showed him the screen.

Tiago blinked. "Speak of the devil."

Yep, pretty much. "I need to get someone to cover this shift for me."

Tiago already had his phone out. "I got that part handled. Just go pack up your shit in the cabin so when it's time to go, you're ready."

Nodding, he headed down into the cabin and did just that. Tiago was right, it was time to figure things out with Hope, to finally sever ties. But he also knew how hard this would be for her with her dad dying.

He wasn't going to let her go through it alone. Because he knew she wouldn't call any of her friends, would simply suffer through losing her dad and not tell anyone. She was so damn determined to take on the world alone, but that wasn't happening.

Not for this.

It was okay to need people and he simply wished she understood that.

CHAPTER 4

Appreciate the ones who show up for you
when you don't even ask.

Hope stared at the front doors of the community center, dreading having to go inside. She'd been sitting out here in her car for the last twenty minutes watching far more people go inside than she'd expected to see.

Her father had outlined his wishes. He'd been cremated and had requested a service at a local community center he apparently hung out at a lot. Everything about his death was so over-the-top organized it was making dealing with his death, her own fallout of emotions, even harder.

She couldn't be angry at him about this part because he'd handled everything.

His AA friends had been serious about taking over because Chelsea and her friends had sent out the announcement to everyone in town; the food and everything for the reception and even who would be speaking at his funeral was all handled. She was glad they hadn't asked her to talk because she had no idea what to say. But she also had nothing to *do*, nothing to keep her mind busy. Part of her had briefly debated just leaving. Ditching this whole thing altogether and blowing town.

Hell, she could just drive away right now and be well within her rights.

She didn't owe him anything... But still, some weird guilt settled in her chest.

"Fine, I'll just say good-bye officially," she murmured to the empty car before stepping outside into another oppressively hot day.

It was one hundred and four and rising. Her sunglasses fogged up the moment she shut the car door behind her, so she slid them off and made her way to the front doors.

She squinted against the sunlight, had barely adjusted when she stepped into the center. Maybe she could get away with sitting in the back—

"Oh, honey, there you are." Chelsea was waiting in the entrance area, standing next to a table with a stack of funeral programs. "Your husband is already here. He's sitting at the front in the section designated for family."

Hope's mouth went dry at the word *husband*. No way Bradford was here. There had to be a mistake. But she simply nodded her thanks and took the program, her chest tight as she made her way up to the front of the aisle.

Simple folding chairs had been set up on a basketball court with a large aisle separating them.

And sure enough, Bradford was sitting in the front row. She'd know the back of that dark head anywhere. That head had been between her legs multiple times, and oh, she was definitely going to hell for thinking about that right now.

What on earth was wrong with her?

As if he sensed her very loud thoughts, he turned and immediately stood when he spotted her.

Her heart stuttered. She wasn't sure how it was humanly possible, but the man was even better looking than she remembered. And yeah, definitely going to hell for paying attention to that right now, but she was only human.

The dark suit he had on was clearly custom made, but she only had eyes for that face. With a jawline that would make angels weep, a five o'clock shadow accentuating it, and dark unruly hair he'd let get too long, the man made her entire body wake up. Even his longer hair looked good, because nothing he could change about his appearance would take away from that raw sexiness. He was walking, talking sex appeal, a gorgeous man who had to know what he looked like, but somehow didn't seem to realize it. Or maybe he just didn't care about the effect he had on women. And some men.

The suit might be custom made, but it still pulled a little on his biceps. And she knew exactly what he looked like naked. People weren't supposed to look better without their clothes on, but he did. A walking god among mere mortals. He shouldn't be real. He was too damn perfect.

It was one of the reasons she'd been so desperate to keep her distance. She didn't trust her own judgment around him and that was terrifying.

Men who looked like him shouldn't be so funny and just plain fun. And kind and generous. He'd once gotten into a ridiculous dance-off with some cook on the base he'd been stationed at. The whole thing had been wildly entertaining to everyone, herself included. He had charisma, but not in a creepy way, because she distrusted "charming" people for the most part. But with him, it was like he exuded sunshine and she simply wanted to soak it up.

The man was dangerous to every part of her, but especially her heart. He owned it, even if he didn't realize it.

Before she knew it, she was standing in front of him, her throat dry, heart thudding. "Bradford."

He pulled her into a gentle hug and kissed the top of her head. "I'm really sorry about your dad. I know you two had a complicated relationship."

Throat still dry, she swallowed past the growing lump. Him being here completely stripped her bare. She'd been ready to face this alone, but having him right next to her was everything. "Thank you for coming." She hadn't realized how much she'd needed him. Or a friendly face. But mainly him. Walking away from him had been one of the hardest things she'd ever done—if not *the* hardest. She hadn't even been able to make herself file for divorce.

"Most of the guys are here too," he murmured, nodding toward the back.

Surprised, she looked past vaguely familiar faces of men and women she knew from growing up in this town: farmers, people from the church she'd gone to, and others. But at the back she spotted Rowan, Tiago, Ezra, Hailey and a bunch of women she didn't know, but who were clearly with the men. She also vaguely recognized some guy from the news—billionaire Jesse Lennox.

Stunned in more ways than one, she allowed Bradford to lead her to one of the fold-up chairs and sat next to him. The family section was going to be very small—just the two of them. Because she was the only blood family left.

For some reason that was what triggered the wave of tears.

Bradford was right there, sliding his thick arm around her and pulling her close. Even though she wanted to ask why he was really here, she couldn't find any words as she laid her head on his shoulder and let the tears fall.

She had the mean thought that her father didn't deserve her tears, but he was dead and gone. It felt so petty and she hated herself in that moment. She also hated that she couldn't say any of the things she'd kept bottled up for years, that they'd never really talked—that she'd never known him as a sober person.

And that she would never get the chance now.

The funeral itself was longer than she'd expected, with people from his AA group talking about him, how much he'd helped them, other farmers who said that even though he hadn't had a working farm in a decade, he'd still been there for them.

Finally Chelsea got up, her eyes damp with tears as she took the small microphone.

"Hank Berkley was one of a kind and I'll forever miss him. Y'all know what I used to be like. After my daughter died, I fell into a dark hole of despair, but Hank helped pull me out of it, helped get me sober." She looked down for a moment, wiped away some tears before she looked back out at the crowd. "I'll miss you, Hank."

For a blip of a moment, Hope felt a weird jealousy that her father had been there for the relative stranger talking in a way he'd never been for her. But it was impossible to be jealous of a woman who'd lost a child. She found herself glad he'd helped Chelsea right now because she could only imagine what kind of despair she would fall into if something like that happened.

After Chelsea set her microphone down, one more person spoke, and then blessedly it was over. Hope felt like she was suffocating, listening to all these stories about a wonderful man she'd never known.

No, she'd known a very different, very selfish version of him.

And it broke her heart. She hated the longing that swept through her for something that she would never have now that he was gone. He'd given the best of himself to other people instead of her.

"Come on." Bradford guided her out a side door before she could think about protesting, but once they were outside, she was grateful, even with the heat and humidity beating down on them. "Didn't think you wanted to walk through all those people and deal with condolences."

"Thank you." Squinting against the sunlight, she looked up at him. Felt that punch to the stomach all over again. He was so beautiful. So strong and solid. But he wasn't hers. Not really. "And...again, for being here. Is everything okay?"

"What do you mean?"

"Why are you here? Other than the obvious?"

"For you, dummy," he muttered, making her half smile. "That's the only reason I'm here. I saw the obituary."

"Oh." She cleared her throat. Hated that she was always expecting people to disappoint her. To be fair, they usually did, but she shouldn't have assumed he was here for any other reason than this. "Thank you."

"Stop thanking me. Come on, the reception's next door and its balls hot out here."

She snorted at his words. And despite the years since they'd seen each other, when he slid his arm around her shoulders, she found herself sliding her arm around his middle, grateful for the support as they walked along the cracked sidewalk behind the community center to the attached cafeteria next door.

"I can't believe your friends are here too," she murmured as they stepped into another rush of icy air-conditioning. The kitchen was already filled with food and a bunch of older ladies who smiled at them as she and Bradford let the door shut behind them.

They probably should have gone in the front, but it was easier to avoid the crowd this way.

"Hope Berkley, I'm so sorry about your daddy." Mrs. Annabelle Harper had to be in her seventies by now, but still moved in that same agile way Hope remembered as she rounded one of the industrial metal countertops. At one time she'd run the local hardware store with her husband, but Hope wasn't sure if that was still the case.

"Thank you, Mrs. Harper."

"You can call me Anna, hon." She pulled Hope into a hug, then eyed Bradford as she stepped back. "Who is this handsome man?"

"Ah—"

"I'm her husband." Bradford's voice was deep and smooth and she swore Mrs. Harper's cheeks flushed pink when he held out his hand. Yeah, he had that effect.

"Well, good for you darlin'," she said, glancing back at Hope. Then she gently patted her arm. "We'll be bringing the food out there in just a minute, but let me know if you need anything. Today and for however long you're in town."

Nodding, Hope smiled at some of the other women who looked vaguely familiar (probably from the church she'd been forced to attend as a teen), then headed through the swinging doors into the large cafeteria.

There was a gaming area on one side of it that wasn't in use at the moment, and clusters of people walking in the main doors. The AA group had been serious about setting up because there were a bunch of round tables, all covered in tablecloths with nice centerpieces, and a memorial with her dad's picture set up in one corner of the room.

"I feel like a fraud being here," she muttered.

"You were his daughter." Bradford's voice was low, steady. "Sounds like he turned his life around and would have wanted you here."

"Yeah, maybe." He'd left her a letter—one she still hadn't opened. She wasn't sure if she ever would. She could only imagine it was an apology, but what if it wasn't? Would that make it worse? *Ugh.* "Also, husband?" She glanced up at him to find him looking down at her with an expression she couldn't read.

"It's true, isn't it?" Now there was a challenging look in his gaze.

It was true only on paper. She'd never found the courage to divorce him. "Bradford—"

"Hope."

She turned at the sound of the sheriff's voice. Jeez, she hadn't even heard him approach. "Sheriff," she said with a polite nod. He nodded back, then looked at Bradford with clear curiosity so she said, "Sheriff Crow, this is my husband, Bradford." Felt weird to say the word *husband*, but he'd already told a roomful of white-haired church ladies. Everyone in town would know by the end of the day. And a small (large) part of her liked saying the word.

He blinked. "Oh, hadn't realized you'd gotten married."

She simply nodded and kept her polite smile in place. It wasn't like she'd told her father, they hadn't had that kind of relationship. "Any news on the guys from Wednesday night?" Hope knew she should have checked in with the sheriff sooner, but she'd been going through some of her father's things. Some of her mother's belongings as well, stuff she hadn't even realized he'd kept. She'd also been working on a story, but for the most part she felt like she was simply trying to tread water in her childhood home.

It wasn't like she'd expected her dad to live forever, or that they'd even had a good relationship, but everything was upside down now. She felt a little lost, untethered to everything. Her last blood relative was gone.

"I spoke to both of them. Jed says he and your dad had some handshake type of deal about a boat. I called bullshit and directed him to talk to your lawyer if he has an issue. If he bothers you again, just call me."

"I will," she murmured, glad when someone called for his attention.

"Someone bothering you?" Bradford asked, a bite to his tone.

"Not really. Just some guy showed up Wednesday night saying Hank owed him money." She rolled her eyes. "I scared him off with Hank's old shotgun." She couldn't call him *Dad*, hadn't for a long time.

Bradford's frown deepened, and he looked like he was going to say something, but his old unit approached then.

To her surprise, Tiago, then Rowan, then Hailey, and Ezra all hugged her one by one, murmuring condolences. She couldn't fight the tears that rolled down her face as they embraced her.

She hadn't expected to have anyone here, and to have all these kind faces from her past show up to support her was almost too much. She wasn't a crier by nature, but today was the exception to the rule of her life.

"Thank you all so much for coming," she said when she stepped back. "I can't tell you what it means that you showed up."

"Of course. Come on, I got us a big table." Rowan, a giant teddy bear of a man, had his arm around a gorgeous redhead he'd introduced as his wife, Adalyn, who Hope vaguely recognized from one of her assignments in Afghanistan.

She sat with them, grateful when a plate of food appeared in front of her courtesy of Bradford, who'd been mostly silent, but a rock-solid presence.

She never should have walked out of that hotel room on him. A thought she'd had so many times when it was just her all alone in her sad little condo. She'd never even slept with anyone after him, which was probably ridiculous.

But she'd never been big into sex anyway. For her it was all about trust and there weren't many people she could or would trust with her body. There was too much intimacy in that. Bradford had been different, had made her feel like she could be the best version of herself.

So of course she'd run, because that shit couldn't last. He would have left her eventually, would have gotten sick of how often they were separated—would have realized she wasn't really that great.

She mostly sat and listened as the others talked, leaning into Bradford as if she had every right in the world until Mrs. Harper (it felt too weird to call her Anna!) approached and asked for her help in the kitchen.

"I'll be back," she murmured, squeezing his knee and wishing he would stay for longer than today, but knowing she would never ask him to.

He had his own life and friends and that didn't include her, no matter how much she might wish otherwise.

CHAPTER 5

*When you have a connection with someone, a
real connection, it never goes away.*

"She still looks the same," Tiago murmured, his arm around his fiancée, Fleur.

The others murmured and started talking among themselves as Hope headed for the kitchen.

Bradford resisted the urge to follow her, mainly because Adalyn nudged his foot with hers and said, "Sit still."

"I'm not doing anything."

"I know, but she's not going anywhere."

Yeah, he knew that was what his issue was deep down. Or maybe not so deep down. He'd been taking classes at Tulane and had just finished a couple beginner psychology classes. The content was fascinating, though some of it was pretty obvious. Still...all the shit Tiago had been calling all of them out over the past decade-plus was spot-on.

They'd always messed with Tiago about being "evolved" and "philosophical" but the man was the most settled and sane of all of them.

"Well, I know that look." Adalyn's tone was dry.

"I don't want her to be alone." Hope had looked so damn lost when he'd seen her walking to the front of the chairs and his heart had broken a little to know that she had no family left.

He didn't either—not family he wanted to know anyway. But he had people he considered closer than the blood he'd been born into. Hope didn't.

He wanted to be that for her, but she'd thrown walls up and created distance when things had gotten to be too much for her.

"Have you told her that you're staying at her place yet?" Now Adalyn was grinning at him.

"Nope, and it's going to stay that way. She'll figure it out when I don't leave."

Tiago groaned slightly across the table. "You're making a mistake."

"This is one time you're wrong. The only mistake I made was letting her run before." Not like he'd had a way to stop her back then. But he could have pushed harder to get back into her life once he'd gotten out of the Marines. He'd been a coward though, and now he realized that if he never pushed, he'd never get what he wanted—what they both deserved. And if she truly didn't want him anymore, then he'd walk away and leave her alone for good.

But she'd never been loved properly, never had anyone be there for her, something he understood now. So that was going to be him, no matter what. He'd be there for Hope as long as possible.

Because he wasn't walking away this time. It didn't matter that he'd thought about serving her divorce papers—that he'd actually had them drawn up. Screw that. He'd burn them tonight.

Hope belonged with him. He just had to break down her walls and get her to believe him. The only way he'd ever walk away was if he exhausted all options with her.

CHAPTER 6

You deserve people who see your worth.

"I feel like I keep saying thank you, but seriously, thank you for helping bring all this food back. I feel a little bad accepting it all." Hope stood back as Bradford put another couple casseroles into her father's deep freezer in the mudroom. She'd put two in the refrigerator but the rest had to be frozen.

She was thankful he was with her, even if being in his presence had her emotions all over the place. Nerves had settled deep inside her with him so close, smelling so good, and god, she had to stop looking at him and thinking about what might have been between them.

"You shouldn't. This is what people do. And who knows how long you'll be here. It'll be nice for you not to have to cook." Bradford had long discarded his jacket, so he was now in a crisp, button-down white shirt with the sleeves rolled up to his elbows.

And apparently she was really into forearms. Because whew, the muscles on him.

Oh that was right, she still wanted her husband, a man she should have gotten an annulment or divorce from years ago. But here they were, that same chemistry crackling in the air between them. At one point she thought she'd imagined it, but it was the same now as it had been then.

There was simply an energy between the two of them that couldn't be contained.

"There were a lot of people at the reception," he said as he slid the last casserole into the freezer. His warm, lemon and spicy scent that reminded her of cardamom wrapped around her, made her think of that weekend in Vegas.

She snorted softly. "Yeah, all those stories were about a man I never knew. He helped so many people in town after I left but couldn't get his life together for my mom and me." Hope knew she sounded bitter, but didn't care.

She *was* bitter, if she was being brutally honest with herself. It sucked that she had missed out on the best parts of her father.

"I'm sorry," Bradford murmured as they stepped back into the kitchen.

It was surreal but nice to have him here. She'd put on a pot of coffee and poured herself a mug even though it was late. At this point, she was so exhausted she'd be sleeping soon with or without it. And one of the church ladies had given her a coffee crumb cake she was about to destroy. "You want some?"

The half smile he gave her had that same familiar tension coiling low. It was like butterflies launched inside her whenever he was around. "I'll never say no to coffee cake." Then he pulled open the fridge and grabbed some whipped cream.

"I like the way you think. Where are you staying anyway?" she asked as she pulled out two plates. Her father might have updated the place to make it more modern, but everything was still in the same relative place as it had been when she was growing up. She was surprised by the pictures he had of her around the house. Seeing them was bittersweet. He even had some of her from the last few years from online articles.

"I had a room in that motel off Main Street, but I'll be staying here tonight."

She stilled, then glanced up at him from cutting the crumb cake. "Is that right?"

"I figure I could ask, but I know you're not going to kick me out. And I'm not leaving you tonight. So here I am."

Having him here in her space, being alone together was hard enough. Him staying over was not happening. "Jesus, Bradford. I'm not like...suicidal or whatever. I'm fine."

"I didn't think you were. But I also don't think you should be alone tonight. You lost your dad."

"I lost him a long time ago."

"True enough. But you don't *have* to be alone. So you're not going to be. You deserve to have someone here in your corner." His jaw was set firmly and she knew there would be no arguing with him.

And what was the point? She didn't want to be alone tonight, though she would have never asked him or anyone else to stay. Unexpected tears welled up like a tsunami, no stopping them.

He let out a small curse and was around the island top before she'd even wiped them away, pulling her into his arms.

His thick, powerful arms. She'd missed him so much.

"Sorry," she muttered against his hard chest as she hugged him back. God, he felt incredible. Even better than she remembered. And he was being so sweet even after she'd walked away and hurt him.

"Please don't apologize for crying." His words were a deep rumble. "Especially not on the day of your father's funeral."

She gave a watery laugh. "When you put it that way." Her words were a little garbled with her face pressed against his chest. He'd always had a way with putting her at ease without even seeming to try.

It was why he'd been her favorite when she'd been embedded overseas for that short time with his team. Not that she'd have ever told any of them that, but Bradford had just been...her person.

In more ways than one. And then she'd done what she always did, she'd run.

Regret pierced deep, a cut that had never properly healed and likely never would. She wished things could be different—that she was a different person. But she didn't know how to love, barely loved herself. How could she ever accept it from him?

At that thought, a fresh wave of tears popped up and she allowed herself to cry, and for him to hold her.

God, he even still smelled the same, all minty lemon cardamom. Fresh. Even in the desert the man had smelled like this more often than not.

Eventually she pulled away, felt a little zing of heat from his fingertips when he gently wiped away her stray tears. But she couldn't fall into that trap of wanting him so bad she couldn't think straight.

She'd allowed herself to do it before, but now she was older and wiser. Or at least older. "So how long are you planning to stay?" she asked as he finished cutting and serving them cake.

He gave a shrug.

"At least tell me what you've been up to." She had to resist the urge to moan around her first bite.

"Working in New Orleans for a consulting company."

She eyed him across the island where he was leaning against the countertop. He was as irresistible as ever. "Consulting is vague."

He lifted a broad shoulder. "Security mostly... I'm enrolled at Tulane too."

She found herself smiling at him. "I love that for you. I know you always wanted to get a degree. So what are you studying?"

"I haven't decided yet. There's a lot to figure out—which feels ridiculous to say when I'm heading toward forty. I've mostly been taking psychology classes, which are interesting. Mostly because I get to screw with Tiago now, beat him at his own advice game."

She let out a startled laugh. "Oh my god, is he still the same?"

"He's worse, but the man is always right, so." He shrugged again.

"His fiancée seems nice. She's...Rowan's wife's younger sister... did I get that right?"

"I'm impressed you remember all that."

"Well it's sort of my job to remember details," she said with a smile. But it was a fair observation—she was surprised she'd remembered too. Today had been a big blur. The two women looked alike though.

"How's work going anyway?" he asked.

"Eh."

He blinked at her in surprise. "Trouble at work? After that whole thing with you on the news I thought it was okay now."

"That stuff is fine..." It had just been a misunderstanding with the Feds and one of her colleagues. "I don't know." She wanted to tell him that she'd been thinking about making a change, maybe leaving journalism altogether. But now wasn't the time for it. He was too good a listener and she needed to keep her head on straight around him.

If she wasn't careful, she'd end up right where she'd been before—in his bed and falling for him.

***

"I wish I could've been there today. Or yesterday, I guess." Thea's voice was sincere over the phone line.

"I know." Hope was sitting in bed in the room that had once been hers. Thankfully her father hadn't saved everything or kept it the same as it had been years ago. Now it was a perfectly lovely guest room she guessed someone with an eye for design had decorated. Lots of creams, blues, throw quilts and airy curtains over the window nook that overlooked the backyard and land beyond.

Probably someone from his AA group had been in charge of decorations, if yesterday was any indication. There had been about an equal number of men and women in the group.

"I appreciate it, but it was unnecessary." And her friend had finally taken a vacation after a couple years of nearly working herself to burnout. Thea was the only one Hope had told about her dad dying. She didn't work in the office anymore anyway. She never really had. As an investigative journalist, she was mostly remote, but at one time she'd had a small desk and checked in when she'd been in town.

Things were so different from even ten years ago. She was different. Wanted a change.

"Any idea how long you'll stay?"

"No. Part of me wants to stay for a while, and..."

"Write that book you've been talking about for a year?"

"Maybe," she said with a laugh, then smothered the yawn that wanted to bubble up. It was almost one in the morning and she'd been unable to sleep so she'd started working on one of the handful of stories she had in progress, but that weren't complete. "My father left it to me in the best way possible so it's not going to go into probate, and the house itself is in great shape." It was spacious, and it was quiet out here in the country. Four bedrooms, three baths, a room that could double as an office if she wanted.

Lately she'd been thinking she needed some quiet. In more ways than one.

"It's such a big change," she finally said when Thea didn't respond.

"Change can be good."

"I know."

"It's also scary," Thea continued.

"Gah, I know. I'm just worried that if I step away from work, I won't be able to come back to it if I fail at writing a book."

"First, you're not going to fail. And why can't you just do both?"

"Because I'm exhausted with my job." The words were out before she could stop herself. "Which you already know."

"Yep, I just wanted to hear you say it. Quitting a job is not the end of the world. Even if it's part of your identity. It's okay to change and to grow and to want better or just plain *different* things for yourself. And if you decide you want to come back to it, the world is always on fire. You'll have no shortage of crap to write about."

"I don't know whether to laugh or cry at that. Or do both." It was true though. "Thank you for listening to me ramble at one in the morning." She'd texted Thea to see if she was awake and her friend had called back immediately. Hope had thought about walking down to Bradford's bedroom, but that way lay trouble.

"You don't ever have to thank me for that... I'm quitting," Thea blurted.

She sat up in bed. Only a dim lamp on the nightstand illuminated the room. "What?"

"Yeah. I'm going back to teaching. I miss it more than I thought possible. I'm tired of trying to convince myself that I love this job. And I miss the community that comes with teaching. I know some people love working remotely, but I hate being so isolated. I want to be back in the classroom with kids who are fun and curious and still think the world is a good place. I can't be around all this dumpster fire anymore. It's destroying me mentally."

"I'm so happy for you." They'd both been unhappy for ages and had been talking about making a change. "Wait, is that why you're using up all your vacation days?"

Thea snickered. "Hell yeah. When Mark quit they tried to push him out without letting him use up his benefits, so I decided to take what I've earned."

Good for her. "So how is Oregon anyway?"

"Gorgeous. Green everywhere. The cabin I'm in is wonderful and I've done nothing but hike, read, kayak, read some more, and relax. And there's this hot guy staying in the cabin next to mine so...we'll see what happens. I might even think about moving out to the West Coast, it's that peaceful."

"I hope you enjoy him and the rest of your time there."

They continued talking for another twenty minutes until Hope was struggling to keep her eyes open. At least she was too tired now to think about crawling into Bradford's bed. Because she had to make better choices with him.

She wasn't sure how long she dozed for, but at a slamming sound she popped up, heart racing. It was still dark out, she realized, and she didn't think she'd been asleep for long.

Quietly, she slid out of bed, slid on her slippers, and grabbed her dad's shotgun. She hoped it was just Bradford, but when she heard glass breaking somewhere downstairs, she hurried out the door.

She avoided the two spots in the floor that squeaked and rounded the corner toward the hallway, her father's shotgun up and ready—and found Bradford on top of someone on the floor, zip-tying their hands behind their back.

"There's another one who ran. Keep your shotgun trained on this one. If he moves, shoot him," he ordered, his expression hard, nothing like the man who'd comforted her only hours before.

She nodded, familiar with this version of him. The badass, deadly one who went from the fun-loving guy who took part in dance-offs to the one who could take charge in an instant.

He hurried past her, racing out the front door, and she spotted a smashed vase on the floor. Looked like it fell over in their struggle.

"This is all just a misunderstanding." The man, who was facedown on the wood floor right next to one of her mother's antique buffet tables, tried to roll over.

"Don't. Move. You broke into my house the day of my father's funeral. I'm not feeling generous right now." And she really had to pee so that was fun. The longer she stood there, she was cursing herself for not grabbing her cell phone, which was likely tangled in her covers upstairs.

But she'd been so focused on getting to Bradford, on making sure that he was okay, that she hadn't thought of it. Stupid mistake.

Luckily the guy didn't say another word, just remained where he was, facedown. She didn't recognize him from when she'd lived here and it wasn't Jed Tanner. So another stranger showing up making trouble. When she heard footfalls coming up the front porch, she swiveled, but immediately lowered her weapon when she saw Bradford stepping through the front door.

"Guy got away, but I've called the police. They're on the way," he murmured, taking the weapon from her.

She opened her mouth to ask questions, but he shook his head so she took his lead and simply nodded. What the heck was going on? First some jerk showed up at her place demanding money, and now whatever this was.

Had her dad owed someone something? By all accounts he'd turned his life around, but there had been a time when he'd never been able to hold on to anything. It was a miracle (in the form of her mother) that he hadn't lost this place before he'd gotten sober.

She didn't believe in coincidence. Something weird was going on. And she would figure out what it was.

CHapTer 7

It's a throat punch kind of day.

"Why is this the second time someone's been harassing my wife at her home?" There was no give in Bradford's voice as he stared hard at Sheriff Crow.

Hope was so used to taking over, especially with her job, but she knew when to step back. And right now Bradford was the one the older sheriff would listen to way more than her. Under different circumstances it would annoy her that the sheriff was taking things seriously only because Bradford wasn't about to let this go. But she liked that he was taking charge...and she also liked the way he said *my wife.*

Though she had to lock down that part of herself. Or try at least. But come on, she was only human.

"I'm looking into it right now."

Even to Hope's ears it sounded like he was trying to pacify Bradford. Ooh, so maybe he wasn't as smart as she'd thought.

"What's there to look into? It's clear that asshole knows you. And we'll be following you down to the station to make our statements. I assume charges will be brought against him."

The sheriff paused slightly, but nodded. "Yes, but just a heads-up…" He looked at Hope. "Patrick Killeen's father owns the farm behind yours and he owns a good portion of land in town. Edward will make a stink about this."

Hope lifted an eyebrow. "Like I care? He broke into my place. Seems pretty cut and dry to me." Though there had to be more going on, considering Sheriff Crow's weird reaction. This was the nonsense she didn't miss about small towns.

The sheriff nodded as he glanced back at the gray SUV with flashing lights pulling away, taking the guy to the station.

"We'll email you the video of him breaking in," she added, because she was annoyed by his underwhelming response.

The sheriff looked surprised at that, but nodded again. "Just send it to me. I'll meet you two back in town." With a sigh, he left.

Bradford turned to her once he was gone. "You have a video?"

Hope pulled up the app on her phone. "Only two cameras. I grabbed them the day before the funeral at the hardware store and installed them. They're not top-of-the-line, but after what happened before I wanted to get a couple up."

He looked at the video on-screen and his grin was practically feral. "This is perfect. But you're right. I'll get you another system set up today. Top-of-the-line."

"That's not—"

"It's happening." Again, there was no give in his voice.

"I don't remember you being this bossy."

The look he gave her, the knowing one that told her she'd loved him ordering her around in the bedroom, had heat rushing to her cheeks.

Oooh, she wasn't touching that one. Because fine, she'd loved it when he'd ordered her around. But only when they were naked. Wordlessly, she turned and headed back into the house to change so they could go deal with all this nonsense. But there was no way she could ignore the reaction she had to him.

The reaction she'd always had to him.

***

"Well that was fun," Hope muttered under her breath to Bradford as they stepped out into the station lobby.

They'd given written statements, but the whole vibe had been off. The officer who'd taken their statements had been warm and friendly, but still, Hope was getting a weird vibe all around. In her experience, she rarely ignored that little radar that sometimes went off, telling her something was wrong.

"I spotted a framed article thanking Edward Killeen for donating the funding for new uniforms and armored vests," Bradford finally said once they were out in the parking lot. There was a hint of sunrise on the horizon. "Sounds like that asshole's dad donates big to the sheriff."

Well, hell. Normally she would have noticed something like that, but she'd been in her head since arriving. "Certainly explains the sheriff's reaction." He'd been way too hesitant about bringing the guy in, which was just plain weird. But he'd accepted their statements and hadn't pressured them into dropping anything.

"Yeah, he probably depends on the guy's money... You hungry?" They'd reached his truck and her stomach decided to rumble loudly at his question.

She laughed and nodded. "Apparently. There's a diner a couple blocks away that should be open now." Because it was five in the morning and sleep wasn't on the menu.

Hope felt that familiar punch of warmth the second she stepped into Cross's Diner and saw Kim Cross behind the counter in a uniform that could have been straight out of the seventies. The brown, orange and yellow had a retro vibe that made her smile.

The older woman hadn't changed at all. Her thick, dark hair was pulled back into a simple braid and she moved like lightning when she saw Hope, pulling her into a big hug. The only thing that had changed about the place was that Kim and her husband Andrew now owned it instead of Andrew's father—who'd passed it on to them.

That was one of the tidbits Hope had gathered from her sporadic, awkward phone calls with her father over the years. The place was meticulously clean, with booths lining the windows and a long bar with screwed-in swivel seats that faced the kitchen.

"I'm so happy to see you! I couldn't make it to the funeral because we were coming back from visiting the grandkids." Her hug was warm and tight and everything Hope hadn't realized she needed.

"Of course, I'm just happy to see you." Kim still smelled like cinnamon and butter, two of the best things in the world, but Hope kept that thought to herself.

"Oh honey, you are still gorgeous. Gorgeous and *smart*," she said, cupping Hope's cheeks with the kind of warmth her mother had, once upon a time. "You look just like her now. God knows she'd be so damn proud of you. The whole town is." Kim nodded to a wall with various framed pictures, including one about Hope when she'd won a Pulitzer for her series on the unprecedented fraud she'd unveiled a few years ago. She hadn't thought anyone in the town even knew about it.

Seeing it on display with pride had something warm settling in her chest. Somehow she found her voice. "Thank you for that."

"I can't believe you're up here so early..." Her voice trailed off as Bradford walked in from parking the truck and a grin lit up her face as she glanced back at Hope. "I heard you got hitched."

She didn't have the heart to tell Kim that it wasn't a real marriage. There was no need to explain to everyone that they'd gotten married in Vegas and... *Whatever.* She didn't even like thinking about it in her own head, let alone explaining to people she likely wouldn't see again when she left.

If she left. Because the thought of staying here and taking the time to write, to give herself a break from the last decade-plus of running non-stop... There was an appeal in that. She didn't want to live in a small town forever, but still... Her mind and body needed a rest.

She shelved that thought as she said, "Kim, Bradford. Bradford, Kim," and found herself grinning when Kim pulled him into a hug.

Bradford, who'd always had a way with people, hugged her back until Andrew, the cook and also Kim's husband of thirty-plus years, called out from the back. "That's long enough, young man! You keep those hands to yourself!"

Snickering, Kim stood back and handed them two menus. "Pick a seat. Our rush won't start for another hour, so you have good timing."

She wasn't surprised when Bradford picked the last booth with a perfect view of the parking lot.

"So what's good here?" he asked, not even bothering to look at the menu. Instead, all his focus was on her and she hated that she cared what he thought of when he saw her.

She'd been in a rush to get out of the house but at least she'd managed to brush her teeth. So that was something. "Everything, really. And since I'm feeling sorry for myself, I'm getting biscuits and gravy with a side of sausage. And bacon."

He laughed lightly. "That sounds good to me."

It didn't take long for Kim to make her way to their table, and when she sat next to Bradford, Hope found herself grinning.

"So, what brings you two out here so early?" Kim asked.

"Someone broke into Hope's dad's place a couple hours ago and we had to file a police report," Bradford said smoothly.

She was surprised he was being so forthright, but it was probably going to get around town anyway.

"I swear, people have no sense these days," Kim said shaking her head. "I take it you two are okay?"

"We're good. Just shaken up," she added, because it was true. Things could have gone very differently. "You know of a man named Patrick Killeen?"

At that question, Kim's expression darkened for a fraction of a moment. "I do. Why?"

"He's the one who broke in. He had a partner who got away. Any idea who that might be?"

Kim glanced past them to the other tables. Only two were taken up right now and no one was paying any attention to them. As she stood, she said, "I couldn't tell you who it might be, but I'll be back with your orders in just a minute."

Hope simply raised her eyebrows at Bradford. It was clear that Kim knew who they were asking about, but she wasn't saying anything.

Or that was what Hope assumed, until Kim dropped off their two giant plates, along with a note tucked under Hope's.

After a glance around, she read it quickly as she cut into her biscuits and gravy.

Patrick Killeen is Edward Killeen's son. He's useless, always causing trouble. He lives in a house on his daddy's property, which butts up against your dad's. Yours now, I guess. He's mean and spiteful and runs around with a man named Ned Hall. They're both no-good, spoiled rich kids.

After that there were coordinates with the words *be careful* underlined three times.

She slid it over to Bradford, who read it with a neutral expression. He tucked it away as the little bell by the front door indicated someone else was walking in. She didn't turn around, but it was clear someone was approaching by Bradford's wary expression.

He had this way of sizing someone up that had always impressed her.

A man with dark hair and a little salt and pepper approached their table. She could tell immediately that the guy had money, given his expensive boots. In his fifties or sixties, he was fit and carried himself in a way that said he expected people to take orders.

He nodded at the two of them politely. "Hope Berkely? I'm Edward Killeen, Patrick's father. I believe there's been a bit of a misunderstanding—"

"There's no misunderstanding." Bradford's voice was ice-cold as he drew the attention to himself. If words could be a blade, his were razor sharp, and Edward Killeen clearly heard the threat in them because he turned all his focus on Bradford, as if Hope didn't even exist.

"My son—"

"Your son," he bit out as if he was digging deep for patience, "broke into my wife's home in the middle of the night with a partner. I can think of two reasons for that. He wanted to steal something or rape her."

The man reeled back slightly. "He would never hurt a woman."

Bradford snorted. "Sure. Whatever you want right now, you're barking up the wrong tree. He committed a crime and we'll leave it in the law's hands. But if you're coming over here asking my wife not to press charges, walk away now."

The older man took a deep breath. "Look, I can understand why you're upset. I would be too. But we can figure this out between the two of us."

Bradford didn't respond, just stared at the man impassively until he stalked off.

"Pretty sure he was trying to bribe us," she murmured before scooping up more of the biscuits.

"Yep. He's going to be trouble," he added.

Yeah, Hope was getting that feeling too. But that wasn't Bradford's problem, this was something she would deal with on her own.

His phone buzzed as she went to ask what he thought she should do, and she definitely saw a woman's name on the screen.

Berlin.

She hated the unexpected punch of...jealousy. Yep, that was what that was. She had no right to care about who he texted with, or dated, or whatever. But she felt it all the same.

She couldn't even be surprised he was dating someone. He was funny, kind and gorgeous. Of course he had someone.

CHAPTER 8

Before

"What's with the face?" Bradford asked when Hope tucked her satellite phone into her backpack after rejecting the incoming call.

She shot him a sideways glance, then slid her sunglasses on as she looked away from him. It was balls hot outside even at eight in the morning here and the sun was already beating down on them.

"Family right?"

"Oh my god, nosy," she grumbled, but she leaned back and took a sip of her water.

His team didn't have anything on the books right now, though they often got called out last minute so that didn't mean anything. "So you get to ask questions, but we don't?"

She turned to glare at him, but then seemed to remember her sunglasses and shoved them up on her head. "That's different."

He shrugged. "Just asking as a friend, but I'll let it go. My own family sucks though, if it makes you feel better."

"In no world would I feel better knowing your family sucks."

Just like that, he fell even harder for her. Because of course that's what she would say.

She turned away from him and looked out on the "lounge" area they'd set up, which was a bunch of crates they'd stolen from somewhere set up in a big circle around a firepit. They'd found a bunch of chili-pepper-themed lights and strung them up around the seating area. It didn't make the desert any less shitty, but it was fun to look at.

"My dad left when I was six. I have some memories of him, but they're hazy. Mostly he just made my mom cry a lot and he seemed big to me. But that could have just been because I was a kid. She tossed all pictures of him so I can't even find out. Then she moved on to a whole string of assholes. Most of them left me alone, but there were a couple who tried to fight me when I was about fifteen." He shook his head. They'd all lost.

And then his mom had lost it on him. She was a tiny thing, but that hadn't mattered, because he sure as shit hadn't been about to fight back. After that, he'd made it a point to be gone most of the time and couch surfed with various friends until he outstayed his welcome. Then once he was eighteen, he'd joined the Marines.

"I'm really sorry, B." She reached out and squeezed his forearm once in that gentle way of hers and he wanted to lean into her touch. Savor it.

He'd have to make this feeling last, because he knew she'd be leaving soon. Something he had to keep reminding himself of.

"It's okay. I mean, I know it's not actually okay, but I found my people." No one else was around yet, but she knew who he was talking about. His guys were his brothers in every way that mattered. They'd all come from different walks of life, but it hadn't mattered once they'd bonded.

"You kinda sound like Tiago." There was a smile in her voice as she spoke.

"Right? Better not tell him though. It'll just make his head even bigger."

She snort-laughed, then said, "I...just rejected a call from my father. I don't know why I feel bad. He doesn't deserve anything from me. But we've been talking lately. Mostly surface stuff, but..." She shrugged, the action jerky instead of casual. "He's my only living relative."

"Ah, that guilt. Yeah, I get it. My mom sent me a few letters years ago. She didn't come to my boot camp graduation or anything, and after a while I realized her letters were basically just sob stories...and her asking for money." Which he had no doubt she would have given to her boyfriend of the week, or wasted on drugs.

"Do you still talk to her?"

"No. And for the record, I don't feel guilty about it. Being related by blood doesn't make up for years of neglect and her being a shitty person. But I'm sorry you're struggling with your dad."

"He's an alcoholic," she said, her voice quiet. "He wasn't always. We had a lot of good years. Until we didn't." She sighed, leaning back in her seat as she stretched her legs out.

An announcement came out of the loudspeakers about breakfast and then some other bullshit that didn't concern him, so he just tuned it out.

"He's seemed better lately on the phone," she said. "It's too much to hope that he's actually sober, but at least he's not slurring when we talk. And he's been getting involved with some local stuff. I guess...it makes me feel a little better to know he's not wasting away on our homestead just drinking himself to death." Her jaw went tight for a moment and he simply watched her profile.

And wished he had the right to comfort her. Even as a friend, but he didn't think she'd welcome any touch and he never wanted her to feel uncomfortable around him.

"I've got a bunch of old pictures of my parents...before my mom died. I can see how happy they were back in the beginning, before me. And then when I was young. But something changed. Or his addiction caught up to him I guess."

"I have...had a cousin who was an alcoholic. He could never kick it, finally wrapped himself around a telephone pole." A complete waste.

"At least he didn't kill anyone else."

"Right?"

"That was always one of my fears too, that my father would kill someone. Though he rarely drank and drove. He'd save all his bullshit until he got home, then just drink himself into oblivion and pass out."

"That had to be hard to watch." His own mom had more than "dabbled" in heroin, so he definitely understood how hard it was to watch a parent slowly kill themselves. But he didn't want right now to be about him so he kept that to himself.

"It was...and you're a really good listener." Her tone was only slightly accusing as she looked over at him.

He lifted a shoulder. "I try."

"Thank you...just for listening. For being such a great friend. I kind of thought you guys were going to hate me when I got assigned to you."

"Hell no. I don't think anyone could hate you. Anyone with half a brain anyway."

She grinned and it was like the sun shone even brighter, a near impossibility here. "Plenty of people hate me when I write about them."

"So what are you going to say about us?"

"I can't tell you that...yet. Though if I'm being honest, yours is definitely a feel-good story, which is so random considering where we are."

Now he laughed. "Random indeed." But he knew what she meant. She was here doing a miniseries of stories on the shift in military culture in general in regard to connectedness with the broader community and combating harmful behavior that had once been tolerated. "For the record,

I can't wait to read your series."

"Really?"

"Yeah, I can read. Hard to believe I have more than rocks in my head, I know."

"Hey! That's not what I meant." She nudged him gently.

"Just joking."

"Yeah well, you do that, put yourself down, and I don't like it."

"Now who sounds like Tiago?"

"Well he's right sometimes," she said. "And you're my friend. So you don't get to talk about yourself like that."

God, he really did like this woman. "Fair enough. I read your series on poverty myths and the working poor and it was solid."

Her cheeks flushed pink. "Oh...thank you."

He noticed that she often got flustered when someone complimented her, as if she didn't know how to take compliments. "We all read your stuff before you arrived. And don't tell Rowan I said this, but I'm pretty sure he wanted to go all fanboy on you."

She laughed. "Now I know you're lying, but thank you."

He savored the sound of her laugh, letting it roll over him as some of the others started to arrive half dressed, coffee in hand.

The moment of privacy between them was over, but he'd replay the time he spent with her later. Because when he was with her, everything inside him was at peace in a way he'd never experienced.

Never even known was possible.

CHAPTER 9

"So how's your wife?" Berlin asked over the phone.

"Stop with that," Bradford muttered as he watched Hope from his truck through the big window of the diner. She was saying her good-byes to Kim so he'd taken the chance to check in with one of his favorite people.

"Well it's true... So I've started a run on both Killeen men—and Jed Tanner and his brother, the first two jerks to bother her. Not much so far on any of them, but I'm just getting started." She sounded a little too gleeful and Bradford almost felt sorry for the assholes.

Almost.

"There's something strange going on," he said, "and we need to figure out what it is. I don't believe in coincidence and there's no way that some guys showed up to her place days ago saying her father owed money, then someone tried to break in last night. Or today." He scrubbed a hand over his face. It was now Sunday morning, the sun already bathing the sky with purples and pinks.

"I don't like any of it either. I'm looking into those coordinates you sent me too, trying to see if I can hack into a satellite or something."

"And that's why you're my favorite," he said as Hope slid into the passenger seat. He pointed to his phone and she simply nodded.

"Of course I am. You better remind Hailey of that. And Gage, for that matter," she added.

"You want me to call them both up and tell them you're my favorite?"

"Yep."

"I'll add it to my list of things that are never going to happen. Gotta go."

"All right. I'll be in touch."

"Everything okay?" Hope asked as he pulled out of the parking spot.

"Yeah, just have a friend looking into the Killeens—and the Tanner brothers. And the coordinates Kim gave you. Did she say anything else when you said good-bye?"

"She just whispered to be careful." Hope's frown deepened. "I don't like that she was afraid to talk about him. Or their family, I guess. There were only two people in the diner when we asked, and they weren't even close by. And she was still cautious."

"She said the son is spiteful, so we'll see what my friend digs up. And she was probably right to be cautious. Edward Killeen knew you were at the diner."

Hope was silent as he pulled down a side street, heading in the direction of her place. "So what kind of friend is this?" she finally asked.

He couldn't tell if that was jealousy in her tone. She'd always been hard to read, and right now she was too locked down, too worried for him to get a solid read on her. "The kind of friend who lives in the gray area and can get information others can't."

"Okay, then. I've got some contacts through work as well, but...I like to use them only for work stuff. This is too personal," she muttered. "So...you want to make our way to those coordinates? I looked them up on my phone and it's somewhere on the property behind my dad's... Ah, behind mine. Hank's four-wheeler is still working. We can take it out in the woods."

"We're definitely going to check them out. I would say I'll take care of it, but I know you too well."

"You're not leaving me behind." Her tone was hard.

"That's why I said we...but we need to change first and gather some provisions."

"That sounds a lot like guns," she said dryly.

"I mean, I'm bringing weapons too, but no. I want to bring a small drone to do some aerial recon first and hopefully grab pictures. Kim didn't give us a lot to go on so I want to send in a drone first." And he wanted to see what Berlin came up with before they ran in without backup. He'd have to tell the others what was going on too—they were still in town from the funeral.

For that, he was grateful. Because it looked like this might be one of their off-the-books jobs. Not that Hope was a job to him, but he would do everything to keep her safe.

***

"You sure we have enough snacks?" Hope said with a laugh.

Bradford tossed in another couple fruit bars he knew that she liked into his "snack backpack."

"Never." Because you never knew when you were going to run into an emergency. Kinda like his friend Mari, who'd been in a plane crash recently. Having a backpack full of food and water had played a factor in helping her get to safety.

"Fair enough... I'm a little impressed your friend gave us live satellite images of the coordinates. And by impressed I mean terrified of her abilities." Her tone was a little off, but Bradford couldn't get a read on that. She'd been through a lot.

"We're all terrified of her."

"So you guys work together?" she asked as they both slid into his truck.

He'd decided to drive his truck instead of using the four-wheeler to access the location. Berlin had found an access road that would be much easier to use to get to the coordinates and it made more sense to drive his vehicle on the main roads. Much less conspicuous. And faster if they ended up needing a quick getaway.

"Yeah, she actually worked at the same location with me in North Carolina, but we both ended up moving to New Orleans when they expanded. All the guys did—Tiago, Rowan and Ezra."

"I love that you're still close with them."

He smiled at that. They'd been his family since he was eighteen. The one he chose every single day. "I know you met Ezra's wife, but a little tidbit I didn't get to tell you—she's the one who got away before I even met him, and they have a now-grown son together."

"I'm so happy for him! He once confessed how he'd lost someone but never spelled out the details. He'd just seemed depressed over the whole thing."

"He did?" Bradford was surprised the other man had opened up at all.

"There were copious amounts of alcohol involved. I doubt he even remembers his little confession to me."

"There wasn't a good way to work their history into the introductions yesterday," he said dryly. God, he loved talking to her like this, even if it was all surface.

Because he wanted to dig deeper between the two of them. But her father had just died and they were trying to figure out who the hell was harassing her—or more specifically, why—so he forced himself to be as normal as possible.

"Man, I'm so happy for him. Looks like they're going to be parents for a second time soon. I mean…I didn't want to say anything just in case, but I assume his wife is pregnant?"

Bradford let out a startled laugh. "Uh *yeah*. She's about a month out."

"I've seen that assumption go very wrong, so unless I see a head crowning, I'm never, *ever* going to assume someone is pregnant. Oh, I think that might be the turnoff." She glanced down at his phone, which had been buzzing nonstop. "You need to grab that?"

He glanced at it—it was Mari and not an emergency. "Nah." Other than the guys, the people who texted him the most were Mari, Berlin, and his friend Violet, who was dealing with some romantic drama.

Hope was silent as he slowed along the two-lane road surrounded by thick woods on either side.

"Doesn't look like anyone's fixed this road in a while," she murmured after about a mile.

Nodding, he slowed even more as he checked the map. "I think we should pull over soon then head out on foot." From the aerial images that Berlin had dug up, there was a whole lot of woods around here and nothing more.

"How far are we?" she asked, looking at the map. "Two-ish miles?"

He snickered slightly. "I see your map reading skills have improved."

"I want to lie to you, but I'm really just more familiar with this area—and I was guessing."

"Well it's a good guess. We're about three miles out."

"Once we cross into Killeen land there's a good chance they'll have cameras," she said. "And we'll be trespassing."

"I'm well aware of what we're doing."

"Okay, just throwing it out there."

He held up a small device and grinned. "This will disrupt any cameras in a twenty-foot radius of us. But we should probably wear balaclavas just to be safe in case they have battery-powered trail cams."

"I seriously hate you right now," she groaned as he tossed her one. She started to pull her dark hair up into a braid and he resisted the urge to capture her mouth with his. He'd had way too many fantasies about her full lips, the way she tasted. "It's a billion degrees out."

"It's either this or risk getting caught on camera." He did have some other options, but it was with high-tech stuff he couldn't tell her he had access to. He loved her, and in his gut, he didn't think she would ever betray him. But he wouldn't risk the people he worked with, his family, by exposing any of them even in a small way. "Before you throw it on, I'll work the drone. See what we find."

"Sounds good." She got out of the truck with him and watched as he prepped everything. "I've never seen a drone like that."

"Yeah, it's next-level."

"Hailey's husband...the tech guy. Is this from one of his companies?"

So she had recognized him at the funeral. Hailey had introduced them of course, but Bradford wasn't sure if she'd known who he was. He should have realized that of course she did.

He shrugged, which just made her sigh.

"Fine, be like that." Her tone was tart, but she sat with him on the back of the tailgate.

It didn't take him long to launch it, the faintest hint of a buzz as he steered it upward and through the treetops. Even though it was still early, the heat was already pressing in on them, so he was glad for the shade.

"It's so quiet," she whispered, even though there was no one but squirrels and birds around. Maybe a few deer.

"And check out this screen."

She leaned in close to him as he held it out, and he tried not to inhale her scent like a demented weirdo. Then he decided he didn't care and just savored having her pressed up against him as he directed the drone in the right direction.

"It's so clear." There was awe in her voice.

"If it senses an incoming attack, it goes into defensive mode and sends out an electric pulse if the attack is another drone. Or the automechanism takes over and it flies itself to safety—to its starting point. So it'll fly back to us if it feels threatened." It had a lot more features, but those were some of his favorites.

They were both quiet as it reached the coordinates, watching the screen as the drone catalogued everything below. Which was basically trees and—

"That's camouflage netting," Hope said before he could.

"It blends really well." He dipped down a little lower, but went slowly, not wanting to attract any attention if there was anyone there.

Nothing happened as he flew it even lower, skimming the top of the netting, knowing the cameras would catch anything for them to analyze later. Still nothing happened so he flew under it and slowly spun the drone, scanning... Nothing.

"I expected to see, like, drugs or something," Hope murmured, the disappointment in her voice mirroring what he was feeling.

"Wait a minute..." He flew closer to the ground. "That's a hatch. A door. That's why there's a camo netting. Whatever this leads to, the owner doesn't want any eyes in the sky seeing."

"Things just got more interesting," she murmured. "We're definitely going to have to go in on foot, see it in person."

"You sound way too happy about that," he muttered.

"I...like working with you." And she sounded surprised by that.

"Fine, we head in on foot, but we're not breaching that hatch until we know more. But we can get a little closer, see what, if any, kind of security cameras they have set up.”

“I didn’t see any on the screen.”

“They might be too small. We’ll find out soon enough.” He didn’t like taking her with him, but knew she’d just follow no matter what he did.

After this recon mission, he was looping in the rest of the crew whether she liked it or not. He still wasn’t sure what was going on, but he wanted backup.

Anything to keep Hope safe.

CHAPTER 10

*Proud member of the Out of Breath Hiking
Club.*

"I thought I was in good shape, but I'm seriously questioning myself," Hope panted as they crouched down behind an oak tree.

"It's the balaclava." But he didn't sound as winded as she was.

And he wasn't sweating like she was. Okay, maybe he was, but she felt like she was dying in this heat and he was all cool and not breathing like a dying bear.

So that was fun. She was putting on her sexiest self right now. *Ugh.*

"Here," he murmured, handing her a bottle of water. "We're not staying long, but we need to keep hydrated."

Wordlessly (because again, she was out of breath) she took it and chugged the whole thing. Sexy? Nope. Once she was done, he handed her a set of very expensive, military-grade binoculars.

"This should be a good spot," he murmured, clearly more to himself than her as he crouched next to the tree, his own binoculars held up to his eyes as he looked in the direction of where they'd seen the netting.

"Not if we want to use parabolic mics."

"You just want to use them because you like eavesdropping." His tone was dry, but amused.

"I really, really do." She held up the binoculars and zoomed in on the spot they'd located before. The angle was different than with the drone, but she could see the top part of the hidden hatch and more of the camo netting. "It's interesting that Kim knew about this place."

"I was just thinking that. Something weird is going on around here."

"Part of me wants to just let it go."

He snort-laughed and glanced at her, his expression incredulous even with the balaclava on. "Like two percent?"

"One percent of me is telling me to let this go." But she'd always loved a mystery. Since she was a kid—thank you, Nancy Drew and Trixie Belden. She looked back into the binoculars. "I'm going to reach out to Kim, see if we can meet up out of the watchful eye of...anyone. I want to invite her to my place, but I'm not even sure I should at this point."

"Have you heard from the sheriff yet?" Bradford asked, still scanning with his binoculars.

"Not yet." She paused at a faint rumbling sound somewhere in the distance. An engine. She couldn't tell which direction it was coming from.

"Someone's approaching." He didn't drop his binos so she aimed hers in the same direction he had, spotted a dusty seventies-era Bronco rumbling up to the covered hatch. It pulled underneath the netting, which covered the vehicle completely, then out got a man she'd never seen before with Edward Killeen, his expression as sour as it had been at the diner.

"Things just got more interesting," Bradford murmured.

She agreed, but wished they were closer so they could utilize the parabolic mics. It was too risky though, she knew that. They were miles out of town with no chance of anyone seeing them. And even if there were cameras around, Bradford had used that handy little device of his, and she assumed it was working since the woods hadn't been stormed by guys looking for them.

"Dude looks like he's constipated," Bradford said.

She laughed lightly. "Yep."

Killeen stomped around to the back of the truck and watched as the other man, in well-worn jeans and a Henley T-shirt, lifted out duffel bag after duffel. The olive green bags were packed full and the guy looked as if he was grunting each time he lifted one of them up, his arm muscles straining.

"Can you take some pictures?" Bradford asked, but she was already pulling out his long-range camera.

He really had come prepared for this. "Why on earth did you have all this stuff with you? I've been meaning to ask." Because he'd come to support her after her father's death—he couldn't have known about whatever this was. Yet he'd shown up ready for a full-on investigation of anything.

"Always be prepared. Scouts' motto."

"You weren't a Scout."

He snorted. "It's a good rule to live by. Ooh, this has gotta be drugs."

She snapped away as the nameless guy climbed down into the hatch, a bag on his shoulder, then returned for more. "It would probably go faster if Killeen just handed him the bags." But it was clear that he was the boss and wasn't putting in any sweat equity.

As she watched, Killeen stepped away from the truck to take a phone call. His body language was hard the entire time, all his muscles pulled taut.

"He's making plans to meet with someone," Bradford murmured as she snapped more pictures.

"You think?"

"I'm reading his lips. Looks like he might be meeting someone tonight. His place. Could be a date or it could be related to whatever this is."

"Drugs," she said, because he was right. "Or weapons, but the bags are the wrong size." They were too compact, and in her experience, weapons tended to be shipped or stored in longer crates, usually with a decent amount of insulation. She mostly reported on white-collar crimes, but when she first started out she'd worked with the DEA for a story and had learned far more than she'd ever thought.

They stayed until the two men left, then thankfully Bradford called it. "I say we get out of here and regroup. And you need to make contact with Kim. I want to see what she knows."

"So...you're going to look into this with me?" He'd been annoyingly vague about how long he was staying in town with her. Whenever she'd pressed him, he'd shrugged. "Don't you have a job to get back to?"

"I'll be staying as long as this takes. This is my new job for now."

That wasn't really an answer, but she didn't want him to leave (not that she'd tell him that) so she didn't push him any harder. It was nice having a partner, someone to have her back.

Moving quickly, they packed up and headed back the way they'd come.

"That was hotter than Afghanistan—and more humid." Her groan might have been a little theatrical as she ripped off her balaclava then cranked up the AC as she swiped the sweaty strands of hair out of her face. If she'd had time to put any makeup on earlier, it would have been gone. "And I need a shower."

"I'd say it's on par." His tone was dry and he still seemed unaffected by the heat. "And yeah, you definitely do."

"Hey!" She threw the face mask at him. "You're not supposed to agree with me."

Grinning in that way of his that had her wanting to take off the rest of her clothes, he simply shrugged and started the truck. "Just calling it like I see it."

"Whatever... Are you sure you don't need to answer that?" Because his phone had been buzzing nonstop for the last couple hours and it was driving her crazy. Was it that same woman still texting him from before? The woman with the sexy name—Berlin. And seriously, why did she care? *You know why you care, dummy.*

He tossed her his phone. "Will you check it for me? I don't want to look while I'm driving."

He was going like five miles an hour down the bumpy access road, but fair. "You're sure you don't mind me looking at your texts?"

"It's clear you want to."

"What?" she practically sputtered.

He shrugged again, his expression maddeningly knowing.

But he wasn't wrong. "Fine, what's your code?"

"Your birthday."

She blinked at him, had to stop her mouth from actually falling open. *That* she hadn't been expecting, and she had no idea what to say to it. His code was... Her. Birthday.

"You have texts from... Oh my god, it's all women." *Don't get jealous, don't have a tone, don't sound annoyed*, she ordered herself. Too late, she was irrationally annoyed. So irrational. But there it was.

"Let me guess, they're from Berlin, Violet and Mari. And maybe Hailey. All happily married or engaged women. Except Violet..." He paused. "But something's going on with her so that might be changing. You can read them if you want. Hell, read them out loud, it'll save me time."

Hope knew she should put his phone down, that she shouldn't care about his life, but... Whatever, she was a journalist after all. She wanted to know everything about his life. "Mari is scary."

"Very true."

"She's talking about dick-punching someone who pissed her off and says that she won't be held responsible for her actions. She asks if you'll be her alibi since her husband won't be a realistic one."

Bradford just snickered as he sped up onto the two-lane highway. "Sounds about right."

"Violet is...telling you about flamingos and the most insane wedding she's ever been involved in. Also, oh no, I don't think I should be reading this. It's too personal."

"What is it? You can't stop now."

"Something about a one-night stand and how she hates herself because she wants more than one. And oh my god, now Berlin is talking about one of her sisters finally making good life choices and how it might be a sign of the apocalypse. You really are just friends with all these women." The relief was almost dizzying. Which infuriated her.

"Told you. Nothing for you to be jealous about."

"I'm not jealous!" Okay, she didn't even believe herself at this point. Of course she was jealous. Bradford was incredible and kind and ugh. *Stop it!*

"Hmm. For the record, I'd be jealous if you were talking to a bunch of men."

"I don't even know what to say to that," she murmured, setting his phone down. She hated that she was so relieved that he wasn't talking to some imaginary girlfriend she'd built up in her head. And he'd even given her his phone code. Again, which was her birthday. She wasn't sure she'd fully processed that yet.

"Are you dating anyone right now?" he asked, and the question wasn't as casual as she guessed he meant it to be.

"No." The word came out more of a snort. She was too busy, had very little to give, and she was still married. Maybe only in name, but that didn't matter to her. It would have felt too much like cheating to hook up with someone else while being technically married to Bradford.

Stupid? Sure, but she'd had more than a taste of him, and it was hard to go back to the nothingness of the "relationships" she'd had before him. She'd somehow convinced herself that she'd built him up in her head, that he wasn't as great as she remembered, but then he'd gone and shown up for her father's funeral without her having to say anything.

And now he was helping her look into the mystery of whatever the heck was going on in her hometown.

And...fine, he was still as gorgeous as she remembered. Maybe even more so. He made it impossible to ignore how wonderful he was. And to forget how incredible their short time together had been.

She'd replayed that weekend over and over in her head so many times over the years, along with all the other times she'd spent with him prior to it. And he *still* lived up to the hype in her head.

But fairy-tale endings weren't for her. He deserved more than what she had to offer. She was too broken inside, had nothing to give long-term. Because everyone eventually disappointed you.

That was just the way life was. And the truth was, she couldn't handle being let down by Bradford, of being disappointed by him. That would crush her in a way nothing else could.

So she was holding the fantasy of him tight in her heart.

CHAPTER 11

Before

Dear Bradford,

I hated leaving you in that hotel room. I wanted to stay more than anything, but knew how things would end. Can I see the future? No, but in the end we wouldn't have worked and probably would have hated each other if we'd given it a shot and failed. Or at least you'd have resented me. Our lives are just headed in two different directions, and deep down I know I'm not good enough for you. I'll screw things up eventually, so it makes more sense to spare you all of that and get out now.

All the things I never told you, but wanted to—you're the best person I've ever known, so giving to your friends and anyone you add to your circle. And I know you're selective, so I'm honored that you included me in yours, even for a limited time. I know we'll never be right together, no matter how much I want you. I never even thought chemistry like that was possible, but you knocked me off my feet in more ways than one.

I won't be sending this letter, but I hope you go on to meet someone incredible. And while the most selfish part of me hates that you'll be moving on with someone who is not me, it's for the best.

You have a big heart and so much to give and you deserve all the happiness. I love you.

All my love,
Hope

CHAPTER 12

*Don't look for someone who will solve
all your problems. Look for someone who
won't let you face them alone.*

"I'm surprised Hope didn't insist on coming with you," Rowan murmured as Bradford pulled his truck into the woods off the side of a well-traveled two-lane highway.

"Her dad's lawyer wanted to talk to her and then she wanted to talk to Kim again. See if she can get more information from her." The only reason he was okay with her being out of his sight was because Tiago had agreed to tail her.

He'd already received a text from Tiago telling him that she'd left her lawyer's and had recently arrived at the diner, so he knew she was safe.

"That makes more sense... So."

"So...what?" Bradford shut the door behind him and pulled out his backpack. All this recon hadn't been on his list of things to do when he'd come to see Hope, but he was glad he'd been prepared.

Everyone who worked for Redemption Harbor Security was like that. Their founder, Skye, probably took things to a level none of them did (she never left the house without C-4, not even to go to the grocery store, and no that wasn't hyperbole) but it was still ingrained into them to be prepared.

"How are things with you guys?"

Awkward? "Good enough. And that's all you're gonna get, so tell Tiago that if he wants to know anything, he'll have to ask me himself. Because I know this shit isn't from you."

Rowan grinned as he hoisted his own pack. "It's mostly Tiago, but we're all concerned too. We've been brothers since we were dumb kids. I care about you. Her too, for that matter. I see how she looks at you, but…I don't know. I just don't want you getting hurt."

"If I do, I do." He shrugged because he wasn't going to worry about that. He was pretty certain that Hope worried about it enough for the both of them. One of them had to just go for it and it was going to be him.

Rowan didn't say anything as they put in their earpieces and slipped into the woods.

"Berlin, you copy?" he murmured. It was half past six, so it was still light out but there were plenty of shadows in the woods.

"Loud and clear. I've got a drone high above Killeen's place. There hasn't been any traffic in or out except that Bronco about an hour ago. I have no idea if he was even driving it since the driver parked in the garage. Since then, nothing. And my battery is about dead anyway. I'm not sure you'll get close enough to gather any real information."

Oh, he would. "You got a backup drone?"

"Of course I do." At the sound of a throat clearing in the background she said, "To be clear, Ezra is the one flying the drone and he wanted you to know that. As if I need to steal credit," she muttered.

"Do I need to head back to base and referee you two?" said Rowan, who, more often than not, *did* referee all of them. Either he or Adalyn did.

There was more good-natured bickering but Bradford tuned it out as they stalked through the thick underbrush, mosquitos and cicadas buzzing loudly in the background.

Berlin had pulled up all the known records for Edward Killeen's property and from there she'd done her magic. He could do basic stuff like property searches, because once you had an address there was a lot you could find if you knew where to search. But Berlin worked a different kind of magic.

So far they knew that Edward Killeen owned at least nine properties in the region. Six were in his wife's name, two in his son's, and he owned about eight spread out around the country. Bradford was certain there were more under aliases, but that was what Berlin had found thus far.

They had a pretty decent aerial layout of where they were headed. And she was right, he wasn't certain they'd find anything this way, but he wanted to get eyes on the ground right now. It was a start anyway, while Berlin dug into Killeen's financials. She hadn't found out much on the Tanner brothers other than they'd been arrested a handful of times for petty crimes. So maybe there wasn't a connection to them and the Killeens. Only time would tell.

There was no way to know what would give them the information they needed so they had to start somewhere.

"Stop right where you guys are," Berlin said into the quiet about thirty minutes into their trek through the woods. "You'll be coming up on security cameras soon so give me a sec…"

She trailed off and he had no doubt she was disabling them.

"Okay, I'm in and you've got about thirty minutes. The cameras are completely down, indicating an error that needs an update, but they'll be up soon enough."

"At the risk of having my head chopped off later, why didn't you just do that thing you do where you create loops or whatever magic you do?" he asked as he started jogging in the direction of Killeen's home. They knew from the aerial photos and coordinates exactly where it was.

"It won't work for this system, that's the easiest way I can explain it. And by doing it this way, even the security system and monitoring company will think it's in need of a reboot. Which it is—it's why I was able to hack in so easily."

Bradford had a feeling that "easily" was just by her standards.

"But after this it will automatically update itself, so whatever you need to do, make it fast. Also, if you can find a cell phone or laptop or PC or whatever, you know what to do," she added.

He and Rowan both grunted because they did know what to do. She'd only reminded them eight times. They were also going to try to plant some small cameras around the house too, and the plan was for Berlin to link them into the Wi-Fi system.

Since Killeen's home and extended property butted up against a palmetto farm, and they weren't certain if the farm was a cover for something, they approached from a different direction.

The guy's house was relatively large, about five thousand square feet, but not what Bradford had seen with some drug runners. But it was more than big enough for the guy and his wife—their son lived in a smaller house farther west on the property on the other side of the palmetto farm.

Bradford really wanted to get in there, but the location made it far too difficult. At least without more aerial recon.

"There's movement on the road. Someone is turning into the main entrance." This was from Adalyn, who was in an SUV a few miles back acting as an extra set of eyes. "Your guy will have company soon."

In other words, they needed to be prepared.

"I didn't see anyone other than Killeen on the cameras inside the house," Berlin added, as if she'd read his mind.

"In the house?" He knew some people had them to watch their pets or kids or whatever, but it seemed like overkill to him.

"One in the kitchen, the other in a game room."

He made a mental note of it and glanced at his watch as he and Rowan crouched down by the tree line.

"Not too much ground to cover," Rowan said. "We can enter from the northwest bottom window." He pointed at the one he meant, but Bradford already knew.

He nodded. His friend was right, it was the straightest shot, and from the plans they had, it connected to a laundry room. "I hate not knowing if there's other security," he muttered.

"Right? Makes me feel like I have a bull's-eye on my chest."

They were wearing top-of-the-line bulletproof vests under their shirts, but yep. He felt the same. If Berlin or the others had seen anyone with the drone, they'd have told them, so it was a good bet that there wasn't any on-the-ground security—at least on the direct grounds near the house.

"Berlin, you see that vehicle yet?" he asked.

"It's approaching slowly, should reach the end of the driveway in about sixty seconds."

He looked at Rowan, nodded when the other man gave familiar hand gestures.

"Okay, Killeen is stepping outside onto the driveway," Berlin finally said.

They took off while they had a chance. Everything funneled out around him as he sprinted for that window at full speed.

It took a precious two minutes to get the window open without breaking it. Then he was inside first, with Rowan quickly following.

"Spread out, stay on the comms," Rowan ordered. "If anything is off, we retreat."

Bradford nodded, already slipping out of the laundry room and into a quiet hallway. They'd already gone over the rooms they'd planned to hit first to plant the cameras and listening devices. It was a crapshoot because Killeen could sweep the place on a regular basis, but it was a risk they had to take.

He moved silently, pausing to sweep a couple generic-looking guest rooms. But once he made it to the kitchen, he got to work. People gathered and talked in kitchens, so it was one of the rooms they'd planned to tag first.

"You're still clear." Berlin said in his ear. "He's staying in the driveway."

He was silent as he worked, placing the tiny bug high up on top of one of the shelves. Then he hid a camera in the corner of a picture with a black frame. If he didn't know it was there, he wouldn't have seen it.

The tech now was next-level and even scared him a bit if he was being brutally honest with himself. There was a reason he swept his own place regularly.

"Time to get out of there. He's walking the guy back to his vehicle," Berlin said.

"Retreating now," he whispered, with Rowan saying the same thing.

He met Rowan at the laundry room door.

"How many did you get?" he asked as they hurried toward the window, careful not to touch anything.

"Three cameras and two audio bugs."

He snorted softly as he slid the window open. They liked to plant more than cameras in case something went wrong with the audio on them. "Same." There simply hadn't been enough time to do more, not without a risk of getting caught. But he'd got one camera in the kitchen, another in one of the living rooms and managed to add one on the back patio that overlooked the massive pool. It blended in with the brick accent wall and if any of them were going to go unnoticed long-term, he'd bet money on that one.

"He's walking up the front steps and there's another car coming up the driveway now. A Mercedes S-Class... Gotta be his wife. Get the hell out of there."

They were both outside now, crouched down by the window. "Are we good to make a run for it?" Rowan asked quietly as Bradford secured the window.

"Yep."

They sprinted back across the grassy stretch of yard and he only dragged in a full breath once they passed the tree line and Berlin said, "You're clear. And with four minutes to spare."

"Let's get the hell out of here," he muttered, not slowing down as they hurried through the woods. He wanted to get back to Hope anyway. He trusted Tiago to watch her, to keep her safe, but it didn't matter.

A compulsion inside him wanted eyes on her, to see for himself that she was okay.

CHAPTER 13

Don't fall for someone not willing to catch you.

Out of the corner of her eye, Hope watched as Tiago and his fiancée (wife? She couldn't remember) slid into one of the only empty booths along the diner window. She thought she'd seen him earlier when she'd left Chelsea's office to go over more paperwork.

Now that her head was clearer, she had questions, and her dad's lawyer had been more than happy to come in on a Sunday. It had surprised her, but the woman had really loved Hank and credited him with her getting and staying sober.

Hearing these kinds of stories about him had shaken her to her foundation, and she wasn't sure if she liked them or hated them. Maybe a bit of both.

She knew that her mom had fallen for him for a reason and there had been good years, but still. It sucked that she'd never seen the best parts of him. That she had to live with the bad memories and regrets instead.

"Hey hon, what are you in the mood for?" Kim stopped in front of her with a smile.

She'd chosen to sit at the diner counter because most of the booths were full. There was no way she'd be able to get any information with so many people around, but she could eat. "Would you judge me if I said I wanted pie for dinner?"

Kim snickered. "How about pie and ice cream? If I remember correctly, peach is your favorite?"

"You really are a goddess. Yes to peach pie and ice cream—and I'll take two of the specials, but to go." She wasn't sure if Bradford would have time to stop and get something, and she wanted to make sure he ate. He was doing so much for her.

"Got it."

"I'm going to grab a seat with some friends if that's okay?"

"Of course, I'll bring your pie to you."

She picked up her drink and headed for Tiago's table. It had been years since she'd seen him, but he looked the same. Even sitting down, he was tall and he had an easy toothpaste-commercial smile as she approached.

She found herself smiling back at him and... "Fleur, right?"

The other woman smiled as wide as Tiago and it was clear to see why the two of them were together. They both had an easygoing energy. The woman had dark hair, green eyes, and in that moment Hope could see how much she looked like Adalyn. Though Adalyn had hard edges that Fleur didn't, they had the same facial features.

"Yes, it's so nice to see you again. And I really am sorry about your father."

Throat tight, she nodded. "Thank you. Tiago...are you following me because Bradford asked you to?"

His dark eyes went wide, but before he could answer, Fleur nodded.

"Oh yeah," Fleur said as she scooped up some of the same peach pie Hope would be devouring in moments. "He said we'd better not let you out of our sight."

"Fleur," Tiago murmured, nudging her gently. "That's not how this works."

The other woman shrugged. "I'd be annoyed if you had someone following me, so I'm not going to lie to her."

Hope grinned as she watched the two of them talk.

Tiago sighed. "We're just keeping an eye on you. Because of...you know."

"I do know. And you could have just asked me." She didn't mind someone having her back. And the truth was, she was surprised Bradford had been fine when she'd told him she had errands to run. This whole protective thing made way more sense to her.

"That's literally what I said." Fleur pointed her fork at Tiago.

Something settled inside her, knowing that Bradford was still looking out for her. She knew she didn't deserve him, but... "So have you heard from him?" He'd told her that he had "something to take care of" and that she should have "plausible deniability," but he'd also hinted at what he was doing. So.

"Yep." Tiago nodded. "He's safe."

"That's all I'll get, huh?" She smiled up at Kim as she dropped off the pie and ice cream with a gentle pat on her shoulder.

"Yep."

"Ah, a man of many words, just like I remember."

Fleur snort-laughed.

"So when's the wedding?" Hope figured that was a safe enough topic, and she was right.

They talked about wedding plans and a lot of light things as they ate. And when Kim dropped off the two to-go bags, Hope said, "Feel free to call me if you lose me."

"Oh, B put a tracker on your car," Fleur whispered low enough only for their table to hear.

Hope paused in getting up, blinked once at the two of them.

Tiago covered his face for a long moment. "Babe, that's not how any of this works."

"Well it's how I work. We've got you. Also…why don't you just take my number?" Fleur already had her phone out as she was talking. "Or just give me yours and I'll text you so you know it's me."

"Thanks." Hope rattled off her number quickly, then stood when she saw the sheriff pulling into the parking lot. "I hope to see you both later," she said, meaning it.

In the parking lot, she smiled at Sheriff Crow as she headed to her car—which was right next to his cruiser.

"Hope," he said with a tired smile. "I'm just getting off work and had the same idea as you."

"Us and everyone else." The parking lot was almost full. She wasn't sure if that was normal for a Sunday, but figured it was a normal thing every day, considering how good the food was.

He grunted in agreement.

"So…anything new?"

He lifted a shoulder. "He's out, of course, and it's up to the prosecutor now whether it goes to trial."

Yeah, she knew how it worked. Forcing a smile, she said, "Okay, thank you. I'm headed home now. Hopefully I won't have any more break-ins." She couldn't quite keep the tartness out of her voice.

The sheriff glanced around then looked back at her. "I don't think he'll bother you again. He's an asshole," he murmured. "But his daddy's got a lot of sway around here. My guess is that he was at your dad's place for kicks, thinking no one was there. The kid has got rocks in his head."

Yeah, she wasn't so sure about that. "He never said who was with him?"

"Nope."

"But you know?"

"I can guess," he finally said.

And clearly he wasn't going to tell her. It was so damn frustrating. "Okay, well I'll see you around."

"You're staying in town, then?" His eyebrows rose slightly, which made sense.

It wasn't like she'd spent any time here since she'd split years ago. She lifted a shoulder. "We'll see what happens." He wasn't telling her anything, so she wasn't telling him shit either. Sure, she understood he had to play politics, but she didn't have to like it. "Have a good one."

She waited in the parking lot until Tiago and Fleur paid, then left only once they were in their own vehicle. Might as well make it easy on them to follow her, even if they did have a tracker.

It was clear that the sheriff wasn't going to do anything about the Killeen family, and she wondered if the rest of the town knew about their exploits. Which, after this afternoon, she was guessing had to be drugs. No one had a random bunker in the woods and shoved duffel bags in them if they weren't doing something shady.

If she hadn't planned on staying before, she was now. Because this was a mystery she had to solve.

CHAPTER 14

Your girl knows you asked us to follow her... Fleur told her. Bradford read Tiago's text, which was followed by a shrug emoji. Okay, then.

He sent back a thumbs-up, hoping she wasn't mad about it. Not like he'd have let her leave without someone watching out for her, but he still didn't relish the idea of her being pissed at him. Another barrier to overcome was the last thing he needed with Hope.

"This could be interesting," Berlin called out from the kitchen of the home she and the others were renting. Her husband was still back in New Orleans helping handle a job for the Feds, and she'd only been a little cranky without him.

Bradford headed into the spacious farmhouse kitchen and found Berlin where he'd left her before, sitting at the massive island top.

Rowan was currently cooking something for everyone, and the scent of marinara and whatever else he was whipping up made Bradford's stomach growl. Adalyn and Ezra were both cleaning their pistols at the breakfast table, and...he wasn't sure where Hailey and her husband were.

She also bought you dinner, just fyi, came another text, this one from Fleur. *And I couldn't lie to her. I like her! Sorry, not sorry.*

His heart did a weird little flip at the thought that Hope had bought him dinner. *Thanks for letting me know.* He'd be skipping dinner here because he would rather share it with her.

"Are you paying attention?"

He looked over to find Berlin staring at him, her expression hard.

"So much for not being cranky," he muttered.

That got a raised eyebrow from her, but she turned back to her laptop.

He sat next to her as she turned up the volume. The quality of the cameras was decent, but it was the audio that really mattered.

"I don't understand why I have to go out of town." Patrick Killeen was sitting at the island countertop similar to the one in their own rental, looking like a petulant child as he stared at his father across from him.

"I need you to be in New Orleans, and your mother needs a shopping trip. You'll make sure that you're seen at a lot of places, make big tips wherever you guys eat, visit any art gallery your mother wants, and don't get into any trouble. Do you understand me?" More than annoyance, there was something a lot like contempt in Edward's tone.

"Dad—"

Edward held up a hand to silence his son, then turned as a pretty blonde strode into the room. "Hey hon, beautiful as always."

He'd been married to Tara Killeen for almost thirty years, and if his financials were any indication, he was faithful to her. At least according to Berlin's research. The man liked to spoil his wife with lavish vacations and shopping trips, and as Bradford watched the two on-screen it seemed clear that they were both affectionate after three decades together.

For the next five minutes they watched as the wife and son said their good-byes, then finally left.

"I don't like that he wants his son out of town," Bradford said as he watched Edward pull out a bottle of whiskey, pour a small glass.

"Giving him an alibi is what it sounds like," Adalyn said without looking up from the kitchen table.

Most definitely.

"Looks like he might have company," Berlin murmured a few minutes later as the man set his now empty whiskey glass down.

On the split screen, Bradford watched as the same guy he'd seen in the woods with Killeen stalked into the kitchen with clear familiarity.

"Well?" Killeen asked.

"I've got things handled. How long is Patrick gone?"

"Just headed out, and the plan is for them to be in New Orleans through Wednesday at least. He knows what to do."

"You're sure about this?" the man asked.

"That's Dale Watsky," Berlin whispered as they continued talking. "Former military, weapons expert."

Huh.

"You find Hall yet?" Killeen asked.

"Yep."

Ned Hall was Patrick's best friend, the one suspected of being with him the night Patrick broke into Hope's place.

"He doesn't suspect anything," Watsky added.

Killeen was silent for a long moment, then nodded. "All right, it's a solid plan. But there can't be any room for error."

"The woman might not even be a problem." Watsky's tone was neutral.

"She should have let things go with Patrick," Killeen snapped. "All she had to do was drop it."

Watsky nodded. "Yeah. Maybe."

"Maybe?"

Even through the screen, Bradford could see the man didn't like that.

Watsky held up his palms. "I'm just saying. She's not from here... She doesn't live here anymore. It's not like she knows who you are. And Patrick did break into her dad's place." Another pause, then, "And she's a journalist. Not a nobody either. She won a Pulitzer. People will notice if she dies."

Dies? Everything inside Bradford went still. Apparently he was going to have to kill this bastard. Slowly. Painfully.

"That's why we have to do this right. I'm sure she's pissed off a lot of people over the years. Even if we don't get everything right, there will be plenty of suspects—and Patrick is out of town. Nothing will come back on us.

Watsky simply nodded, but Bradford could see he didn't like it.

And it was taking all of his self-control not to storm out of here, hunt down Killeen, and put an end to him for good. Just put a bullet in his head and call it a day. It was clear he was coming for Hope and had a plan to do it.

"Fine, but it feels too public and not worth our time," Watsky added, clearly not done with the conversation.

"Since when did you start questioning me?" Killeen snarled.

"I'm not questioning you. I'm trying to keep you—our *operation*—safe. We've got a great thing going, and Patrick..." He trailed off, clearly not willing to say more.

"Jesus, I know." Some of the wind seemed to leave him as he grabbed his bottle of whiskey and another glass.

Watsky took the other glass offered and they silently sipped for a few minutes.

"I'll keep him in line," Killeen finally said into the quiet. "Let's just handle the woman, then after that I'll get him in line."

"What about the husband?" Watsky asked as he set his glass down.

"Just some asshole. Works for some security company as an analyst or something in New Orleans. He won't be a problem."

"Glad to know our covers hold," Bradford murmured.

Berlin sniffed. "Because I'm a genius."

He grinned at that, despite the turmoil roiling in his gut. This asshole wanted to kill Hope and it wasn't going to happen.

"He might get in the way," Watsky said.

"Nah. If you do things right and lure her away from the farm, everything'll be fine. You sure you've got that part covered?"

"Yeah." It was clear that Watsky still didn't agree with whatever Killeen wanted, but he was still going along with it. "She'll get the text tomorrow afternoon to meet at the lawyer's, then..." He made a sort of explosion motion with his hand. "We'll pin it on Ned. Shouldn't be hard to make it look like he did it."

Okay, so it was clear that the plan was to kill her then.

For a moment, Bradford saw red, wanted to head right to her, pack her up, willing or not, and haul ass out of town. But he knew how that would go over.

Killeen nodded. "Ned's a dumbass. And if the Tanner brothers hadn't spooked her the other night..." He shook his head and downed his glass.

So Edward did have something to do with them going to her father's house. But why? The same reason that Patrick had?

"We're going to handle this." Rowan's voice cut through the quiet kitchen, and Bradford looked up to find his friend watching him carefully.

"I know."

"You sure? Because you look homicidal right now."

"Probably because that's how I feel. But I'm not going to run off and do something stupid." *Probably. Definitely.* "I'm going to head out. Keep me updated." He'd seen enough, and he wanted eyes on Hope.

Hands too, but at the moment he was certain that wasn't on the table. They might be married, but it was in name only. For now.

"I'll let you know if anything else pops up... Maybe you guys should just stay here tonight?" Berlin asked, her tone cautious.

"I'll ask her, see what she thinks." But Killeen's "plan" wasn't until tomorrow anyway, so he doubted she would want to leave.

Berlin nodded and the others were quiet as he left, which was just as well. He didn't want to talk right now, he simply wanted to see Hope.

CHAPTER 15

Before

"Come on, I swear I've got it this time. Just do it," Hope insisted.

Bradford snorted, knowing she would miss again, but opened his mouth anyway—because he would do anything she asked him—as she threw a corn nut at him. He winced when it nailed him in the eye. "I feel like you're doing it on purpose at this point." He tossed it in his mouth even though it had landed in the dirt.

"Oh my god, gross." She threw a handful of them at him in mock horror.

"This is one of the least-gross things I've had over here. Have you tried the MREs?"

"Ugh, barf, good point."

A rocket detonated in the distance, shook the ground and they both paused before he lay back on the old beach chair that had just shown up one day outside their quarters. It was the two of them right now next to the MGPTS—Modular General Purpose Tent System. The others would be back soon, something he was ignoring. He wanted Hope all to himself for as long as possible.

She set the corn nuts down and stretched out next to him on a mismatched beach chair with green and white bands barely hanging on to the aluminum frame for dear life. "Can't believe I leave tomorrow."

"Yeah." He'd been obsessing about it, though he kept that to himself. "I'm glad we met."

"Me too." Her voice was soft. "I know I shouldn't have favorites, but I'm glad I got assigned to your team."

"Well, we are the best." He gave her a lopsided grin and thought he saw heat in her gaze.

But she quickly turned away, casting her eyes up to the dark sky blanketed with countless stars. "And so very humble."

He chuckled around the pain in his chest. He hadn't expected Hope Berkley at all, none of them had. She'd just been some journalist they'd been instructed to show around, to answer questions for... They'd all been cautious about meeting her. But then she'd shown up the first day with treats (a surefire way to a bunch of Marines' hearts) and authenticity.

That was the thing that had gotten him, how real she was. And kind. Not nice, but truly kind. There was a difference.

"You gonna forget about us?" he asked as the ground shook again.

She didn't even seem to notice, or maybe she'd just gotten used to it like him. But she'd been like that from the beginning. Nothing seemed to faze her, which was impressive in itself.

"I don't think that's possible." Her voice was whisper soft and he thought she was going to say more—

Then the guys returned, all wearing makeshift birthday cone hats on their head.

Tiago was carrying a cake with the words *We'll miss you!* and a smile as he approached.

"You guys!" She hopped up from the chair as Rowan tossed one of the paper hats to Bradford. "Did you know about this?"

"Of course," he said with a laugh. Though their timing sucked. He'd just wanted a couple more minutes with her.

Lies. He wanted all the minutes with her.

But she'd be leaving in the morning, and despite what she said, he had a feeling they would lose touch.

How could they not?

They lived in different worlds, and soon she'd be back stateside, writing her miniseries about them and the culture here and moving on to the next one.

He wasn't sure where he'd be in a month or two, only that they had orders to ship out soon. They were headed back to California, and then...who knew.

Didn't matter really. He would follow orders, because that was what he did.

But for tonight, he pasted on a smile as Hope handed him a piece of cake, her smile brilliant. He would enjoy what time he had with her and hold on tight to the memories.

"You're sneaky," she murmured, nudging him with her hip. "Oh my god, and this cake is so good. I would marry this cake."

"Right?" Ezra had the same reaction. "I don't know how Tiago does it, but he has the best connections."

"I can't help it if everyone loves me." Tiago sniffed, only a little obnoxiously.

Bradford half listened as the conversations went on around him, but most of his focus was on Hope. The woman he'd fallen for when he'd least expected it.

The woman he would have to live without.

CHAPTER 16

*Why are you holding on to a past that didn't
even make you happy?*

Bradford had already texted Hope so she would be expecting him, but he still called out as he stepped through the front door. "It's me."

"In the kitchen," she answered.

Hot anticipation simmered inside him at the thought of seeing her again, after being separated for only a few hours. He wanted to resolve this distance between them, even if he had no idea how. The only thing he was certain of was that he had to keep showing up and he couldn't let her run when she wanted to.

Because that was her instinct: to bail when things got hard.

She looked up from her laptop when he stepped inside and gave him a tired smile. She'd changed into pajama bottoms and a sweatshirt she'd stolen from him. The sight of it on her made his heart stop for a moment. He'd let her borrow it one night years ago, and when she hadn't given it back, he hadn't wanted to ask for it.

But she'd kept it. That had to mean something. *He* had to mean something to her. Right?

Somehow he kept his voice even. "Getting a lot of work done?"

"Eh. Just noodling on a story. And I sent a PI friend of mine information on the Killeen family. He's not associated with my paper, but a friend. I know you've got Berlin, but maybe he'll find something too. Did you eat yet?" she asked, sliding off her stool.

He shook his head. "Fleur said you got me dinner."

"I did, and I waited for you… To be fair, I did have pie at the diner to tide me over." Her mouth curved up slightly as she went to the fridge and pulled the boxes out.

"You and pie," he said with a laugh.

"The best food there is."

He poured glasses of water for them as she plated their food—patty melts and French fries. His mouth watered at the sight. "I'm going to have to hit up her diner again."

"I could live there," she said as she slid the food into the microwave. "The place was too crowded so I didn't get to talk to Kim. Tell me you found something good, hopefully?"

Good? Not exactly.

He quickly recapped everything, noticed the surprise in her expression as he told her about the conversation between Killeen and one of his guys. Then he said, "It's clear he wants to kill you and blame it on someone." Even saying that out loud had him grasping onto his self-control. He knew he couldn't just go and kill the guy—even if it was exactly what he wanted to do.

"Yeah, all that sounds super murder-y. Jesus," she muttered. "Definitely not the first death threat I've gotten, but none of this makes any sense."

He knew she'd had death threats because of the nature of her job. But it was mostly trolls on the internet who were a lot braver behind their keyboards than they were in real life. Not that it was okay. He hated the shit she had to deal with.

"He's pissed at you, but yeah, this seems over-the-top. If we can figure out why he sent the Tanner brothers here and why his son broke in here in the first place, maybe it'll help us figure out why he wants to kill you. Not that I'll let anything happen to you."

"I know you won't." The smile she gave him was so trusting, but he could see the worry lingering in her eyes. "Do you think we should leave now?"

"No. If I did, I'd have had Tiago pack you up and toss you in his trunk."

She narrowed her gaze at him. "As if I would have argued about leaving when my life is in danger."

"I'm just saying."

Her mouth quirked up again as she shook her head. "Okay, so we stay put for now."

"Tonight only. And full disclosure, Tiago added a few more cameras outside. There are a lot of them. Berlin has them set up so that if anything bigger than a small animal triggers them, it'll send an alert to my phone."

"Yeah, it kind of sounds like Patrick won't have a good alibi until tomorrow anyway. I think I'll pack up my stuff tonight anyway so we're ready to go."

Good, he'd been planning to suggest that. His things were mostly still packed, but he always traveled like that. Being ready to run at a moment's notice was ingrained into him.

"So what are you working on?" He slid his food onto a separate plate so she could take hers to the island top.

"It's...complicated. I mean, no more than other things I work on. But it's a tale as old as time. A man in power abused his position to hurt women, young women in their twenties with very little work experience, and the people on his team covered it up. I think it's even worse because the women who went to work for him did so because they believe in the things he allegedly stands for." She took a deep breath and he could see the frustration in her blue eyes. "I actually liked the guy too."

"Oh."

"Yeah, he's very charming, and the things he says that he stands for align with my personal beliefs. Unfortunately, he's just another predator hiding behind the good things he does."

"I'm sorry. What's holding the story up?"

"I don't even know if I want to write it. I mean, I *do*, but I'm well aware of what the fallout could be on the women who come forward. So I haven't been pushing them hard to tell their stories. I honestly don't know if it'll help. Young, bright-eyed, twenty-year-old me would have been indignant that someone didn't want to tell their story."

"But you've lived in the world long enough to understand why they don't... Anything I can do to help?"

She gave him a ghost of a smile as she picked up half her patty melt. "Maybe I'll come up with something. For now, three of the women I've talked to have actual proof, but not the heart to go public. Or maybe not the stomach, because they know there would be consequences for them." She shrugged. "We'll see what happens."

He loved how big her heart was, but it still hurt to watch her take on so much without taking care of herself.

They were silent as they ate, but it was a comfortable silence as they both settled in for the night. He was exhausted, but wanted to do another perimeter check even though they had cameras and a security system. With Hope's safety, he wasn't taking any chances.

After they'd finished, she sat back in her seat and said, "So...how exactly did you get the information on the Killeen family? More spying?"

"You really want to know the details?"

She arched an eyebrow. "You worried I'll narc you out?"

"No." That was one thing he definitely wasn't concerned about. "Fine, but you're losing plausible deniability. A friend and I broke into their place and planted listening devices and cameras."

She blinked once, but he couldn't tell if it was in real surprise. "You brought one of your coworkers?" she asked carefully as she stood, taking her plate.

"That a problem?" He wasn't sure why he was pushing, and tried to temper his tone. But something about her body language was off.

"I didn't say that."

He followed her to the sink with his plate, nudged her out of the way so he could load up the dishwasher. "You're not *not* saying it either. What's the deal?"

She scrubbed a hand over her face. "Nothing. This just feels like things spiraled so fast and I hate that I don't have a clear picture. I don't like not knowing what's going on, especially in my own life! And now strangers are involved—"

"Not strangers."

"You know what I mean."

"Maybe. But we all tried to stay in touch with you," he added, unable to keep the bite out of his tone. Apparently he wasn't holding back, even though he told himself he should.

She turned away from him then. "I know. I know! I just...I suck, okay."

Well, hell. "No, not okay. And I'm calling bullshit." He tugged on her hand to keep her from walking away. It was past time they hashed this out. He wasn't letting her run from this conversation.

To his surprise, she turned back quickly, so he used her momentum and tugged her flush against him until they were inches apart. "You don't suck. You're just a coward sometimes," he growled.

Her pupils dilated as she glared up at him. "I'm not a coward! Just a realist."

"Whatever you've got to tell yourself to sleep at night. You ran from me years ago. And you even ran from the others when they would have been your friends for life. You're a runner, Hope. Might as well own it."

She gritted her teeth as she continued to glare at him, and for a moment he thought she might lean up and kiss him.

He wasn't strong enough to turn away from her, but he also wasn't going to initiate anything. Not this time. She'd been running from him, and probably her past, for years. He couldn't force the issue too hard and make a misstep now. He'd pushed his luck just by confronting her. But she was worth it.

"I want to wipe that smug look off your face," she finally managed to grit out.

"Pretty sure you want to do something else to my face."

Her pupils dilated again, this time with something wild and heated, but she abruptly turned away from him and stalked from the kitchen in a few long strides.

Still running. The words were on the tip of his tongue, but he held back.

"I'm not running!" she tossed over her shoulder almost as an after-thought.

"Sure seems like it."

She growled in frustration as she stomped up the stairs.

Good, he was under her skin. Was only fair, since she'd lived under his since the day they'd met.

Now every time she contemplated running, she'd think twice. And maybe she'd eventually stop running altogether.

***

Hope sat up and punched her pillow, rolled over, then punched it again. *Coward? Ugh.* "Screw him," she muttered, then immediately felt like a jerk.

But whatever, she wasn't a coward... Except...maybe...she was. And it was like he'd seen straight into her soul years ago and never left. Which was part of the reason she'd run from him in Vegas.

"Maybe I'm a coward. But it's a protective mechanism," she whispered into the quiet.

And there was nothing wrong with wanting to protect herself. That was just normal human behavior. People always disappointed you. *Always.*

Her father. Her mother. The few boyfriends she'd had.

She should just march right down to his room and...what? Knock on his door and...maybe hook up? Right about now she felt as if she could crawl out of her skin and it was all his fault.

Maybe if they had sex again, it would help scratch the itch that had been destroying her since she'd walked out of that hotel room in Vegas. Not that she actually believed that. Not anymore. She'd had him before, and if she went down that road again...she didn't think she could walk away. Or *run*.

But if she did go see him, then left his room—which she inevitably would—he'd call her a coward again... "Oh my god, you're spiraling." Groaning, she rolled over and shouted into her pillow.

Why was being a human so damn hard? Just why?

It was like the world had gone mad, with people trying to hurt each other all the time, mostly for no reason. And the voices of reason were just ignored. Someone was plotting to try and kill her right now for absolutely no reason that made sense.

Closing her eyes, she rolled over and stared at the ceiling. This wasn't about Bradford calling her a coward (well, maybe it was a little), but where her brain was lately. She was thinking about leaving her job, one she'd been doing forever it seemed. Her work had been part of her identity for so long.

It had been the one thing she could dive into and use to ignore her own life and problems. If she was helping tell other people's stories, helping shed light on the wrongs of the world, then she didn't have to deal with her own crap.

She was just up in her head about all the changes coming her way. And her dad dying without them having resolved anything. Everything was so messed up right now.

She simply needed…nothing she could put into words. Not even to herself. There was nothing simple about this situation or what she wanted.

So she closed her eyes and tried to sleep even as it pulled away from her. Tomorrow someone would be trying to kill her, apparently. She couldn't be sure, of course, but that conversation between Edward Killeen and the guy who worked for him was beyond ominous.

And giving his son a strong alibi? Yeah, she needed to shelve all the other nonsense in her brain and just focus on staying alive.

Not worry about a future with a man she loved but could never have.

CHAPTER 17

I'm not as mean as I could be—and I think people should acknowledge that.

Bradford paused at the bottom of the stairs at the sound of two distinct voices coming from the kitchen the next morning. Frowning, he hurried, only to find Hope pouring a mug of coffee for Berlin.

Who looked quite smug.

"What are you doing here?" he demanded.

"Well, good morning to you too. I was just telling your wife about what we found yesterday—and what I've found in the last few hours while you slackers were sleeping. Not you," she added, looking at Hope. "This is mostly reserved for Bradford."

He liked the whole "wife" thing. It had taken an act of will not to go to her bedroom last night. "Why are you picking on me?" he muttered as he stalked to grab his own mug of coffee. "And how did you get in here without alerting me?"

"I'm going to pretend you didn't ask the second question." She sniffed slightly but then her expression turned feral. "And I'm just messing with you... But I found something and figured I'd stop by and meet Hope properly. Also, I'd like to install some cameras inside here before we head out."

"Wait, what?" Hope blinked, clearly still waking up as she looked at Berlin.

"Killeen's guy is going to make a move sometime this afternoon," Bradford said, because he'd already planned to install cameras as well. He and his people needed more information—like the names and faces of whoever Killeen was sending after Hope—because they were walking dead men. "It sounded like they're going to target you in town, blame it on that guy Ned Hall. But when you don't show up to your lawyer's office, they'll likely send guys here. They'll have to change their plan."

And again, it was taking everything in him not to just hunt Killeen down and end him. But that would only solve part of the problem. They needed to find out if Edward Killeen himself had a boss, how deep this threat ran, and who else he worked with. It sounded like it was Killeen running his operation through his farm, but there could be more to this. And Bradford wanted all the details before they moved on the guy. Otherwise there could be blowback on Hope and that was the last thing he wanted.

"Exactly, and we're going to try to catch whoever is after her on video. Get proof," Berlin said. "That's why we need cameras inside your place."

Hope nodded slowly. "Yeah, that makes sense. I keep wondering if we should tell the sheriff—"

"No," Bradford and Berlin said at the same time.

Hope held her palms up. "I get it. It's not my instinct to call the cops either, but Crow was friends with my dad." She paused. "Of course, he hinted he wanted me to drop the charges against the son. Fine, yeah, okay."

"If we do bring anyone in, it'll be a couple Feds we know," Berlin added as Bradford pulled out a stool and sat next to her. "Anyway, I know where Edward Killeen is going to be today, and I figured you'd want to tail him. You guys can do it while we put cameras up here."

"Who's this *we*?" Hope murmured.

"Friends just waiting for me to give the go-ahead," Berlin said. "Basically everyone who showed up to your dad's funeral."

Hope nodded, looking a little surprised.

Bradford got up and pulled out eggs and sausage from the fridge as Berlin continued. "Last night Killeen made a few phone calls, and has lunch plans a couple towns over. I don't know if it's part of his own alibi or what, but I don't think it'll hurt for you guys to tail him."

"He'll recognize me." Hope poured another cup of coffee, then topped off his, which made him smile. "I want lots of cheese in my eggs," she whispered to him.

At least she didn't seem angry at him for his comments last night. To be fair, he wasn't sorry and he stood by them. But still, he didn't want friction between them—not that kind anyway. Aaaand he had to cut those thoughts off. Now definitely wasn't the time for that.

"Nah, you can wear a wig and you'll be fine. He's not going to be looking for you anyway," Berlin said.

And she wasn't wrong. In his experience, people saw what they wanted to. "Killeen might be more aware than most people though."

"I know, but wigs and a few other little changes should make a big difference. And it's not like you'll be driving one of your own vehicles. Look, if you don't want to go—"

"No," Hope said quickly. "I want to follow him."

Berlin gave Bradford a smug look because of course she did. He didn't want Hope going, but he also knew he couldn't stop her. Something Berlin had obnoxiously pointed out.

He turned back to the stove. "So we'll follow him, and you guys will plant cameras here. We're also going to drop our bags off at the rental." He looked at Hope, who nodded.

"I'm going to go pack some of my toiletries," she said, stepping away from the island top. "But I'll be back down to eat."

He nodded, smiling until he heard her upstairs. Then he swiveled on Berlin, who'd added rainbow highlights to her hair sometime in the last twelve hours. He was pretty sure they were clip-ins or something.

"What are you really doing here?" he whispered. Because they hadn't talked about this at all. She was supposed to come later once he and Hope were gone.

Berlin shrugged. "I wanted to talk to her, meet her in person. I'm the only one who doesn't really know her. She likes you, I can tell."

She'd better more than just like him; she'd freaking married him and never filed for divorce. "I'm not having this conversation."

"Fine, but you asked and I'm being honest. You're my friend so I want to get to know her. Also, the others wanted me to come in first and see what the reception would be like, if she'd be okay with planting cameras."

"And they figured *you* would be the least threatening option?" They weren't wrong. He adored her, but still, he had to give her a little grief.

"Hey!" She was indignant. "I am a freaking delight and people love me."

"Fair enough. So you find anything else?"

"Eh, sort of. Mostly Hailey and I are still combing through his financials. Oh, Gage is pitching in too since he has some down time."

"Oh." That was unexpected. And nice. Gage was one of the founders of Redemption Harbor Security, based out of their original office, and a scary genius. Bradford was pretty sure the NSA had tried to recruit him.

"Mostly I think he's going a little stir-crazy at home."

Yeah, Bradford could see that. His wife had given birth recently, so he'd been spending all his time at home supporting her. Considering the man was obsessed with his wife and new baby, Bradford doubted he hated being home. But their friends and family had been a huge help as well, so yeah,

Gage probably had some down time and needed to be doing something to keep his brain stimulated. "Whatever the reason, I'll take all the help we can get. And in case I haven't said it, thank you for this."

She shot him a hard look. "Please don't ever thank me again for helping you. You're my family in every way that counts."

He cracked another egg. "Never going to stop thanking you." She'd been an unexpected friend later in his life, an absolute weirdo who he was grateful to call his family.

"So...did anything happen between you two?" she whispered.

"Again, I'm not having this conversation." Mostly because nothing had happened. "Freaking nosy."

"Fine, but you're no fun."

"You know, I can't hear that enough." He glanced at his cell, saw another text from Rowan.

Are you cooking? We're starving. Can we come in? Adalyn is hangry.

"Wait, are the others *here* here?" he asked Berlin. He'd assumed they were still back at the rental waiting for her to give the go-ahead.

"Oh, like a mile down the road. I just told them you were cooking if they were hungry."

Snorting, he texted Rowan back. *Come on over.*

He really hoped that Hope didn't mind the intrusion, but at the same time he was grateful to have his people here. It meant she was that much more protected. And fine, they could act as a temporary buffer while Hope digested everything he'd said last night. He knew her, knew she was mulling over his words.

By the time he finished cooking everything, everyone had crowded into the kitchen. Hope finally returned, her eyes a little wide as she took in all the people and the food.

"I owe you more groceries. And..." He slid a plate over to her with the omelet he'd made just for her. "Extra cheese."

She took the plate with a soft smile. "You don't owe me anything. Besides, I think I have like twenty gifted casseroles in the freezer anyway. I just remembered them. We should bring some with us when we drop off our bags. I can share them with everyone."

He nodded, wishing he had the right to kiss her. Hoping he would again soon. And he loved that she was sharing with his friends—and knew that if she just opened herself up, she would fit right into his world and make it *their* world. "Good idea."

***

Hope watched in fascination as Adalyn, a gorgeous redhead married to Rowan, ordered everyone around with a familiarity that said she was definitely the boss.

Hope knew she shouldn't be surprised—none of the guys had ever been sexist assholes, a rarity in her experience—but she still kind of was. Rowan had been the team leader back when she'd been assigned to the group, but Hailey had... Well, she'd sort of bossed them around too. But that had been different because she'd been in Intelligence and had mostly ordered them to "be safe" and "stay alive" over the comm lines.

"Okay," Adalyn said, looking at Hope and Bradford. "Rowan and I will be driving separately, but we'll head out about ten minutes before you in case anyone is watching the main road. You're sure you're good with this?" She motioned to the others, who were laying out little cameras and random tools all over Hope's now Lysol clean island countertop.

"I mean, please don't put cameras in my shower or anything, but yeah, this is good."

The woman blinked, then let out a surprised laugh. "Definitely not. Okay, we'll be heading out now." She nodded once at Bradford. "Keep your comms on and let me know when you've parked."

"Will do. See you soon."

"So...do I get to put my wig on now?" His friends had come with a bag of disguises, and while this whole thing had anxiety stirring inside her, she liked the idea of going incognito.

With a half smile that hit her square in the heart, Bradford nodded. "Come on. We'll let them do their thing and get ready upstairs."

She'd already brought her bags downstairs, so she followed after him. It didn't take long for her to put on a short wavy blond wig, a red Nike sports visor and Jackie O-style sunglasses that wouldn't look a bit out of place in this weather. She just appeared to be a woman running errands in athletic gear. "If I didn't know it was me, I wouldn't glance at me twice," she murmured at her reflection.

Bradford had on a similar visor, his with a local sports team logo. His clothes were the same style as hers, as if he was going to play a round of golf somewhere. And he'd dusted something in his hair that had given it a salt-and-pepper look with lots of salt. It was like looking into his future in another decade or so, and he was just as hot as a more mature version of himself.

You won't be with him then, a nasty voice whispered at the back of her mind. God, she hated herself. The idea of not being in his life sliced deep but... She really was a coward. Why couldn't she just take the risk? It was so much easier to write other people's stories than actually live her own.

He nodded once at their reflection as he pulled out his own sunglasses. "We'll blend just fine."

Once they were on their way, in a Jeep they were borrowing from one of his crew as another layer to keep them from being noticed, she said, "I like your friends. I like that you've found a real family." She wasn't sure if she should say anything, but whatever, she was glad he had such a solid group of people around him when he'd had no one he could depend on growing up.

"Thank you," he murmured. He started to say more, then his phone rang. Berlin's name was on the screen. "Hey, you're on speaker."

"Found something interesting. Didn't pop up the first go-around, but Killeen's wife owns the coffee shop he's going to be at today. As well as most of the shops on that same strip. It's buried pretty deep and I have a feeling that Killeen is the one who set it up, but she's the actual owner. I don't know if it means anything yet, but wanted to let you know."

"Thanks."

"That's interesting," Hope murmured after he'd hung up the phone. "I'm getting the feeling that there's a bigger puzzle we're not seeing. These are shops that they own, towns over from here. So they, or he, owns these huge chunks of real estate." And she could feel that familiar buzz start up that this could be a great story—without the part where someone wanted to kill her. "Though I still don't understand why Killeen wants to kill me."

"Sometimes people don't need a deep reason." Bradford's fingers tightened around the steering wheel, his knuckles going white. "But yeah, I agree."

On instinct, she reached out a hand and squeezed his forearm.

His muscles relaxed under her touch and she *might* have trailed her fingers along his forearm as she dropped her hand. She liked touching him, missed him in a way she didn't want to fully accept.

"I like when you touch me," he rasped out, taking her by surprise.

"I like touching you," she admitted, the words just falling out.

And now he was gripping the steering wheel even tighter.

What was wrong with her? She shouldn't be telling him that. Shouldn't be admitting anything when it came to him. But she'd sensed from day one that Bradford would be her greatest weakness.

CHAPTER 18

"This is the most boring part of the job," Hope said as she took the iced coffee Bradford handed her, tried not to suck it all down. But it was like walking on the sun out here. Summers in Louisiana were not for the faint of heart.

Rowan and Adalyn were in the coffee shop across the street, because even with their disguises, she and Bradford had opted to keep some distance. Smarter to be backup rather than get caught on cameras or run directly into Killeen.

So they'd grabbed drinks from an adorable pink-and-teal food truck parked across the street that sold coffee, pastries and even ice cream. Considering how hot it was outside already, she was thinking about getting one.

"Right." He took his own coffee then dropped a tip in the bucket before he fell in step with her.

Even though it was early enough not to be melting heat yet, there still weren't a ton of people out on Bohn Street. Luckily they found a shaded bench underneath a crepe myrtle and sat, just a random couple enjoying their coffees and taking pictures and videos with her cell phone.

"Anyone look familiar to you?" he asked, his voice low enough so only she could hear.

"No, but that doesn't mean anything. I didn't recognize over half the people at my dad's funeral, and this is a couple towns over." It was unlikely she'd run into any familiar faces. She hadn't been home in so long that she barely knew anyone anymore.

"I think this might be him," Bradford said as he took a sip of his coffee.

A giant truck pulled into a spot a couple slots down from the coffee shop, and yep, Edward Killeen got out, his expression intense as he stalked toward the front door.

"He didn't even look around or anything. He's not worried about anyone watching him." Hope took a sip of her latte. No one was paying them any attention anyway. Most people were ordering their drinks from the nearby food truck, then heading on their way. They would need to move in a little bit too if they wanted to plant a tracker on his truck before he left.

"He's talking to one of the waitresses." Adalyn's voice came over the comm line. "And...oh, these two are more than friends."

Hope's cell phone buzzed and she saw that Adalyn had sent both her and Bradford a group text... A picture of Edward Killeen with his hand gripping a dark-haired woman's hip in a very possessive manner. They weren't making out or anything, but they were way too close to just be friends, or employer and employee. The woman was looking up at him as if he hung the moon and he was staring down at her as if he wanted to screw her right up against the countertop.

"Picture really does say a thousand words. Bet his wife won't like this," Bradford said.

"Unless they have an open marriage." Hope didn't get that. She would never have shared Bradford.

Bradford just snorted. "Somehow I doubt it."

"They're heading to the back now," Adalyn said. "I'm trying to get into their camera system."

"You guys really just don't care about breaking the law, do you?" Hope murmured.

Bradford turned to her, and even with his sunglasses on she could see his surprise. "Does it bother you?"

"Hell no." Maybe it should, but in her experience, the people she went after didn't follow the letter of the law so why should she? It didn't make sense to play by an arbitrary set of rules and let assholes off the hook because they were playing by a different set than the rest of the world. To bring stories to light, she'd had to bend the law more than once and she was fine with it. As long as she could still look at herself in the mirror in the mornings, she was doing all right. "I mean, I have some lines I won't cross, but this isn't one of them." And this guy wanted to kill her, so screw him.

"Any more on that story you're sort of writing?" he asked.

She was aware that the others were on the comm line, so she kept it vague. "Maybe. One of my sources sent me a video this morning. It's pretty damning. I'm not sure what I'm going to do with it yet."

"She doesn't want to tell her story?"

"Not yet. But I think she wanted me to have the evidence, as if she thought I was unsure of her story. She's a tough one to read so I don't know. She literally sent it with a short note telling me to watch, that's it." Hope had been talking to three women, and this was the one she'd approached cold, based on a tip from one of the man's other victims. "She could just be working up to it. It happens that way sometimes."

Or more often than not. People were scared to come forward, to put their lives on display for the rest of the world to judge and plaster their opinions all over the internet. It often took time to mentally prepare. And even then, there was only so much preparation a person could do. "If I was unscrupulous, I'd just leak the damn video and sit back as it went viral. Hell, she could have done that if she wanted to, but she sent it to me instead."

"You think the video would go viral?"

She snorted softly. "No doubt. Even with all the trash today online, this one would rise to the top quickly." He was a well-known man—the governor of Mississippi. Someone whose name had been floated as a potential VP in another decade plus. So yeah, a video of him slapping one of his interns when she'd rejected his sexual advances, then tearing at her shirt—and only stopping when he was interrupted—would go viral. Of course, some people would say it was fake even if it was authenticated.

People would judge the victim, analyze the woman's entire life, her choices, what she'd been wearing the day she'd been attacked.

"You okay?" Bradford squeezed her leg gently, clearly having read her expression.

She gave him a small smile, nodded. "Yeah. Just...wishing the world was a better place, that's all."

"Me too..."

They both paused as Adalyn said, "Okay, I'm in. Sending you a live feed of what I've got."

Hope scooted a little closer to watch his screen, trying not to pay attention to how good he smelled. Or what being so close to him did to her. But his scent alone brought up so many memories of being tangled up with him in the sheets, of lounging in bed just talking and laughing with each other—

No, focus!

She forced herself to watch the feed, which was just an empty hallway. The angle of the video was from up high, set in a corner of a long hallway. There were a few doors, two of them open. "Any sound?"

Bradford increased his volume as Adalyn said, "None yet. Not sure if it has that capability."

A whole lot of nothing happened so she glanced around the street, seeing if anything looked off. Not that she actually expected it to, but still. She wanted to be aware of her surroundings, even if she was confident in her disguise—and having Bradford next to her.

Bradford made a soft humming sound and she glanced back to see… "Oh my. You think he forgot about the cameras?"

"Maybe he doesn't care," Bradford murmured.

"They're not live," Adalyn said. "Well, he doesn't think they are. I'm using the recording function now to get all this for later."

Killeen had the waitress pressed up against a wall. Her legs were wrapped around him, and they were making out pretty hard as he slipped his hand under her skirt.

She was grinding against him like an overzealous porn star.

"Kinda glad we don't have any audio," she whispered. "So ridiculous."

Bradford snickered, then glanced around, likely making sure no one else noticed what they were looking at.

Nope, no one was paying them any attention as they went about their lives. And the tree gave them decent cover from any prying eyes.

Killeen went down on his knees as he flipped the woman's skirt up and… There was more grinding, more over-the-top thrusts and likely moans Hope was so grateful she didn't have to hear. The whole thing was per-formative. And then… "Barf." She looked away as Killeen pulled his dick out.

"Maybe we'll learn some moves," Bradford said around a laugh.

Oh, his moves were just fine.

"I need brain bleach," Rowan muttered, the first time he'd spoken over the comms.

"Whatever, this is fantastic," Adalyn said. "Because now we've got something to use against him with his wife. If she finds out he's cheating on her, she might turn on him."

Hope kept her gaze averted as the two of them continued gyrating against the wall. "What's the point of doing it out in the hall for anyone to see? Don't they care about her coworkers?"

"Maybe that's their kink." Bradford shot her a sideways glance. "Maybe they like the thought of getting caught."

"More likely Killeen likes the thought of someone seeing him banging a woman half his age." Men and their stupid egos.

Bradford laughed lightly. "You're probably not wrong." He looked back at the screen, then winced. "I've seen enough of this guy's dick."

"You and me both." This from Rowan.

As they started cleaning up, a message popped up from Berlin on Bradford's phone. *They're definitely using the coffee shop and other businesses to funnel money. I'll have the details later for you, but his wife is hella rich on paper since she owns these places.*

Interesting indeed. "I'd love to out him to his wife," Hope whispered. "Just blow up everything, since he wants to, you know, *end mine*."

"No shit." Bradford squeezed her thigh gently and didn't take his hand away immediately.

And she hated that she wanted to lean into him, to tell him that he could leave his hand there. Maybe...hooking up again wouldn't be a terrible thing. They were stuck together because of this mess and she'd missed him so much. Missed everything about him, including the things he did with his talented mouth and fingers and...

She forced herself to shut down all the images that wanted to surface. It was already hot enough outside; she didn't need to burst into flames in public.

But...maybe they could hook up and try to get each other out of their systems? Move on for good. Yeah, that was just wishful thinking.

"You ready?" Bradford murmured.

"Yep."

They both stood and casually strolled down the sidewalk to the crosswalk. As they reached it, they tossed their empty cups in the recycle bin, then continued on their way.

As they neared Killeen's truck, Hope pulled up her phone, pretended to take a call as Bradford slipped between his vehicle and the one parked next to it. He bent down as if he was tying his shoes, slipped a magnetic tracker up inside the undercarriage, then walked on without missing a beat.

She waited on the sidewalk until he joined her a minute later.

"He's still in the back," Adalyn said. "Might be here for a while. You two are good to go if you want."

"I think we'll stick around until he heads out," Bradford said, eyebrows raised as he looked at Hope.

She nodded in agreement. Finding out what the Killeens were up to was her main priority right now.

CHAPTER 19

"You sure this is a good idea?" Hope asked, trying to keep the worry out of her voice. *And failing.* Even though she knew she was safe now that they were at the rental house, she was still nervous.

"I've done this before hundreds of times. We're just going to try to get one of these guys to talk. That's it." Bradford sounded so sure of himself, which of course he was. She knew how much experience he had.

Still... "I don't like any of this. We should just let them break into my place..." She paused when her cell phone buzzed. Her heart rate kicked up when she saw the message, so she held it out to him.

Hey Hope, this is Chelsea. I've got a new number. If you have time, could you stop by my office in an hour? I need to go over some things with your dad's estate. In court now, can't talk. But I'll see you then?

"This is exactly what Killeen said he was going to do," she murmured.

"Text the number back," Berlin murmured from the kitchen table where she had a couple laptops set up and was monitoring all sorts of things, including Hope's phone.

"And this is exactly why I'm going to your place," Bradford said quickly. Then, surprising her, he kissed the top of her head and headed out of the kitchen to meet the others, who were already geared up and waiting for him in one of the SUVs.

She couldn't argue with him, not when some of his friends were still in the kitchen—watching her. Probably judging her.

"Sit with Berlin," Hailey gently ordered. "I'm going to make us all tea."

It was only Hope, Berlin, Hailey, and Hailey's husband, Jesse. Magnolia was upstairs resting—and no wonder, since she was so pregnant. Fleur was with her, keeping her company and watching "trashy TV" according to her.

Hailey's husband was sitting at the island top on his own laptop, working away and talking quietly into his phone via Bluetooth. He'd been working from practically the moment Hope and Bradford had arrived back at their rental place, but he was still friendly.

Biting back a sigh, Hope sat at the oversized table in the kitchen nook that overlooked a large backyard and pond.

"He's really good at his job," Berlin said, her smile soft. "Promise."

Okay, so not judging. His friends really were kind. "I know. I'm just worried."

"They've got this. Adalyn will make sure they all come back in one piece."

Hope simply nodded and looked at the screens. It was weird to see images of her dad's home—her home—on-screen at various angles. "Thank you all, for helping." She knew they were doing it for Bradford, but she was still grateful.

"It's no problem. We all like a mystery, and we love Bradford." Hailey set a cup of tea in front of Hope and then sat across from her and Berlin. She had a tablet in front of her she'd been working on, but she glanced over as her husband raised his voice. "Uh oh," she whispered. "He's going into Scary Jesse mode. Someone's about to get fired."

Her husband stood then, phone in his hand as he stalked from the room.

"Aww, I was hoping to hear him get mean," Berlin said without taking her eyes off the screen.

Hope felt weird sitting there with nothing to do, especially since she didn't know these women. Sure, she'd met Hailey years before, but she didn't actually know her the way she did Bradford.

"So is that them on-screen?" There was a small map in one corner of one of the screens, with a handful of dots moving along at about forty-five MPH.

"Yep. They've got trackers embedded in their vests and in their shoes. Just in case. We like to be prepared."

She wanted to ask more about what they did as a company—it was clear that they were way more than a security company—but never would. She would ask Bradford later, but she couldn't imagine them telling her anyway. And she wanted to hear it from him.

"This is good tea," she murmured into the quiet, feeling off-balance with these strangers as she worried about Bradford. She would never forgive herself if anything happened to him because of her.

"Thanks." Hailey smiled at her. "I've read your work over the years. It's really good. I loved that huge piece you did on fraud, obviously. But my favorite one is your ongoing series about corruption in local government and how it affects the broader community. It's been really eye-opening."

"Ah, thank you."

"I imagine it's hard to write about that all the time. To know how much money is being mishandled and the damage it's doing on a consistent basis—with no end in sight."

"Wow, yeah, it really is. And I'm not complaining, but yes, it's been very emotionally draining. Probably worse in the last couple years. It feels like there's just so much noise out there right now and it's hard to get people to care about things on a local level. I think that's the most frustrating thing of all. People will post all over social media, but then not actually get involved or even vote. I'm... I find myself getting jaded."

Hailey nodded. "I can definitely understand that. But you're doing good work, just FYI. What you're writing matters."

"Thank you... I might be taking a break soon," she said, mainly because she wanted to tell someone other than her friend Thea and Bradford.

"Good for you," Berlin murmured as she worked on something on her computer. "You're going to burn yourself out otherwise."

Surprised, she glanced at the other woman.

"What? I've read your stuff too. It's bleak as shit. But that's why we do what we do." Her mouth curved into what Hope could only describe as a feral grin as she started clicking away.

"She just found something," Hailey whispered conspiratorially. "We're about to be invisible to her for a couple minutes at least."

Smiling at Hailey, she felt something ease in her chest. These women were really kind. Way more welcoming than she'd expected. "I've read about some of the new things you, your husband, and his friend, or partner I think, Constantine Pierce, have been doing the last few years. It's impressive."

"He gets all the credit," Hailey said with a smile.

"Don't be all modest." Berlin still didn't look up from what she was doing, but she was smiling.

"Fine. Since we've gotten married, I've used his money—"

Berlin cleared her throat.

"Oh my god, *our* money, stop interrupting," Hailey shot Berlin a pointed look before turning back to Hope. "We've started a charitable foundation whose main goal is to combat food insecurity, specifically with kids. But also with families, especially single-parent households. Too many kids aren't being fed enough, are going to school hungry, and frankly I think that's bullshit. Both Jesse and I grew up in the foster system so we know firsthand how tough it can be. We're trying to work with local schools for now to make sure all kids are getting fed breakfast and lunch and... I'm about to go off on a tangent." Her cheeks flushed pink.

"No, I love hearing about this. Is it weird if I ask to talk to you later and maybe do a story on this? Like an in-depth one on the two of you, about your program?"

"She would love to," Berlin said.

"Oh my god, you're driving me nuts today," Hailey muttered. "And yes, I would love to. I think she just misses her man," she whispered conspiratorially to Hope.

"I can hear you and I do... Okay, here we go. The team has arrived and they're setting up outside. They're going to hang back and see what happens, who shows up."

Any levity disappeared as Hope turned and focused on the screens.

"I'll catch anyone inside your house though, which might come in handy later if we can get their faces on-screen."

Hope knew all this, they'd been over it before, but she was still glad that Berlin seemed to be walking her through everything again. All of this was so overwhelming.

It was one thing to write stories about others. She was always on the periphery, the narrator or storyteller. This wasn't a story, it was her life. And it was hard to sit back and wait for some strangers to break into her childhood home. But she was trusting the process of all this. Trusting Bradford.

It was clear they knew what they were doing. And she knew she'd be lost without them. Hell, she'd have likely headed to Chelsea's office today without question, and she didn't even want to think about what that would have looked like.

CHAPTER 20

Bradford watched from the cover of trees as a single SUV parked about a mile from Hope's place. He and the others were spread out, with him closest to the end of her driveway.

Her family home was a couple miles back from the road, so if she had been home, it was unlikely she'd have heard these guys arriving.

He was in camouflage, up in one of the oak trees, watching through his scope as four assholes got out of the SUV, one by one.

While he wanted to be point on this, Adalyn had very firmly told him to get his head out of his ass. She was right, as always.

He wasn't going to let his anger at the situation get in the way of clear thinking. So Tiago was tasked with keeping an eye on the main road entrance, Bradford was at the halfway point, and Adalyn, Ezra, and Rowan were at different points closer to the house.

They'd talked about waiting inside the house, but no one wanted to leave any evidence behind if things went south. Much easier to clean up outside as opposed to trying to clean blood off Hope's kitchen floors or cabinets.

Not that he wanted it to get that far. But they always thought ahead. They had to.

As he sat there watching the suspects pop the hatch then pull out multiple weapons apiece, he had to steady his breathing. He couldn't think about what would have happened if Hope had been here alone. That way lay madness.

At a buzzing sound in his pocket, he glanced down at the burner he'd brought for this mission. They were all linked by comms, but had decided to go relatively dark in case the enemy had access to their radio channel.

The text message was from Adalyn, telling everyone that she had access to the other guys' radio channel and to turn to it.

He quickly switched over his feed, but kept himself muted just in case.

"We move in fast, take care of this. It has to look like a robbery," a dark-haired man with a clean-cut face said. So he was the one in charge of this. No visible tattoos, looked like a normal guy Bradford wouldn't glance twice at on the street, except for the vest and tactical gear. "For whatever reason she didn't show up to her lawyer's. If the husband is here, we take him out too. We can still pin this on Hall if necessary."

Not likely.

"What about a rape if it's just the woman? That might sell this better." There was amusement in one of the guys' voices.

Oh, Asshole Number Two had just signed his death warrant, Bradford thought as he zeroed in on him via his scope. Blond hair, scruffy beard. Some kind of tattoo on his neck. Yeah, he'd remember that face.

It would be so damn easy to pull the trigger. Just a couple pounds of pressure, then boom.

Don't. Do. It. A text from Adalyn.

He responded with a thumbs-up, because that was about all he had in him at the moment. He might be pissed and want all of these guys dead, but he wouldn't screw this up.

He couldn't.

"Man, shut the hell up with that. You know the orders."

"I'm just playing. Jesus. No one can take a joke anymore about any-thing."

The other two were silent, but they all pulled on balaclavas, which told Bradford they had a decent amount of training.

"I hate these stupid things," Asshole Two muttered.

"Then why don't you wait in the SUV?" the one who was clearly the leader growled before stalking off.

The mouthy one didn't say anything, but fell in step with the other three as they hurried down the drive.

"Split up. I'll take the front, Weezer, you take the back. Blue, Red, you know what to do."

There were grunts of agreement, but he couldn't see anyone anymore.

Am I clear? he texted the group.

And got a thumbs-up from Adalyn.

I'm planting a tracker while they break in, Bradford added.

Once he received the go-ahead, he quickly climbed down from the tree, and after another scan from the shadows of the oak, he made his way to the SUV. Instead of just slapping one directly under the carriage, he crawled under and slid one in where it wouldn't be found easily.

The magnetic tracker was strong enough to withstand almost anything.

"Where the hell is she?" A male voice came over the radio as Bradford rolled out from under the truck. The jerk who'd joked about rape before.

"Quiet." The leader.

"She's obviously not here. This is ridiculous."

"Then we wait a little longer. If we don't get her, the backup team in town will."

So they had more than one team in place? He'd made the assumption that when she didn't show up to her lawyer's, whoever had been sent to kill her would simply come here. And he'd also assumed that Killeen would send two guys max.

Four men for a single civilian woman seemed like overkill, but Killeen must be factoring in Bradford's presence too. The guy didn't seem to know anything about him, based on the audio they'd captured, but they'd likely sent two men for Bradford, two for Hope.

"I don't like this. Her vehicle is still here but she's not." A new, raspier voice. "Something feels off."

"I'm with Blue on this. I don't like this at all."

"God, and you two say I'm a whiner."

"Someone shut him up," the raspy voice growled. "Hey…I saw a flash of something. Scope maybe."

The four men went silent.

Visual? he texted.

Setting sun must have given away my location. On the move, Rowan responded.

Disable their vehicle, Adalyn ordered.

Bradford gave a thumbs-up, then got to work disabling the fuel pump. He'd done this far too many times on different missions over the years. He wasn't sure what the plan was anymore, but since they'd potentially been made, they had to keep these guys here until law enforcement could arrive—if Adalyn made the decision to call the cops.

He was against that, but four guys on Hope's property in tactical gear, caught on cameras they didn't know about? That wasn't going to look good for any of them—and he had a feeling the mouthy one would turn on the others. Maybe even Killeen.

This could be the break they were waiting for.

Bradford heard a gunshot in the distance, cursed. *Shit.*

Using the woods and the growing shadows from the setting sun surrounding the long drive as cover, he sprinted in the direction of the shot.

As he moved, he spotted one of the masked men racing through the trees right at him. This was not what he'd expected or wanted.

Before he could make a decision, the man went for his holstered weapon.

No other choice.

Bradford raised his rifle, had it against his shoulder in milliseconds, and pulled the trigger before the other man had fully raised his arm. He preferred his SIG, but there'd been no time to pull it out.

The man sprawled on the ground.

Keeping his weapon up, he hurried to the fallen man and kicked away his weapon. He didn't even have to check his pulse. Not with the hole in the guy's head.

Suddenly Adalyn's voice came over the comms. "They're all down. B, you good?"

He hadn't heard any shots so the others must have used knives. "Yep. Tango down here too."

She was silent for a long moment, then said, "Everyone convene at the front of the house. We have to move fast with this."

"Still keeping watch," Tiago added. "We're clear for now."

Even though it sounded like all four men were down, he kept his weapon up and his senses on alert as he headed to the meeting point.

There was one dead man on the front steps. He couldn't see the other two, but knew they had to be nearby.

"We have limited options," Adalyn said as Bradford approached their team.

Everyone's expression was grim.

"He pulled his weapon on me first," Bradford said, even though she would already know it.

Adalyn nodded. "Same with everyone else."

"Stupid," Rowan muttered in frustration. "Guy came at me with a knife."

"Unless anyone objects, I want to take fingerprints, and photographs of their tattoos and faces. Then move the bodies and SUV. We'll have to disable any tracking on the SUV."

"Berlin will want to dump their phones," Ezra added.

"It looks like they're all burners and I don't think we should take the chance of them being tracked. I say we put them in the SUV, move it, then kill all the electronics at once when it's far away from here. I want to screw with Killeen now. He won't know what happened to his guys and no one will be reporting a break-in. If he is tracking them, he'll only know that they came here, then left. And that's it."

"What are we doing with the bodies?" Bradford asked. He didn't love this idea, but it made sense. They had no idea who to trust in this town, and if they called the local cops on this... They would all get brought in and have to answer some very awkward questions. And he didn't trust the local sheriff anyway.

Nope, they couldn't get on anyone's radar. Sure it had been self-defense, but it didn't matter at this point. Whoever had sent these guys, maybe Killeen's boss if he had one, would then know Bradford and his team were involved with Hope.

It was an easy decision.

"We'll store them in a freezer for now. I've got...a location in mind." Adalyn's voice was dry. "But we'll have to transport fast."

He had a feeling he knew where she was talking about. Redemption Harbor Security had various storage units all over the southeast, rented under one shell corporation or another. Nothing that could be tied back to them.

They kept stores of weapons in some, random antiques in others, and freezers in more than a handful of them. Because these were definitely not the first dead bodies they'd dealt with.

"Why don't you and Rowan transport the bodies and the rest of us will clean up here, make sure there's no trace of their tire tracks, forensics, anything." Not that Bradford thought Killeen would report these guys missing, but they needed to make it look like the men had come and gone. Or maybe not even arrived at all, depending upon if they had been tracked.

Adalyn nodded and they all got to work. He wasn't sure how much to tell Hope about this. Berlin was monitoring the interior of her house, but he wasn't sure what she was letting Hope see.

He shelved all of that for now. They had a job to do, and he wanted to get it done fast in case backup arrived.

CHAPTER 21

"Yikes, these are some nasty guys." Hope looked at what Berlin had pulled up on-screen after running the tattoos, faces, and fingerprints of the guys Bradford and his team had killed.

He was safe, the only thing that mattered.

Though, it was sort of weird that they'd had a place to hide the bodies, but Hope was going out of her way to not ask questions right now. It went against her nature, but she knew when to be curious and when to keep her mouth shut. They were trying to protect her.

"Yep. The fact that they get tattoos to announce their affiliation is stupid, but also helpful," Berlin said as Hope stepped back from her screen.

The four dead guys were all affiliated with some fringe group that believed in what amounted to anarchy and absolutely no government. They basically wanted individual militias where they lived—which made no freaking sense. But she'd learned that sense didn't often play into the weird fantasies these nuts had.

"Any link to Killeen?" she asked.

"Not that I can find online. Yet. But if there's one, I'll find it."

Hailey cleared her throat much in the same way Berlin had been doing to her earlier.

"Fine, Hailey is helping too."

Hailey sniffed a little, but grinned as she went back to her computer.

"Would you guys mind if I headed to my room and crashed for a bit?" Bradford was supposed to be back soon and she'd done nothing but worry about him since he'd been gone. She needed to decompress.

"Of course," Berlin said. "We'll probably pop a couple of those casseroles in for later."

"Sounds good." But she was mostly mentally checked out at this point.

She just wanted to see Bradford, to hold him and know he was okay. He'd texted her and she knew from Berlin that he was fine, but seeing him would hit on a different level.

After stripping down, she took a hot shower, which refreshed her somewhat, but that worry was still buried deep even when she finally emerged from the bathroom in a swath of steam... And found Bradford sitting on the pink cushy chair by the window.

"Hey." She was moving before she was conscious of it.

"I'm gross and sweaty," he muttered as he stood.

That was when she saw that he'd even placed a towel underneath him so he wouldn't get the chair dirty.

"I don't care." She pulled him into a tight hug and was grateful when he held her close, burying his face into her towel wrap.

"You smell good," he murmured.

"You don't."

He let out a startled bark of laughter as he pulled back. "You're not wrong. I need to grab a shower, then I'll tell you everything."

She already had some of the details, had heard a shot, so knew something had gone down, but nodded as he disappeared into the bathroom. As she heard the shower start, she moisturized her arms and legs with lotion she knew Bradford liked, changed into lounge pants and one of her oldest, softest sweatshirts, then lay flat on the bed. She didn't bother taking the towel off her hair, because her comb was in the bathroom and she was too tired to mess with it.

So much had happened since she'd returned home, and she felt like she was coming down from a high or something. Maybe not a high, but… She closed her eyes as she heard the shower continue, pictured his wet, naked body, and tried not to think about what his reaction would be if she decided to join him.

It was just a fantasy, not something she would do, but…they'd showered together before and she'd enjoyed it, thank you very much.

Hope wasn't sure how much time passed, but when she felt the bed depress slightly she opened her eyes and rolled over to find Bradford sitting on the edge, gazing back at her. He had on lounge pants but no shirt and she wanted to trace her fingers over his muscular back and the intricate tattoos covering his arms.

"You can go back to sleep," he whispered as he grabbed a Henley.

"No, I didn't mean to drift off." Yawning, saw it was nine o'clock so she'd only been dozing for half an hour. Even though she was still waking up, she wanted to tell him not to put a shirt on. Hell, she wanted to crawl over to him, straddle him, then take his pants off.

"You hungry?" he murmured.

"I'm not sure." She tried not to stare at him, but it was impossible not to drink in all his hard lines. He'd killed to protect her. That knowledge was buried in her brain now and she couldn't turn it off.

"How about I bring you some food? I think everyone is doing their own thing this evening. And I'd like some down time with you."

Her heart rate kicked up at his words—she wanted to spend quality naked time with him. Knew that if she gave him a hint that was what she wanted, he'd have her pinned against the bed. Or wall. Or any flat surface. But...no. *No, no, no.*

She cleared her throat and stood. "I'll come with you. We can eat then retreat back here." She didn't want to let him out of her sight. She might not have seen anyone shot, but she'd heard a gunshot over the live feed and it had thrown her all the way back to Afghanistan when she'd been assigned to his team.

She'd worried about him and the others then as well. But deep down she'd always worried more about Bradford, no matter how capable he was. That hadn't changed, clearly.

Now...she wanted to thank him for what he'd done for her. Wanted to grab onto him and never let go. But she was terrified of what would happen if things didn't work out.

Though, the more she thought about it, she already didn't have him in her life. If she gave in to this, and lost him...she was right back where she'd started.

***

"You want me to sleep on the floor?" Bradford asked as they stepped back into the bedroom. The rental didn't have enough rooms for them to sleep separately—not that he wanted that.

She gave him a dry look as she slipped under the covers. "We're both adults."

Yeah, both adults who wanted each other—and were still married. She might be trying to keep walls up with him, but he'd seen the way she looked at him earlier. He was hanging by a thread at this point, barely holding back the need to strip her and pin her underneath him on the bed. "Just checking. Glad you said no, because I'm exhausted."

Her eyebrows drew together as he got in next to her, and in a surprising move, she reached out for him. He didn't bother even pretending to hold back, simply pulled her close as that desperate need to touch her took over.

"I was so worried about you," she murmured against his chest, a tremble in her voice.

He loved the way she fit against him so perfectly, the way their bodies fit together. He gently rested his hand on her hip when he wanted to do a whole lot more. But she needed to give him the go-ahead this time. "I'm fine." He'd already told her more than once, but didn't mind soothing her again.

She'd had a lot thrown at her in a short period, right around an incredibly vulnerable time.

"I'm a little weirded out by how fine I am with you guys making those bodies disappear."

He snorted softly. "We'll make sure they're found eventually." They might have to reach out to one of their Fed contacts, but that was a problem for the future.

He simply wanted to savor the present while Hope was in his arms and not worry about any of that shit. And god, she smelled and felt like heaven. That familiar rose oil scent of hers wrapped around him, threw him back to their time in Vegas.

"Berlin told me that Chelsea is fine, likely has no idea someone was pretending to be her," she murmured against his chest.

"Yeah, from what we can tell she has nothing to do with this. They just used her name since she's one of your few contacts in town. It was a smart gamble."

"Yeah, I probably would have gone to her office if I hadn't known what was going on." She was silent for a long moment, then said, "I want to go see Kim tomorrow. She had those coordinates. She definitely knows more. I'll ambush her at her house in the evening when she gets off work."

"Ambush is a strong word."

She laughed lightly. "Seems fitting because I'm not going to tell her." Her grip around him tightened and she scooted even closer until their bodies were flush—and she had to feel his reaction to her now.

Because it was unavoidable with her around.

She stilled for a moment, then rolled her hips against his erection in a slow but very clear invitation.

And just like that, everything else ceased to exist.

"Hope," he managed to grit out. They couldn't do this. Not until he was certain it was more than just physical for her.

"Bradford." Her tone was breathier, inviting.

"We can't...do anything." *Right?*

"Why not?" She leaned back slightly, their faces only inches apart as she looked at him. Her bright blue eyes were dilated, her lust clear.

And it matched his own. "Because..." He had reasons. Really, really, good ones. "You'll just run from me again. And you have nowhere to go right now. It'll mess up the dynamic."

"Not running," she rasped out.

She was lying to herself, then. "Tell yourself that," he whispered as he slid his hand down between her legs so that he was cupping her mound right over her pants. Apparently he had no self-control, even if he wanted to pretend otherwise. Not where she was concerned anyway. "We're not having sex," he managed to get out as she rolled her hips against his hand.

Now who was lying to themselves? Because she might not run tonight, but she'd run later. And he had to have her so damn addicted that she never wanted to run again.

"Okay." She didn't look like she believed him, but that was fine.

"I'm just going to get you off," he growled as he dipped his head to hers, claiming her mouth. Because screw that—if she wanted some relief, he would give it to her.

"I'm getting you off too," she snapped back against his lips.

And fine, he sure as hell wasn't arguing with that.

As they kissed, he could feel himself falling again. Or maybe he'd never stopped falling for her. But her familiar taste, the breathy little sounds she made as he nipped her bottom lip—

He slid his hand up her shirt.

Because he knew she wasn't wearing a bra, and if he was getting her off, he was going to enjoy every inch of her.

She moved faster than him, stripping her shirt off before he'd fully got to palm even one breast.

"Hell," he growled before pinning her to the mattress. He'd missed her so much. Not just the physical stuff, but her, all of her. "You're so gorgeous, it hurts to look at you sometimes."

She covered his mouth. "No, you can't say all this sweet stuff," she whispered.

He nipped her hand. "I'm going to say it. Because I mean it. You're incredible, Hope."

She got that same look she always did when he gave her compliments, as if she wanted to argue or simply didn't know how to take them, but he didn't give her a chance.

Instead he kissed her again as he palmed her breasts, rolling her nipples into tight little points exactly the way she liked it. Oh so slowly, he ran his thumbs over the hard buds, savoring the way her kisses grew more erratic and the way she wrapped her legs around him, digging her heels into his ass.

"Faster," she demanded against his mouth, urgency riding her likely as hard as him.

"So impatient." He gently bit her bottom lip.

"Yes, absolutely I am." She tugged at the bottom of his shirt, practically ripped it over his head. Then she sighed as she raked her gaze over him—and followed with her fingers in soft little sweeps over his bare skin.

His muscles went taut at her gentle touch. No one touched him the way she did, with a sweet reverence he felt to his bones. But he pulled back when she tried to slip her fingers under the band of his lounge pants because he was staying in control. "Nope."

"You make me crazy," she rasped out.

Good. Because he'd barely started. And he needed to keep his pants on if he was going to maintain any semblance of control. Because god knew she wasn't going to help either one of them on that count. "You're going to lie back and hold on to the headboard while I taste exactly what I've been missing."

She sucked in a breath at his words and commanding tone, because she loved it when he told her what to do—but only in the bedroom.

She squirmed against the bed as she did exactly that, gripping onto the headboard as he leaned down and sucked one nipple into his mouth, her moans everything he needed as he teased her. He switched between breasts until she was panting and demanding more.

If only it took pleasure and orgasms, he knew he could keep her tied to him. They'd always had chemistry. But she needed more from him: to feel safe, to know that he wasn't going anywhere.

Laughing lightly against her taut abdomen, he kissed a path down her stomach as he tugged her pants off—and found that she had nothing on underneath.

The sight of her spread out for him, her legs parted, had him harder than he'd ever been. He'd planned to tease her a little more, but god, he needed to get her off with a desperation that bordered on obsession.

Sliding one finger along her slick folds, he groaned at how wet she already was.

Demanding, in pure Hope fashion, she arched her hips against him, trying to make him go faster. As he slid his finger deeper, he crouched between her legs and could feel the tension coiling in her as she dug her heels into his back.

"I've missed you," she rasped out.

She'd been so honest with him when they'd been naked together before, more so than any other time. He wasn't sure if it was because they were both literally bared to each other in those moments, but he'd treasured her realness with him in their intimate moments.

"I've missed you too." He didn't stop teasing her as he murmured the words against her clit.

As he increased his pressure, he added another finger, and neither of them talked after that. He teased and pleasured her with his tongue and hand until he felt her inner walls tightening around his fingers faster and faster.

When she slid her fingers through his hair, clutched onto his head, he knew she was close. He sucked on her clit—and she came hard and fast against his mouth and fingers, with her entire body.

"*Bradford.*" She moaned it like a prayer as her climax hit.

The way she said his name sent a shiver of pure pleasure down his spine. His cock pushed against his pants, his balls pulled up tight as he finally lifted his head to stare up the length of her body.

She watched him, looking a little dazed, but only for a moment before she grabbed his face and pulled him to her, kissing in that full-body way that made every single brain cell leave his head.

He loved the feel of pinning her to the bed, of them being skin to skin, and when she slid her fingers down his pants and gripped his cock, he didn't stop her.

Because this was Hope touching him and he was at his breaking point. As they kissed, she began stroking him until he lost control, coming on her stomach in long, hard strokes that completely wrung him out.

As he came down from his high, she gently let go of his erection then pulled him close, clearly not caring about the mess.

He didn't care either, just wanted to hold her, lose himself in her.

"We're not done," she whispered, kissing him softly as she wrapped her legs around him, holding him close.

He wasn't sure if she meant tonight or in general, but he knew he wasn't done. Wasn't walking away from her. Not after this. It was too soon to tell if anything had changed for her, but he was going to make it impossible for her to leave by the time all this was over.

CHAPTER 22

"She's fine. You can see her," Berlin murmured.

Still staring out the windshield at the sidewalk of Main Street, Bradford still didn't like letting Hope out of his presence. Was that a realistic thing to expect? No. Also, he didn't care. He was irrational and unreasonable when it came to her. "I didn't say anything."

"You're vibrating with energy."

"We're all vibrating with energy."

"Oh my god," she muttered. "Wait, there he is."

Edward Killeen had just stepped out of the hardware store and was striding down the sidewalk, looking half distracted as he headed in the direction of Hope's attorney's office.

Bradford texted Hope, who was waiting in the café next door. *Go time.*

A moment later, Hope stepped out of the café and slid her sunglasses on. She was carrying pepper spray in the pocket of her pants and... Fine, Adalyn was watching Killeen through her scope across the street where she was hiding on top of a building with a clear shot of the sidewalk. If Killeen made one wrong move, she would put a bullet in him.

Was it over-the-top? Yes. And again, he also didn't care. At all. He would have preferred to be right next to Hope, but they were trying to get Killeen's reaction to seeing her in the flesh. And Adalyn would have no problem pulling the trigger.

But more than seeing his reaction, they wanted to see what he did next—who he called. They needed him to unlock his phone.

Bradford watched from the SUV. Saw the moment Killeen spotted Hope walking down the sidewalk toward him.

The guy's body tensed but he didn't go for a weapon, just watched her cautiously. He was stunned that she was alive.

To give her credit, Hope didn't even act as if she saw him, just kept on walking and only stopped when she reached her attorney's office.

Killeen stood there for a long moment, looking as if he was going to follow her.

Bradford had his hand on the door handle, could reach him before he even thought about heading into the lawyer's office behind Hope.

"Hold on," Berlin murmured.

But Killeen turned away and pulled out his cell phone—unlocked it to make a call.

"Here we are. Cover me," Berlin whispered as she slipped out of the passenger seat. She waited until Killeen passed by her, but kept up her pace.

Bradford moved out after her, literally just being her backup in case Killeen realized what she was up to. But Berlin was so damn good, he doubted Killeen would realize anything was off.

The man had unlocked his phone and that was all Berlin needed. But she had to stay within a certain distance of him while she mirrored his phone.

Bradford had a fake coffee cup in hand and a shopping bag he'd stuffed with a towel to give it a shape as he kept a few paces back from Berlin.

Killeen had paused outside a dog grooming shop that advertised their prices right on the window, as well as a display of "puppy treats" that looked more like cupcakes for humans.

Berlin stopped in front of the shop and pretended to take a picture of the prices before she peered inside for a closer look. Bradford sat on one of the nearby benches lining the main strip, glad there was a decent amount of people out on a Tuesday morning. Mostly dog walkers and joggers, but it was right after ten and a lot of shops had just opened up, so more people were starting to park and make their way onto the sidewalk.

Made it a lot easier for him to blend in.

Though Killeen wasn't paying attention to either him or Berlin as he angrily spoke into his cell phone.

When Berlin turned away from him and headed back the way she'd come, Bradford knew she'd gotten what they needed.

Without looking at her, Bradford got up and headed back to the waiting Jeep—one of their company vehicles—and found Adalyn sitting in the back seat, the vehicle already running.

He slid into the driver's seat, and moments later Berlin was in the front passenger one.

"We've got him." She sounded smug—as she should. "Might not matter if this ends up being a burner, but I've now cloned his phone." She set the phone into the stand in the cupholder, then pulled out her laptop from the footwell.

He texted Hope just to check in and got a message back that she was good, so he could breathe clearly again.

After they'd fooled around last night, he'd simply held her as they finally drifted off to sleep. By the time he got out of the shower this morning, she'd been gone.

Well, she'd been downstairs. But it had felt like she was putting distance between them.

Still didn't regret last night, even if he should. She hadn't been weird, exactly, but he'd still sensed her putting those walls back up as they'd eaten breakfast and gone over the plan for today.

Which was simple enough—clone Killeen's phone and see who he called after spotting Hope. Because his guys had disappeared last night. Just poof.

Into the ether with no contact.

Killeen wasn't going to let that go. But they needed to know if he had a boss and who he was working with.

The other part of the plan was to get Kim alone and get some damn answers. Unfortunately that was going to be later tonight when she got off work. And Bradford was going with Hope whether she liked it or not.

"I don't give a shit, I just saw her with my own two eyes walking around town. What the hell happened!" Killeen's voice came through the laptop loud and clear. "This was supposed to be taken care of."

"He's talking to this number. Looks like a burner," Berlin murmured as she shifted her laptop slightly to show the phone number. "Caller isn't far from here."

Bradford eyed the map, saw the little dot was relatively close to Hope's place. Maybe a neighboring farm?

"I have no idea where they are," the unknown man said. "Haven't heard from any of the guys."

"No one checked in at all last night?"

"Not last night or this morning. I already told you I'd contact you when I heard from one of them."

"This is bullshit."

"Look, I can get another crew together," the unknown man said. "No one connected to you at all."

"No. Hell no. That's not the point," he snarled. "Something weird is going on. Four armed men didn't just disappear."

"Maybe she killed them or something?" The man's tone suggested he didn't even believe that possibility. "Or maybe that guy with her?"

Killeen's sigh was filled with derision. "Yeah, a journalist took out four of our guys. There's no way. Are you screwing with me? And if something happened, her husband would have called the cops. Did they even hit her place?"

"I swear to god they did! Weezer contacted me about half an hour before they were rolling out, said he'd be in contact as soon as it was over. Then I never heard from him."

"Why didn't you tell me last night?"

"I already told you. I fell asleep."

"Bullshit. You got high is what happened. I don't know why I thought I could trust you to handle something like this."

"That's not—"

Killeen ended the call with a savage snarl. He didn't wait long to start texting.

Bradford watched as the mirrored messages popped up on the laptop.

How's New Orleans?

"That's his wife's number," Berlin murmured.

Having a great time. Patrick wanted to stay out so we didn't get in until almost two. I'm exhausted this morning but nothing a café Americano can't fix. This was followed by a few laughing emojis. Then, *I miss you!*

I miss you too. Busy with work, will call this afternoon.

His wife texted a bunch of kissy-face emojis and Killeen didn't respond.

"I don't think they have an open marriage," Bradford murmured.

"Nope," both Berlin and Adalyn said almost in unison.

Bradford really hoped they got to use that video of Killeen and the other woman against him. "Who's he calling now?"

"Hmm, this isn't a burner," Berlin said, pulling the new number up. "Belongs to a woman named Edith Phillips. She's ninety-two... Okay, this isn't her on the phone." Berlin started working on her computer, likely looking up potential relatives as Killeen's voice came over the phone line.

"I've got a job for you."

"Hit me," a male voice said.

"I need you to follow Hank's daughter."

"The reporter lady?"

"Yeah. Just tail her around. I want to see where she goes, who she talks to, whatever. And don't let her see you."

"Anything I'm looking for in particular?"

It was clear by Killeen's sigh that he was fighting for control. "No. I just want to know what she's up to. Try to get a picture of her husband too. I need more details on him. He's been a ghost. She's at Chelsea Ortega's office now. No idea how long she's gonna be there."

"All right, headed out now. I'm not too far. I'll try to place a tracker on her vehicle if I can. What's she driving?"

"I'll send you the details."

"Okay."

Moments later, Killeen texted the make and model of the vehicle Hope had driven that morning—her actual car—to the same number.

She'd parked out of sight of her lawyer's office. Bradford and the others had driven into town in a Jeep with tinted windows and a lot of rubber ducks on the dash.

"I think we might need to return to her house," Bradford said. "It'll look odd if she loses this guy. And we can't have him tailing her back to the rental."

"We'll take him out before then," Berlin said.

"No... We don't want them to know we're on to them." Adalyn was silent for a long moment. "Yeah, let's have her go back to her dad's. Bradford, you'll go with her, obviously. Then maybe she tells a friend in town, or Kim or the sheriff maybe, that she has friends coming to support her after the loss of her dad. That'll be us. Killeen will find out she's got company. He won't make a move on her if she's got a house full of people with her—and if he does, we'll just take care of him. Right now he has no idea what's going on with her. We need to keep it that way until we figure out who else is involved with…whatever this is."

Bradford nodded slowly. "Yeah, keep him guessing, keep him confused." He texted Hope, letting her know to head back to her place after talking to her lawyer. He'd be following whatever guy ended up tailing her. And if the man got too close, Bradford would end that problem fast.

"We'll need to find out for sure," Berlin said. "But I think that caller might be a man named Alden Phillips. He's twenty-seven, lives with Edith, takes her to her doctor's appointments and anything else. At least according to all her social media posts about him. He doesn't have much of an online presence, but he was in the army, got out last year, and does handyman-type jobs. He has an online social media page for that with his portfolio, but that's it."

"You pull up his army file?" Bradford asked, still watching for Hope to exit her lawyer's office.

Berlin shook her head. "Still working on that. I'll have it by tonight."

"What's he drive? Or what does his grandmother drive?"

"Nothing in his name but…Edith owns a gray Subaru Outback."

"I see a gray Subaru, might be our guy," Adalyn murmured from the back seat right before she slipped out of the vehicle and headed in the direction where it was parking.

He glanced down the street at the incoming traffic. "We'll get a tracker on that car if possible… I want to get down in that bunker. See what the hell Killeen is hiding down there." And then take him down.

CHAPTER 23

You don't need the whole world to love you.
You just need one person.

"Look, there's no pressure to sell. I think Hank would have liked it if you stayed. Or at least held on to it. But I also know that he wouldn't have wanted to pressure you about anything. I'm just passing along some of the numbers I'm seeing." Chelsea sat back in her chair, looking every bit the professional lawyer this morning in her black jacket and pale blue camisole underneath.

Hope glanced at the various numbers people had told Chelsea they would be willing to offer for her dad's—her!—land.

"No real offers yet. These are mostly what people have been telling me they're thinking about if you decide to put it up for sale. I believe about half of them."

"Is that why you have poop emojis next to some of them?"

Chelsea grinned. "Yep. They're the stinkers. But the others, I think you can take at face value."

Hope noticed that Edward Killeen was on there too, and tried to keep her voice casual. "Edward Killeen? The guy whose son tried to break into my place?"

"God, what a screw-up." Chelsea straightened slightly as she sat up and leaned forward. "I don't particularly care for Edward, but I like his wife. I don't know how they went so wrong with that son of theirs. I call him a kid sometimes but he's a grown man," she said, shaking her head in clear disgust.

"His offer is pretty decent."

Chelsea shrugged. "Yeah, he's been buying up a lot of land around here."

"You know why?"

Another shrug. "I don't know. I heard a rumor that they might be building a highway through here in a few years. They've got ten years to make it happen. But...I don't know. The money from the sale of all the land can't be that good for what he's offering. I have my suspicions about him... I think he might be wanting to build more beverage manufacturing plants. There's big money in that. Or start another farm. Which brings money to the town, so I can't complain."

But she didn't look totally on board with Killeen either. "How did my dad feel about him?"

"Edward Killeen? I don't know. Okay, I guess. Something happened between them years ago but whatever it was, they patched it up. I might not love the guy, but he puts a lot of money back into the town."

"You hear anything about the charges against his son?" She was still waiting on anything and figured her lawyer would have a lot more insight than anyone else.

"Yeah. You probably won't like it, but he's not going to jail. He'll end up doing community service. Which the little shit deserves at the very least. But he won't serve any time—his dad is friends with the judge and it's his first offense."

"His *first*?"

"First time being charged with real evidence." Chelsea's tone was dry.

"What do you think he wanted when he broke into my place?" Because Hope was still trying to figure that out.

"Who knows? To cause trouble. To steal stuff he doesn't need." She shook her head slightly and her gaze strayed to a picture of her and a teenage girl with a big smile, framed on one of her shelves.

"Is that your daughter?" Hope asked softly.

"Yeah." Chelsea's voice got a lot softer too.

"I'm sorry, I shouldn't—"

"No. It's okay. I can talk about her now. About…what happened. And I know you had a lot of issues with your dad. Rightfully so. But he was there for me after I lost her."

"I'm glad he was," she said, and meant it. No one should have to lose a kid.

Chelsea nodded, her mouth pulled tight as if she was fighting emotions. "I'd never even been a drinker before. I never did the 'wine after work' thing, and for happy hours I usually just drank sparking water or Coke. But once I lost her…I fell into alcohol. Or maybe I dove right in is more accurate. I also never understood how anyone could become an addict before I lost Gabriella. That was her name."

"Beautiful name for a beautiful girl."

She gave a small, sad smile. "Yeah, I named her after my abuela. Alcohol—vodka was my drink of choice because it's hard to really smell—was my best friend for a while. It was the only thing that dulled my senses. In the beginning I just drank at night. I'd get blackout drunk, but I always woke up and made it to work so I told myself I didn't have a problem. Then slowly I started taking a little nip at lunch just to tide me over until I got home. It took the edge off, but it wasn't long until I was having a shot with my coffee in the morning." Chelsea shook her head in disgust. "I was an absolute mess. I thought no one knew about my problem, but I was also a fool."

"And Hank really helped you get sober?"

"Oh yeah," she said with a laugh. "Helped me detox, then forced me to go to AA meetings with him five days a week at first. And he showed up at my place on the two off days to bug me. I used to call him a menace, and he told me he was retired with nowhere to be so I could just deal with it... Fentanyl is what killed her," she blurted.

Hope blinked once. She was well aware of the out-of-control opioid problem, specifically with fentanyl being added to other drugs. "I'm really sorry."

"One of her friends got MDMA—Ecstasy—and they all decided to try it." Chelsea shook her head, raw pain clear in her dark eyes. "They were all just sixteen-year-olds on spring break, wanting to have a good time. It was a stupid choice, but they were kids... Only one of them survived."

Hope wasn't sure what to say other than she was sorry again.

"Anyway...you didn't ask to have all that dumped on you."

"No, stop. Thank you for telling me. That's a lot of trauma. Too much. But I'm glad you're sober now." And so damn sorry she'd lost her kid.

"It's been ten years now. It doesn't actually get easier. The pain, I mean. I don't care what people say. But you learn to bear it. And that's enough out of me. I just wanted to talk to you about the offers and let you know that if you end up deciding to sell, you've got a lot of options."

It was clear she was done talking about her daughter, so Hope nodded. "Thank you for letting me know. And thank you for being so wonderful after my dad died. I was dreading coming here, but you and your group have made things bearable. I might actually stay for a little while."

"Well I kind of love that. I'd love to see you outside of office hours. Maybe grab coffee or dinner or something."

"I'd love that too. And do I owe you anything, or...?"

"Oh, no. Hank took care of that. He basically prepaid me out of the estate. And he was very generous in case you're worried." She gave a ghost of a smile and started to stand.

So Hope took the cue and followed suit. "I might have some friends coming to visit for a while," she said, since Bradford had just texted her. Apparently something was going on and she needed to tell people that she had people coming to stay with her to keep herself safe. "For moral support."

Chelsea nodded as she walked her out into the front of the building where her assistant was quietly talking on the office phone. "The place is huge enough. I told him more than once he could turn your homestead into a B&B or something. But he just laughed."

After wrapping up with Chelsea, Hope stepped back out into bright sunlight, the oppressive heat once again rolling over her as she headed to her car. She slid her Bluetooth in her ear and called Bradford. "Hey, everything okay?" she asked as she walked past the parked Jeep without looking inside to see if he was there.

She knew that he was, felt his intense gaze on her. And she was grateful he had her back. Last night had been unexpected but wonderful. And she hadn't run from him this morning, as his accusing stare over breakfast had implied.

She'd simply been hungry and he'd been in the shower. Ugh, whatever, she had to stop defending herself *to herself*. She'd done nothing wrong.

"Yeah, but someone is going to be following you."

"Someone?"

"Someone not us. I'll explain everything once you get back to your place. Just drive that way like normal. A gray Subaru Outback is going to be following you, but we'll be following him in case he tries something."

"Got it." She wasn't sure what her life had become, but she didn't hate

Bradford's presence in it. Not one bit. Because if someone was following her with the intent of hurting her, she knew he would have her back. "Are you going to join me?"

"Yep. I'll see you soon."

She was counting down the seconds until she saw him again.

CHAPTER 24

"Thanks for the update, Sheriff. Oh, before I forget, I've got some friends coming to stay with me for a few days. If you see any strange vehicles heading to my place, that's why," Hope said.

"Oh, that's nice you've got friends coming. You need support right now. Wish I had better news for you, but I'll talk to you soon."

"Yeah right," she muttered to Bradford only after she'd hung up the phone. The sheriff had called to tell her what Chelsea already had—Patrick Killeen was basically getting a slap on the wrist. Which wasn't a huge surprise, but it still annoyed her since she knew he and his dad wanted her, you know, *dead*.

They were back at her place, along with Adalyn and Berlin, who were currently working on something in the living room.

"Between the sheriff and Chelsea, word should spread that you've got friends staying over," he murmured, that simmering heat still there in his eyes.

And she wasn't sure what to do with it.

Or him.

Or herself.

She knew what she wanted to do right now—but that wasn't happening with the others in the house. "Stop looking at me like that," she whispered.

"Not looking at you like anything." His voice was just as low, his eyes heated.

"When you whisper, we can't eavesdrop!" Berlin called out from the other room.

Bradford shook his head, but grinned.

"You've got a nosy group of friends," Hope said in a normal voice.

"Heard that one," Berlin called.

Bradford's grin grew for a moment, but then he straightened as he glanced down at his phone. "You ready to get out of here?"

"Yeah, we need to get going. What about that guy who followed me?" Alden Phillips.

"His tracker hasn't moved," Berlin called out again.

Thankfully Adalyn had managed to put one on his car. After following her here, he'd parked down the road about a mile off the two-lane highway. He'd see her if she headed back into town, but not if she headed west.

"We'll take one of the other vehicles just in case," Bradford said, grabbing a set of keys from the countertop.

It didn't take long to get on the road, and even though she felt a little bad ambushing Kim like this, she needed answers. Because she couldn't live like this, wondering when Edward Killeen would send someone after her again.

"We ever going to talk about last night?" Bradford asked as he made his way toward Kim's home.

Thankfully Kim was out in the country too instead of in a neighborhood, so it was easier to approach her home without being seen. "What should we talk about? The orgasms we gave each other? Because they were nice." And she wanted a repeat.

"First, they were great."

She let out a startled laugh as he pulled down a little side road, kicking up dust as the car rumbled along. "Fine...agreed. They were great. *Fantastic*. And I don't know what else to say."

"What do you want from me, Hope?"

She wasn't sure how to answer that, because she wasn't sure what the hell she was doing with her own life. "I don't know," she whispered.

"Try and verbalize it." His voice was soft.

"I...I like you, Bradford. I always have." More than she should. Though it was more than like. She'd fallen hard for him, even if she couldn't get the big L word out past her tight throat. Because love messed everything up. Made everything worse. Made you stupid.

"I like you too, Hope." His voice was rough and gritty now.

She had no idea what to say, but it seemed he didn't either, because he was silent until he pulled off the side of the road two miles later, tucking the car out of sight from any random passersby into a small break in the woods.

Though she doubted anyone who didn't live down this little road would wander by. There were only three people who lived off this unpaved road and two were retired. According to Berlin's sleuthing (and Hope's own knowledge of the locals), they didn't venture out after six.

"We can head in on foot from here," Bradford said, pointing at the woods.

"Or we can just...walk there from here." She nodded in the direction of the dead-end road where the Crosses' mailbox was visible. Their house was over a little hill but she knew it was there, had been there multiple times over the years when growing up.

"I don't know enough about her neighbors. They might have cameras."

"I kind of doubt it, but okay." So she followed him into the woods, and what should have been a seven-minute walk from the car to Kim's place took half an hour until they were at her back door.

Hope knocked lightly and waved at the small camera positioned above the frame. So maybe she'd been wrong about people out here not having cameras.

The door swung open moments later. Kim was wearing a long robe, her hair was up in a turban and she had some kind of mud mask on her face. "What on earth are y'all doing here?" she asked as she stepped back to let both her and Bradford enter her kitchen.

She'd made changes in the last decade-plus so it was more modern. Soft gray cabinets, cream-colored walls, new-looking appliances, and the place smelled like fresh apple pie.

"We knew Andrew was at work and wanted to talk to you without anyone seeing." Hope shoved her hands in her jeans pockets. "Sorry, I probably should have called but you were kind of weird about talking at the diner."

Kim nodded and motioned for them to sit at her kitchen table. There were six quilted dark blue and white placemats in front of each seat. "I didn't want to talk about anything at work. There are always people around and..." She sat across from them with a sigh. "Y'all hungry? I've got pie."

Hope was going to say no, but Bradford grinned and leaned back. "I wouldn't say no to pie."

The woman winked at him and stood again. "I knew I liked you. And you two will just have to deal with my green face because this is my night off and I'm pampering myself."

"We interrupted you," Hope murmured. "And we parked out of the way down the road so your neighbors wouldn't see."

Kim nodded as she opened her fridge. "Neither Mrs. Burleigh or Ms.

Wise would have heard or seen you. They're both in for the night."

"I kind of can't believe Ms. Wise is still kicking," Hope admitted. "And do you need any help?"

"Nope, you two sit. And you're not kidding. But she's still getting around and volunteering at the pet shelter two days a week. Andrew and I check on her most nights."

They were quiet as she busied herself getting out what looked like blackberry pie, three plates, and ice cream. Hope's mouth was watering as Kim started plating everything.

Once everything was served and Kim had started a pot of fresh coffee, Hope said, "You want to tell us about the coordinates?"

Bradford was quiet as he dug into his pie, clearly fine with letting her take the lead.

"Not really, but I'll tell you what I know. Your father thought Edward Killeen was up to something—he gave me those coordinates. Said it proved that Killeen was running drugs. Or hiding them, I should say. But he was also convinced that Edward was growing them too. Said he had a big heroin operation going right under everyone's noses."

"Heroin?" Bradford murmured.

Kim shrugged. "It sounds farfetched to me. But some days…I don't know if he was right. Hank had been motivated in a way I hadn't seen him the last couple years."

"Motivated?" Hope asked.

"Maybe that's the wrong word, but he was excited about something. Don't get me wrong, he'd been doing a hell of a lot better since getting sober, especially since he was mentoring people. He had a purpose. But the last couple times I saw him at the diner, he seemed almost, well, excited. He told me that he'd found something, but wasn't sure who to trust."

"You think it had to do with Edward Killeen?"

"Yeah. Or I assume it did. Once when I was closing up the diner, Hank confided in me that he'd been watching Edward and his son, gathering proof."

Oooh, she liked the sound of that. "What kind of proof?"

"He wouldn't tell me exactly what, just that the man was growing and storing drugs. He gave me the coordinates and told me only to tell someone about them if something happened to him."

"Did you tell anyone but me?"

"Nope." She sighed, having barely touched her pie. "And I debated telling you at all, especially since you'd just lost your dad. I didn't know what the coordinates went to, but a quick search told me it was on Killeen land. From there I could figure out that it was something worth looking into. I'm too old to be playing detective and...the town has been doing well the last decade. And that's in large part to the Killeen family. He or his wife own half the stores downtown and a couple of the restaurants. Not to mention the two biggest beverage manufacturing factories. People love their family—well, they tolerate his son—because of how much he's helped the town grow.

"You think the sheriff knows about Killeen? Assuming he is running drugs?" Bradford asked.

"I have no idea. It's hard to believe that Crow would look the other way, but some of his deputies might."

"Any other people we shouldn't trust?" Hope asked.

"Honestly, I wouldn't trust anyone. Except maybe Hank's AA buddies. They're all close and would do anything for each other."

"Do you know why Killeen would want Hope dead?" Bradford asked, dropping the heavy question like a grenade.

Kim blinked, but didn't look surprised by the question. "Your land, maybe. He tried hard to get your dad to sell a few times." She pushed her half-eaten pie away and leaned back. "Is that why Patrick broke into your place? Everyone's been talking about him getting community service." Her mouth kicked up in amusement. "Glad he finally got some sort of punishment for all his bullshit."

"We're not sure why he broke in," Bradford said before she could. "Just trying to figure it out since the cops were useless. You know anything about the Tanner brothers? They stopped by Hope's house before Patrick did."

"Useless bastards," she said with a shake of her head. "I know they've done some handyman-type of work for people, but they're thieves. They never take much, just petty stuff. Still." She shrugged. They did a decent amount of work for Edward at one time, I do know that. Helped him build a couple barns and some stuff to do with his palmetto farm. At least that's what I heard."

Hope didn't look at Bradford, but made a note of it. She wasn't sure what else to ask Kim.

It wasn't as if she was going to tell Kim about the break-in and the four dead guys they were hiding in a freezer somewhere.

"While I don't think the sheriff is necessarily corrupt," Kim continued without any segue, "Crow definitely looks the other way where Patrick Killeen is concerned. But I think that has more to do with the fact that Edward donates so much to the local force. I honestly don't know if he's involved in...whatever the Killeen family is into."

Hope nodded again, knowing they were coming to the end of their conversation. Kim didn't know as much as she'd hoped, but it wasn't nothing.

"Who was my dad close to? Someone he would have confided in." Hope had wanted to ask Chelsea, but wasn't sure she could trust her with this. She didn't know her well enough. But she'd known Kim forever, had found refuge over at her place more than once over the years when it had gotten to be too much at her house. She'd always been welcomed with a big hug, warm pie, and a quiet place.

She rattled off a list of names. "Those were the people he came into the diner with after AA meetings. The ones I know for sure he was close with."

Hope recognized the names, two farmers, and one had owned a local grocery store that had closed a few years ago. She filed them away and made a note to reach out to all of them even as she tried to figure out what she should say. She'd seen two of them at the memorial so might use that as her opening.

She wasn't sure about Mr. Rivera's whereabouts though. He hadn't been at the memorial and she vaguely remembered her dad saying something about him moving. He'd been kind to her family back in the day though.

After they wrapped up, she gave Kim a quick hug, and she and Bradford headed out. Instead of trekking through the woods, they simply walked down the dirt road instead.

"You think she's holding anything back?" Hope asked once they were in the car, the door shut.

"No." Bradford's answer was immediate. "I think she knows that Killeen is running drugs and just doesn't want to say it, but no, I don't think she was holding anything back. She seemed..."

"Frustrated?"

"Yeah."

"Join the club," Hope muttered as she started the car and pulled out. "I feel like we're spinning our wheels trying to figure this shit out."

"Well we know a little more. If he's growing poppy fields, and actually has an operation...local law enforcement has to be involved. Doesn't have to be the whole force, but Killeen would have to have someone in his pocket."

"Yeah, I was thinking that too."

"So that's something. We know we can't trust the cops."

Sighing, she nodded, but was silent as they headed back to her home.

CHAPTER 25

*Your person will make you realize why you
had to wait.*

There was only one vehicle in front of Hope's place when they arrived. "I thought the others were supposed to be here?"

"They are..." Bradford frowned and pulled out his phone, but it rang before he could make a call. It linked to the car's Bluetooth system as he answered. "Hey, we just pulled up."

"I know. I didn't want to bother you while you were at Kim's," Berlin said. "I've been monitoring Edward's phone and cameras and he's making another move on Hope tonight."

"What, I thought—"

"I know," she said, cutting him off. "We thought Hope was safe, but we're all leaving now. Apparently he didn't hear the rumor that she had people visiting her. I've printed out some plane tickets and a few other travel-related things and I'll be leaving them in the printing tray. It's over-the-top but hopefully once whoever he sends here sees it, they'll assume she left town."

Hope had a lot of questions and it was clear that Bradford did too, but she knew that now wasn't the time. "What about my bags?" she asked.

"Already packed up. They haven't left yet, but you guys need to turn right around and leave."

"Who's in there with you?"

"It's just me...wrapping up now."

"We'll wait for you."

"Bradfo—"

"Berlin, I'm not leaving you behind."

"Neither am I," Hope added. "Do you need help bringing anything out?"

"No...fine, come on. It sounds like his team isn't rolling out for another ten minutes."

Bradford cursed and jumped out of the car, Hope not far behind.

"Did she say ten minutes?" she asked as they hurried up the front steps.

Bradford threw open the door to find Berlin grinning at them. "Oh my god, they're not really rolling out in ten are they?"

"Nope." Her grin grew even wider. "They're waiting until about midnight. They want to make sure it's quiet out here. I just wanted to see you run."

"You're a monster." His tone was dry.

"All right, let's see this setup," Hope said. She was glad that they had time before another round of assholes showed up. "And I'm probably getting ahead of myself, but I want to expose these guys. I know we can't with the last four...obviously. But we've still got the cameras up. I don't want to keep hiding. I want to do something."

Berlin looked a little feral as she turned her smile on Hope. "What are you thinking?"

***

"Is it weird that I'm excited about watching this?" Hope whispered to Bradford, even though they were both wide-awake and watching the laptop screen.

She, Berlin and Bradford had added a couple more cameras hours ago, before they'd laid their trap and headed out. Now they were back at the rental. She wasn't sure if anything would come of this or if this alleged team would even show up—

"Someone's coming," Bradford murmured.

She glanced over at him, wondering if he'd decided to go shirtless to make her crazy.

They were both sitting up against the headboard, and while she was in her pajamas, he was wearing boxer briefs and nothing else. Yep, he was definitely trying to make her crazy.

It was only partially working, because now an SUV was slowly moving down the driveway. Thanks to the night vision capabilities of the cameras, she could see one... "Two SUVs? That seems like overkill."

Bradford lifted a broad shoulder. "Four of their guys disappeared without a trace."

"Fair," she whispered again. "Not sure why I'm whispering."

He snickered slightly. Neither SUV parked right up on the house, but about halfway down the drive. Then two teams of four men each got out.

One guy made a bunch of hand motions to the others.

She leaned in to watch them fan out. "So he's like the team leader, right?"

"Essentially, yes. And if I had to bet money, he's got military training."

"These guys seem different than the ones the other night. More organized, I guess."

Bradford nodded, his expression tense as he watched the screen.

She couldn't take her eyes off him for a long beat. She might hate the situation, but she liked being with him. She felt...safe with him. Truly, utterly safe in a way she'd never felt with anyone else. Or anywhere else. Though the location had nothing to do with it.

It was being with him that changed everything.

He was the game changer.

The reality of that dawned on her and she had to turn away from him before it could sweep her under.

"So why do you think he has military training?" she asked, even though she was pretty sure she knew.

"The hand movements—he's giving orders without words, something you've seen."

"Yeah. I wasn't sure if that was, like, universal though."

"Not really. It's used in all branches, but these guys move like a unit. No talking, not even now." He chin-nodded at the screen again.

She watched as two men carefully entered her house, looking for any traps, while two others stood guard on either side. Two more moved into the front and back, and then the last two slipped into the woods. Or maybe they were headed out to her dad's shop, which she hadn't even ventured to.

"They're all wearing balaclavas too," she murmured.

"That's a Spec Ops thing too. But it's also a criminal thing, so we can't be totally sure about the training."

She snorted, then straightened as the two men inside began a careful sweep, going room to room.

The one she'd dubbed the leader had a small flashlight and was now looking at some of the paperwork they'd left behind. Instead of leaving it in plain sight, she'd tucked it away in one of the kitchen drawers.

A half-ripped plane ticket, which she thought was overkill (who printed their tickets anymore?), and a travel guide with some highlighted parts in the city she was supposedly flying to—Orlando, Florida. A massive place no one would find her in.

In the bathroom she'd cleared out most of her toiletries, but not every-thing. She'd also left some clothes behind so it would look like she was coming back. She wasn't even sure if these guys would notice, but they'd wanted to make this as authentic as possible.

For the finale, she'd written a note to an imaginary woman named Carla thanking her for checking on the house while she was gone and asking her to leave the mail on the kitchen countertop.

"He sees the note to Carla on the fridge." Bradford sounded smug, likely because it had been his idea.

"Let's just hope they buy it."

Half an hour later, the two men inside headed back outside. Then the leader guy motioned with his hands for everyone to move out.

And Bradford was right, they even jogged like a team, all in unison. Back at one of the SUVs, the lead guy shoved his balaclava up and pulled a cell phone out.

She was really glad that Bradford's team had added more cameras.

"She's not here," he said to whoever was on the other line. Likely Edward Killeen.

Before she could voice that, her phone buzzed with an incoming text from Berlin saying *Click on this link*.

When she did, a small screen popped up to reveal Edward Killeen in his kitchen in casual clothing, on his cell phone.

"...the bitch couldn't have just disappeared. And I had someone watch-ing her place—no one saw her friends show up and she never left."

"I don't know about any of that, but she's not here. There are a couple of sets of tire tracks though. I can take some pictures."

"Don't waste your time. What did the house look like?" Edward asked.

She focused back on the screen, feeling like she was watching a tennis match.

"Clean, but not too clean. Signs she might have headed out of town. To Orlando, specifically, with plans to visit Disney. Some lady named Carla is supposed to be checking in on her place."

"Carla who?"

"I don't know, it's the name on a note from the fridge."

Killeen was silent, his expression contemplative as he sat there at his island countertop, a glass of what looked like whiskey in front of him.

Finally the other guy motioned for his men to return to the SUVs as he spoke into the phone. "This is a waste of our time and resources."

"Says who?"

"Says me," the man snarled. "We've got a good thing going and you're getting paranoid. If Hank had anything on you, we'd have found it. We searched his place top to bottom before."

Her heart rate kicked up at the mention of her dad.

"Not if he gave it to her. I'm telling you, my instinct on this isn't wrong. Something is off with her. And she's a reporter."

"Journalist," she murmured to herself.

"So what?" the man asked.

"She could be here writing a story about—"

"Her dad just died. There's only one reason she's here. And I've put myself and my men at risk for nothing. I don't like exposing myself like this."

"Four of my guys disappeared and no one has heard or seen them since."

"Weezer and those assholes are probably wasted in Atlantic City. You'll hear from them eventually. That's what happens when you pay morons up front," he added, and it was clear that this was a conversation they'd had before.

"Something is going on. I'm not wrong about this."

"I was willing to give you the benefit of the doubt, but her dad didn't have shit and neither does she. And you made a mistake by sending the Tanner brothers out here to check his shop again. It spooked her..." He paused, his body language tense. "Please tell me this isn't about her not dropping the charges against Patrick?" There was ice in the guy's tone.

"Jesus, no. That's just what I told Patrick and Dale."

Dale Watsky, she remembered from Berlin's information.

"Why not tell Dale the truth?"

"Because he doesn't need to know all the ins and outs of everything. And my suspicions about this bitch don't concern him. He needs to stay focused on other things. Now just plant some cameras and get out of there. I want to know exactly when she arrives back home. Because I'm not wrong about her. Something is off."

"Fine." The man hung up without another word, then motioned to the only man who hadn't gotten back into the SUV. "We need to plant a few cameras, couple bugs."

"Shit," Bradford muttered.

"What happens if they find ours?" she asked.

"That's what I was thinking... The cameras are well hidden though."

Heart racing, all she could do was watch as the guy slid his balaclava back on and headed back inside with the other man. His body language said he wanted to be anywhere but there.

The two men moved quickly, placing a camera in the kitchen, one in the living room, and another in the bedroom that was clearly hers.

"Perverts," she muttered.

Bradford snickered. "Or more likely they think you'll be talking on your phone in that room."

She gave him the side-eye.

"Or, you're right and they're definitely perverts."

"I like when you tell me I'm right," she murmured, looking back at the screen. She felt almost detached as she watched them, as if this wasn't her home.

Once the two men were done, they headed back outside, their body language clear. They were annoyed.

"We searched the old man's place more than once," the second man who'd been helping plant the bugs said.

"I know. That's not what this is about," the leader murmured as they reached the SUV. "Edward's starting to get paranoid about everything."

"Those are some seriously good cameras," Hope whispered, not wanting to miss any of the conversation. "Their conversation is so damn clear." She wanted to ask where they were from, but had a feeling it was from Hailey's husband. Or one of his companies, to be more specific. She knew that the guy was into next-gen tech. Stuff she probably *didn't* want to know about, now that she thought about it.

Bradford only nodded instead of responding, still watching the screen

"I don't care what he says about her. Killeen is just pissed that his baby boy is doing community service."

"We should take care of that asshole," the other man said. Which earned a snort-laugh of approval before they slid into the SUV.

"You think Berlin will get anything from the license plates?" She hadn't been paying attention when they'd arrived, but when they turned around she tried to get a good look at the plates. They were moving too fast though.

"Maybe, but I have a feeling the plates will be fakes anyway."

"Yeah. If they went to this much trouble to come kill me... Eight freaking guys. And what the heck were they talking about with my dad having something on Killeen?" It was rhetorical because obviously Bradford didn't know.

"There's clearly more going on than the issue with his son, though he seems like a big enough asshole to want to kill you for that alone. I want to kill him and be done with it," he grumbled as he leaned back on the bed.

She tried not to stare at all that bare skin, at the way his stomach muscles flexed with his movements. Somehow she forced herself to turn away. "I'm going to grab some water before I crash. You want anything?" She couldn't look at him again as she slid out of bed.

If she did, she was about to make a bad (or really good) decision and proposition him for the rest of the night. And you know, into the morning.

Why had she thought sharing a bed was a good thing?

"Nope, I'm good." He sounded all relaxed, which just annoyed her.

She felt as if she could crawl out of her skin and he looked as if he could roll over and sleep at a moment's notice.

CHAPTER 26

The people who show up for you during the bad times and the good times, those are the keepers.

By the time she returned to their bedroom, she was even more keyed-up and annoyed. Mostly with herself.

When she stepped into the room, Bradford was texting on his phone and she wasn't sure why it bothered her so much. *Okay, lies.* She knew. She wanted all his attention on her while simultaneously wanting to bury her head in the sand.

So healthy.

He set his phone down when she closed the door behind her. "Your phone went off a couple times. I wasn't sure if I should answer it."

"Thanks," she murmured, glad he hadn't. Having someone else answer her phone after building up so much trust with the people she was writing stories on wouldn't have been the best. When she saw Lex's phone number on her missed calls, she held up a finger to her mouth. "It's my PI friend. I'm going to put him on speaker but don't let him know you're with me."

Bradford nodded and sat forward slightly as she got into the bed next to him.

Lex answered on the first ring. "Hey. You okay?" There was concern in his voice, surprising her.

"Yeah. Why?"

He shoved out a breath. "Whatever story you're writing that's linked to this family, walk away."

She raised her eyebrows at Bradford as she responded to Lex. She'd told him that the Killeens were loosely linked to a story she was working on, but had kept it vague. "Why?"

"When I started digging, I got a call from a hacker friend of mine who told me the same thing. Then he sent me an article that I'm going to send you. Sending it to your phone right now."

She clicked on the link to what turned out to be a story out of Arkansas. "I vaguely remember reading about this," she murmured, hating that it hadn't been bigger news. "Fifty bodies found in a mass grave, linked to a potential war between drug dealers." She read out the article title. "There was speculation that it might be cartels, right? They're linked to this? Is that what you're trying to tell me?"

"I honestly don't know. But something happened to an established heroin operation in Arkansas. Right across the border from Louisiana. I only know this after heavy research, but apparently they were linked to some outfit out of New Jersey. Not cartels."

"That's a surprise."

"It's a new world," Lex said. "Anyway, someone came in and cleaned house, killed everyone at what turned out to be a heroin farm. No one took credit for it. But when I started asking around about the Killeen family, a contact of mine sent me this and told me to stop whatever I was doing unless I wanted to end up like these guys. It was his subtle way of telling me that they were behind this."

"Thank you for letting me know."

There was a short pause, then, "You're not going to drop this are you?"

"Of course I am."

"You're a terrible liar. Don't say I didn't warn you." Lex disconnected before she could respond.

Bradford was already on his phone as she set her own down. "I just sent the article to Berlin. That's...a new link."

"A terrifying one." She sat back against the headboard, digesting everything. "If Edward Killeen took out fifty people..."

"He's not going to get near you. He doesn't know who my people are and what we'll do to stop him." There was an edge to his tone that promised retribution to Killeen if she even stubbed her toe.

She shivered and leaned into him. Thankfully, he wrapped an arm around her and pulled her close.

"Can you just hold me right now?" A cold had seeped into her bones as she thought about how differently things could have gone if Bradford hadn't been here, if he hadn't come to see her at her father's funeral.

"Of course." He moved both their phones onto the nightstand and pulled her against his chest while she curled into him. "You always handle things with so much ease, sometimes I forget that you're not Superwoman."

She snort-laughed as she fought back stupid tears that wanted to bubble up. "That's probably the nicest thing anyone's ever said to me," she whispered. And he wasn't wrong. "Being in war zones or dealing with death threats online is, I don't know, different, I guess. This threat is so visceral, so real."

"So close, and it has a face," he murmured, kissing the top of her head.

"Yeah. And that face maybe ordered the murder of fifty people. At least. Part of me can't believe that it wasn't a bigger story."

"It did the rounds. I remember," he added. "But when it was linked to drugs, people didn't care so the story never gained much traction."

"Yeah, that makes sense. If people don't think stuff like that can happen to them, they don't bother to click on the story. It loses steam before it ever gains it."

"He doesn't know where you are, and we know exactly where he is. Just a reminder. He's not going to touch you."

"Thank you." She buried her face in his chest for a moment, soaking up all his strength. Even though she wanted him physically—the understatement of the century—sex wasn't what she wanted right now. She simply needed to be comforted by the man who'd shown up.

The man who was consistently there, whether she asked for help or not.

People might disappoint her, but Bradford wasn't people.

That realization struck her with such force she stopped breathing for a moment. Then she dug her fingers into his side as she curled up against him, and to her surprise—and horror—tears sprung to her eyes.

She hadn't cried in years, not really. And it was like they were all coming up at once with a storm-like intensity she was unable to stop.

Even if she'd wanted to.

But right now, after years of keeping her shit together, of acting like nothing ever affected her, she just wanted to let go and cry. To embrace all her emotions.

So she held on to him, and he held on to her as she finally let go of more than just the present situation, but of everything from her past. Maybe she wasn't letting go, but she was allowing herself to grieve her lost childhood, her mother, her father and even Bradford.

She wasn't letting him go though, wasn't running anymore. That much she knew.

CHAPTER 27

I'm comfortable with morally gray.

"What is all this?" Bradford stopped in the living room, staring as Hope, Berlin, Hailey and Rowan all turned back to him as they finished taping up various printouts on the living room wall.

The others were all either on the couches or standing and looking at the giant wall of maps that they'd created. It was an oversized map of Hope's land and all the surrounding lands, plus various satellite images linked to certain properties.

"The satellite images are new," he murmured as he stepped forward.

After Hope had cried herself to sleep last night, he'd gotten a little sleep himself. When he'd woken up, she'd been gone, but to his surprise she'd left a note telling him that she wasn't running, but getting coffee and breakfast and hadn't wanted to wake him. He was surprised he hadn't woken up, but he must have needed the sleep. And it mattered that she'd left that note, even if she was just going downstairs.

"Got a text from my Lex around four this morning. He sent three of these. Not sure where he got them from. I think he felt bad about hanging up on me last night," Hope murmured.

"I need the info of whoever he's working with," Berlin grumbled. "Because that's NSA-level shit."

"She's just mad someone else found something she didn't," Adalyn whispered.

Which earned her a short-lived glare from Berlin.

Hope simply raised her eyebrows at Bradford, a grin pulling at her mouth before she turned back to the wall.

"This is incredible." He still needed coffee, but he scanned all the farms, the layout of the properties, and more importantly, the satellite images.

Berlin continued. "Combined with what I found—"

Hailey cleared her throat.

"Oh my god, I was going to include you and Gage." Berlin lifted a laser pointer that had a poop-face emoji as the red laser, and pointed at one of the images as if she was teaching a class. "Like I was saying. Combined with the satellite images *we* found, land records, and a whole mess of other information, I'm pretty sure we've figured out where these guys are growing their product."

Bradford was starting to see that as he took in the wall. "I'm guessing they store some stuff underground, considering that bunker we saw." And it had to be only one of many, considering how vast this expanse of land was. "Your land is right smack dab in the middle of all his." He'd known it, but seeing it like this created a vivid picture.

"It's not like he gets my land if I die, but…he did say something about Hank having information. I know we can't search the house now, but I think it's worth another look once…Killeen isn't a threat anymore."

"We're going to give him something else to worry about." Adalyn's tone was neutral, but there was a feral look in her eyes as she smiled.

"Oh, please tell me we're doing what I think you're suggesting." Bradford tried to suppress his grin, but failed. This was what he'd been waiting for. It was time to start destroying shit.

"We're doing it."

"Wait, what's happening here?" Hope asked, glancing between them.

"They're going to blow shit up." Magnolia, pregnant and glowing, didn't look up from her book as she read on the couch. "Or that's what I'm guessing."

Bradford gently took Hope's hands in his. "We're going to target their grow operations. With these images from your PI friend, we'll be able to pinpoint *exactly* where they're growing. If we take out enough of their product, they're going to have a whole other problem on their hands and Killeen will forget about you. You will be nothing to him. Or I'm assuming that's the plan?" He looked up at Adalyn, who confirmed with a sharp nod.

"Exactly," Adalyn added. "We're still going to keep you locked down until we've eliminated any and all threats, but we're going to screw up this guy's life so bad that he won't know what hit him. He'll be scrambling to keep his cash flowing and find out who's targeted him. He's going to be very, very busy soon."

"That's...very dangerous." Hope looked at Bradford, then the others, before looking back at him. "Can we talk in the kitchen?" she whispered.

"Of course."

"This is too much," Hope said once they were alone, her voice pitched low. "Too much danger. I know you guys are trained, but I can figure something out. Go visit friends in Canada. Or I've been meaning to visit an old college friend in London for years. I'll just disappear for a while, just go off-grid, but—"

"Hope. We've got this. I swear. We've taken out operations like this before."

She leaned against the countertop and looked up at him. Her eyes were slightly puffy from crying last night, but she was still gorgeous. She'd pulled her dark hair up in a ponytail and her blue eyes popped with emotion as she shook her head. "No. If something were to happen to you..." She trailed off in a whisper. "I couldn't bear it."

Ah, hell. He tugged her into his arms, even though it was clear she just wanted to argue about this.

Thankfully she buried her face against his chest with a groan. "I can't say anything to stop you, can I?"

"Nope. Not where your safety is concerned. You might not agree, but you're mine to protect, Hope," he murmured.

She held him tighter. "So who protects you?"

"I've got my team and I swear we're prepared for all this."

Still holding on to him, she leaned back and looked up at him, her expression fierce. "I get to hear all of the plans. And if it sounds stupid, you're not doing it."

"Okay."

She blinked, as if she'd expected him to argue. "Okay? Just like that?"

"The plan won't be stupid. It never is. We've taken down one cartel, an Albanian criminal organization, multiple trafficking orgs, and disrupted the flow of cash to another cartel just because we wanted to screw with them. Just to name a few of our jobs."

She blinked again as understanding set in. "Okay, then. Let's hear this plan."

Bradford kept his arm around Hope as they headed back into the living room.

"All right," Adalyn said, as if she'd been waiting for them. Then she snagged Berlin's poop-emoji laser pointer with a sigh and pointed at the first target.

He wasn't surprised that she'd picked one with a water entrance. Coming in via water would give them an easy escape (easy being a relative word).

They would also be hitting two more of the suspected growing operations at the same time, via drone strikes with some next-level tech that couldn't be traced back to them.

Rowan strode up to the wall and stared at the various images as he said, "The message will be even stronger if we can infiltrate a couple of his bunkers, take out the current product he has as well as what he's growing."

"I know," Adalyn agreed. "But that's too much of a risk."

"Not if we call in backup," Bradford added. "Raven isn't on a job right now." Raven was code for Skye, one of their founders. He loved Hope, but wanted to keep that information to himself for now.

Adalyn was silent as she thought about this.

"I vote we ask her for backup," Hailey said from the couch where she was shoving chips into her mouth.

"I'm not taking advice from the person eating Doritos for breakfast." Adalyn's tone was dry.

"Hey! These are the new tangy pickle ones," she said with a sniff.

"Is that supposed to make it better?" Bradford asked, looking at her in slight horror.

She simply rolled her eyes at him as Adalyn took over again. Next to him, Hope smothered a laugh as she leaned into him, setting her head on his shoulder in a way that was heartbreakingly familiar, yet foreign.

He loved that she was holding on to him now, not pushing him away—literally or figuratively. Something had shifted between them last night. He'd felt it then and even more so now. She was clearly worried about him. And she didn't have that same look in her eyes as before. He wasn't even sure he could describe it, but the way she watched him now, there was something a lot like hope in her eyes.

And he was never going to let her down. He would fight for his Hope until his dying breath.

Though he really, really didn't want that to happen for a hell of a long time. Because they deserved a future. It was their time, and he was going to grab it.

"I've already called her," Adalyn finally said with a grin. "About three hours ago. She's on her way and ready to blow shit up. She's also bringing her own backup."

Bradford knew it couldn't be her husband, because Colt was on a job in Alaska. So if he was a betting man, he'd guess it was Skye's best friend, Axel. Former Fed turned hitman turned "security expert."

They all lived in shades of gray, something he was more than comfortable with. There was no black and white, not truly. Sure, some things were easy choices, but the world and the people living in it were complicated.

He just hoped that Hope could live with who he was and the path he'd chosen.

CHAPTER 28

Bradford was in the back seat next to Tiago, trying to ignore Skye and Axel, who had just arrived at a small airport about an hour from the safe house.

He didn't like being separated from Hope, but tonight it was necessary. Hell, tonight hinged on a lot of moving parts and they hadn't done nearly enough recon. Normally that wouldn't have worried him—they were more than trained.

Skye was a former spook who'd done more things than any of them would ever know about. She was an explosives expert and could be a ghost when she wanted to. She'd even infiltrated a cartel to rescue someone solo.

Axel, a Marine turned Fed turned hitman... The guy had similar training. But right now the two of them sounded like children.

"...I forget how moonfaced you get over Hadley when you're separated from her." Skye was in the driver's seat as they idled outside a storage center, waiting on Rowan to grab a couple duffel bags of explosives from one of their units.

"Who the hell uses the word moonfaced?"

"It's a solid word."

"Maybe if you're using word of the day toilet paper," Axel grumbled.

"And considering I had to listen to you and Colt talk dirty to each other on the flight here, I'm allowed to miss my wife."

"Oh sweet baby pandas, we were talking about Semtex. Nothing dirty about that." She sniffed indignantly.

"Please. Everything about that conversation had sexual undertones and now I need brain bleach." Axel shuddered, and turned around as if to look for support from the two of them.

But Bradford and Tiago both shook their heads in unison.

"No way, man," Bradford said. "We're not part of this very weird conversation. In fact, we don't even exist until the op starts."

Skye turned back to face them now, a feral grin on her face. "You guys good to go?" she asked, though her attention was on Bradford as she spoke.

And he knew that the question was for him. "I'm focused. Yes, I'm worried about Hope, but this is a job and one I'm good at. I won't forget why we're doing this." To destroy Edward Killeen's life. Hell yeah, he was focused. Some days he hated aspects of his job, but today, getting to go after the livelihood of the monster who'd targeted Hope? Of a man who made his money off the pain of others?

It was a good day.

Or night, as it was.

"I figured, just wanted to check." She turned back around as she switched on her ear comm.

Normally Adalyn or Rowan was team lead for their New Orleans branch, but with Skye in town, one of the original founders of Redemption Harbor Security (and one of the scariest people he knew), she was taking point.

"Everyone check in," she said as Rowan popped the back of the SUV and tossed the bags inside.

"Check," everyone murmured at intervals until they were all accounted for.

"Rolling out now, everyone stay on comms. When I give the signal, we move."

There were murmurs of affirmation, but no chatter after that, not even from Skye and Axel.

It was op time and every one of them took that seriously. Especially on a night like tonight when they were making decisions based on satellite feeds and research. They didn't have any on-the-ground intel, which was usually the best recon.

But there was no time, not with Hope's life in danger.

"Dropping T off now," Skye said as she pulled off the side of the road and let Tiago out.

He pulled out two drone cases, both of which he could leave behind if necessary to self-destruct, but of all of them, Bradford figured his strike was going to be the easiest tonight. It was on the perimeter of Killeen's land and looked like a small territory. Though he'd never say that out loud and jinx them all.

Everyone was quiet until he heard Adalyn come over the line. "E and I are at the drop point, about to head in." Meaning that Ezra and Adalyn were at the perimeter of their target area and would be moving in on foot—via boat. They would be using a drone as well, but had also brought in a backpack of explosives designed to impart maximum damage before they made their escape.

Twenty minutes later, Skye pulled off the side of the road where they'd left a four-door sedan an hour ago, and she and Axel got out. Once they'd grabbed one of the duffel bags, they got into the other car and drove off.

Bradford slid into the driver's seat, and it was just Rowan and him now.

Rowan tapped mute on his earpiece as Bradford drove, so he did the same to his. "What's up?"

"Just checking in with you. I know you're solid. But I also know a lot is riding on tonight."

"We've got this." He made a turn at the next four-way stop, adrenaline already starting to ride him hard. It was always like this during an op.

And they'd been going over their plans all day. Over and over, until everyone was on the same page. He and Rowan would be parking in the woods, then going in on foot to what was a barnlike structure and a lot of camo netting covering what they were guessing was a farm. Killeen was growing something, given all the aerial camouflage and security.

"We're at the perimeter," he said quietly once they'd trekked in about a hundred yards from the road.

"Bravo and Romeo, get on channel two," Berlin said through the comms to him and Rowan. Then once they did, she continued. "I've got eyes in the sky. You're good to approach."

They were too deep in the woods for Berlin to see either him or Rowan, but everyone had on multiple trackers. While they were two little dots on a map to her, she'd also hacked into an old satellite and was guiding them from above.

Tiago was doing his own thing with his drone, Hailey was the aerial guide for Skye and Axel, and Adalyn and Ezra were using a drone as well.

He was glad Berlin was guiding them, had been working with her for a while and trusted her implicitly. Though he trusted everyone he worked with, he and Berlin had a tight bond.

It took roughly forty minutes for them to make it on foot to their destination, mostly because they were looking for any traps—and setting explosives as they moved inland.

Once the trees started thinning and they could see lights in the distance, Berlin said, "You're close and my window is closing. Right now I've got a visual on at least six tangos. Four are outside sitting around a table, playing cards. Two others are rotating around the barn and perimeter as active security checks. Security itself is relatively light, but there could be more that I'm not seeing. They'll have cameras, but the Wi-Fi jammer should take care of that, at least temporarily."

"Copy," Rowan murmured as Bradford pulled up his NVGs.

Crouched by an old oak tree, he slowly scanned the faded red and white barn they'd captured from satellite images. All the doors were closed up, but there was light coming from inside.

Sure enough, an armed man—carrying his semiautomatic far too casually at his side—strolled around the side of the barn about five minutes later.

Bradford couldn't hear him, but could see him on his cell phone laughing at something as he talked to someone. The screen was lighting up his face in the darkness as he walked, making him a perfect target. *What a dumbass.*

"Cocky," Rowan said quietly, his voice pitched low.

Bradford simply nodded. It was obvious that these guys were secure that there was no threat out here. Which would make this part a lot easier. While they waited for the go-ahead, they simply watched and made notes.

It was a quiet night, with a hazy blanket of stars mostly covered by clouds. As he watched, he thought about Hope, wished he was with her. Or could at least check in with her. But that was impossible. They'd all gone dark and were only communicating with anyone directly involved in tonight—there was no room for any outside distractions.

"Skye just checked in, everyone is moving in now. It's go time." Berlin's voice cut through the comm line. "And my satellite is shifting. You guys are on your own. Watch your six."

"We've got this," he said quietly.

Rowan nodded, and almost as if karma or whoever smiled down on them, a dark cluster of clouds moved over the rest of the stars, plunging the night into darkness.

They slid on their NVGs and moved like ghosts across the grassy field toward the back of the barn. If their timing was right, they would have two minutes before the next guard (and he was using that term loosely) made his rounds.

Rowan motioned for Bradford to get low so he ducked into the overgrown weeds as Rowan moved up to the barn, plastering himself against the wall.

Bradford was immobile in the way he'd been trained, remaining still as the guy rounded the corner. They'd heard the guy coming since he was still on his phone.

"Yeah, they moved up the delivery time. No idea why..." He turned slightly, maybe sensing Rowan's movement toward him, and went to shout even as he dropped his phone in an effort to pull up his weapon.

But it was too late—had been too late even before he stepped around the side of the barn.

As Rowan overpowered him, slit his throat in a couple short moves, Bradford was already in motion. He grabbed the guy's cell phone before it had a chance to go dark.

"Yo, White, did I lose you?"

Bradford ended the call, then removed the code to open it and turned down the volume as Rowan dragged the body into the brush. He tucked the cell away for later. Hopefully Berlin would be able to dump the contents and find something useful.

He held up a hand for Rowan—they had roughly five minutes to get this shit done and then get out. With their Wi-Fi jammers active, these guys would start getting restless soon.

Sliding his NVGs off his face, he pulled out a long, thin wire-camera and slid it between two cracks in the closed barn door while Rowan remained alert.

They should have time before the next guy rounded the corner, but they weren't taking chances.

When he saw what was in the barn, he showed the small screen to Rowan, whose eyes widened only slightly.

They hadn't been expecting this at all, but from what he could see the place was stocked with not only packaged heroin, but a stockpile of weapons.

He recognized the weapons' crates, quickly counted twenty. And that was only what he could see. They should have brought in a bigger team for this, but he removed the wire-camera, then pressed one of the explosives against the door, held it for a moment until the adhesive stuck tight.

As they moved along the exterior, they set more explosives. It was a risk that they might be seen, but it was dark and if you weren't looking for them, they didn't stand out.

Once they were finished and had reached the front of the barn, he spotted the second armed guy who did the active rounds heading from the small house where the other guys were playing cards.

Both he and Rowan pressed themselves up against the side of the barn. This was where things were going to get tricky.

"White? What the hell are you doing back there? Better not be jerking off again," the man called out as he approached. "Disgusting asshole," he muttered as he rounded the corner.

His eyes widened as he spotted the two of them, even in the darkness.

Bradford moved first and faster, shoving his KA-BAR straight through the guy's skull. The tango dropped with a soft thud as Bradford wiped off his blade.

No time to hide this guy. Not with the chaos they were about to create.

He turned down the volume on his comm when he heard shouts in the background from one of the other target areas. Sounded like one of the other teams had been faster than them and shit was already explosive.

Rowan held up his hand, then counted down from three.

Bradford pressed the first button from their pack and the forest lit up in a fireball of explosions. It was just a rumble at first, but orange illuminated the sky in a fiery ball of chaos.

The men shouted in the distance, then began running for the tree line, weapons in hand.

"We need backup," one shouted into his phone as he jumped onto a four-wheeler and raced for the trees.

He'd been hoping all four would take off, but one of them sprinted for the barn, his weapon in one hand, his cell up to his ear—likely calling one of the dead men. As he neared them, he cursed, then headed into the barn as he made another call.

"Someone's breached the property," the tango snapped into the phone.

Instead of waiting, Rowan and Bradford took off, sprinting into the darkness toward where the men had come from.

According to the satellite images there were multiple fields on the other side of the small house, and that was their real target. Or main one. He wished they'd had time to inspect the barn, to see about those weapons and maybe get some serial numbers, but there wasn't time.

Adrenaline surging through him, he tensed up when he heard, "Hey, stop!"

In front of him, Rowan palmed one of the triggers, set off the other explosives without a backward glance.

The pulse of the explosion ripped through the night, heat punching through the air even though they were at least a hundred yards away now. He glanced over his shoulder, briefly taking in the destruction and debris falling from the sky before he and Rowan rounded the other building.

There!

They split up in two directions, Rowan moving to the west, Bradford racing along the east end. As they ran through the crops, they sprayed accelerant—the fastest and dirtiest way to kill everything was through fire.

By the time they reached the end of the field, they'd both tossed lighters behind them.

A whoosh went up immediately, an orange ball engulfing the red and white poppies with a savage hunger, destroying everything in its wake.

He didn't have time to appreciate the destruction as the sound of multiple engines filled the air. The backup had arrived, and he and Rowan needed to get the hell out of here before they were found.

Chapter 29

Bradford and Rowan used the cover of night and the dark forest as another four-wheeler zoomed through the trees past them.

Their window for escaping was closing.

They'd been in tighter situations than this, but they had to get out of the woods and to the main road if they had a chance at survival.

"We're heading to pick you up," Skye said through the comms. "According to Berlin, you can make it to rally point six."

"Confirm," he whispered as the four-wheeler grew louder again.

The engine rumbled past him, then idled. He didn't move out from the oak tree he was using for cover.

Rowan remained in place as well, about twenty feet from him. If he didn't know where his teammate was, he wouldn't have spotted him. That was how much camo they had on, from head to toe.

A voice trailed on the wind not too far from him. "I'm telling you, they're not out here. They must have escaped."

The response was crackly and he couldn't make it out, but it was enough to know that these guys were using radios.

"I'll keep doing sweeps," the man finally grumbled.

Bradford watched as Rowan peeled off from the tree, used shadows to disappear from sight altogether.

They were too far away to risk talking out loud or to trust their comms weren't compromised. Even with their Wi-Fi jammers going strong to disrupt any active cameras, they had to be careful until they were out of here.

He crouched low, then slid the wire-camera he'd used earlier around the side of the tree. He didn't like focusing on a screen during an op—not when it lowered his range of peripheral vision—but he couldn't risk getting his head blown off.

A man in a T-shirt and cargo pants was sitting on the back of his four-wheeler, looking down at his phone. The guy was texting.

Rowan was moving in like a ghost, but... *Oh shit.*

Already moving, Bradford shoved the camera into his pocket and slid around the tree, scanning the woods as he raised his pistol. It had a suppressor but might not be enough to mute the shot.

And he wasn't close enough to use his KA-BAR.

Rowan was moving up behind the guy on the four-wheeler who had no clue he was about to die.

Unfortunately there was a man in a balaclava moving up behind Rowan like a goddamn wraith, a long blade in his hand.

Unlike the guy on the four-wheeler, just sitting out in the open like a dumbass duck, the other man moved like an operator, was dressed similar to them as well.

He couldn't warn Rowan either, could only take out this threat.

Blood rushing in his ears, he stepped quietly through the underbrush, following after the tracker—then the man paused, started to turn.

Bradford fired twice, two quick shots into the back of his head.

At the sound, the guy on the four-wheeler cried out, gunned the throttle, but Rowan took him out with his own pistol.

No time to be quiet now.

Bradford scooped up the fallen man's weapons, then quickly peeled off the man's gloves. Though they didn't have time to lose, he needed to know who this man was—because he didn't fit in with the rest of the dumbasses who'd been guarding this farm.

Using the fingerprint device they all carried with them, he scanned the man's first three fingers, knowing that it would transmit to Berlin and Hailey immediately.

Then he jumped up and raced to the four-wheeler where Rowan was already on the front.

"Could be LoJacked," he said as he slid on back.

"I know. Either way we'll get to the rally point faster."

Yep. He held on as Rowan took off, watched as the ATV got up to fifty miles per hour. Oh, they were going to make good time.

At the sound of a shout behind them, he turned around, already lifting his pistol as two men zoomed in from different directions.

The two men were behind them, but gaining fast.

Adrenaline pumping, he aimed at the nearest, fired.

The left front tire exploded, and the vehicle careened off course, slamming into a tree.

The other guy raced around the first, raising a semiautomatic rifle as he tried to steer, but Bradford already had him in his sights.

A shock of pain sliced through his arm, but he ignored it, fired at the man's tires.

"Your three o'clock!" Rowan shouted above the engine and wind as the four-wheeler behind them rocked off-kilter.

Swiveling, he aimed in the direction Rowan had said, saw another ATV coming up on them. There were two men on this one, one driving, the other standing up and— Bradford fired at his chest.

Pop. Pop.

The guy flew backward, and before he'd hit the dirt, Bradford took out the driver.

"I think we're clear for now," he shouted above the engine as Rowan raced past a cluster of trees.

"Two minutes out from the rally point," Rowan called back.

Bradford stayed alert and as they cleared the woods, skyrocketing onto the two-lane highway, he raised his weapon at an approaching vehicle—but dropped his arm when the headlights flashed three times.

Relief that their own backup had arrived surged through him.

They'd caused a lot of damage tonight. Now it was time to get the hell out of here and find out more about the guys they'd taken out. Either "White's" phone or the other guy's fingerprints had to give them something.

As he slid into the back seat of the SUV next to a waiting Tiago, he realized that he was bleeding.

Well, shit.

CHAPTER 30

"How do you guys deal with this all the time?" Hope couldn't sit still as Berlin worked on her laptop communicating with everyone.

Hailey was doing the same thing on her own laptop.

Both women were sitting at the kitchen table and had on headphones. They couldn't hear her as she spoke to Magnolia and Fleur, who were both sitting at the island countertop.

She had a feeling that the two women were only downstairs to keep her company. Because they seemed so calm about Ezra and Tiago being gone on this *very dangerous* operation.

"Honestly I'm too tired." Magnolia leaned back in her chair, rubbed her pregnant belly. "Don't get me wrong, I definitely worry about Ezra, but fate brought us back together. I like to think that she wouldn't be so cruel as to rip us apart now."

"Oh my god," Fleur said with a laugh. "While Magnolia is wonderful, she's lying through her teeth. She's trying to put you at ease. We both worry like crazy. We even have a group text with the partners of this crew—oh, I'm going to add you to it. We send each other funny memes. Sometimes dark ones... It's nice to have others to commiserate with."

Magnolia gave a tired laugh. "She's right, I'm totally lying. I was hoping to make you feel better. But I'm not lying about the tired part. I don't remember being this tired with my first. Probably because I wasn't having a 'geriatric' pregnancy then. All I want to do is sleep, but then I can't get comfortable when I am in bed. So." She shrugged.

"Wait, did you call your pregnancy geriatric?" Hope stared at the gorgeous woman.

"Any pregnant woman over thirty-five is considered to be geriatric." She rolled her eyes.

"I...sort of hate that. It seems like such a hateful term."

Magnolia grinned at her now. "I knew I liked you."

Fleur snickered even as she typed something into her phone. "Okay, now I've added you to our group text."

Hope wanted to tell her that she wasn't Bradford's partner, that she shouldn't be included, but who was she kidding? She *wanted* to be included. She wanted him so badly her chest ached with it. And this was it; she was in this thing even if she hadn't told him. She had to take this chance at life and stop letting the past control her chance at happiness. "Thank you." She shot a glance over at Berlin and Hailey, who were quietly talking into their comms.

Then she looked back at Fleur and Magnolia. She'd already talked to Bradford and Berlin about this and they'd been waiting to execute this part of her plan, but she felt like it was time to just do it.

"I reached out to a friend of mine about releasing that video of those guys breaking into my house. I keep going over the pros and cons of it."

"I say do it," Fleur said around a yawn.

"Yeah." Magnolia nodded. "And I think you guys should release the video of Edward Killeen screwing that waitress. The only con is if the waitress gets caught in the crossfire from online fallout. I mean, I think she sucks for screwing a married man, but I still don't want to expose some woman to a bunch of hatred like that. That stuff can be toxic."

"Maybe...we could just send it to his wife instead?" Hope felt a little mean doing it, but if they were going to blow up this guy's life, they needed to do it right. And they should do it while Bradford and the others were destroying Killeen's heroin.

Which was awesome in itself.

"Ooh, I love that. And you know Berlin will do it." Fleur looked very pleased with the idea.

Berlin turned around to face them as she slid her headset off. "They're on their way back now. And yes, I love that idea. I can send the video to Killeen's wife using an encrypted message. She'll never be able to figure out who sent it but...I almost guarantee she knows who the woman is, considering she's the owner of the café. At least on paper. This might make things very uncomfortable for Edward Killeen."

"It might also give the Feds something to use to sway her to help them," Magnolia added.

Oh, that was a great point. "I've got someone who can release the other video of those guys at my house," Hope said. "Once my coworkers and professional acquaintances get wind of it, this thing will spread. A bunch of masked men breaking into a journalist's home... It's going to piss off a lot of people."

Whether that would fall back on Killeen, directly or not, wasn't exactly the point. It was part of it, because she wanted him to feel pressure from all sides—and to leave her the hell alone. But she also wanted the public to know about it in case something happened to her. And hopefully whoever was working with Killeen would back off once that video was live.

"Do it now," Berlin said. "Unless you want me to?"

"No, I've got this." She needed to be doing something anyway. After grabbing her laptop, she got to work, sending it to her most trusted allies in the industry. Two she didn't actually like on a personal level, but she respected them and their work.

Once she was done with that, she texted her friend Thea, hoping it wasn't too late, considering it was now four in the morning. But she knew that Thea woke up early to jog so she took a chance that it wasn't on Do Not Disturb.

Hey, just wanted to let you know that a video related to me might be dropping soon and that I'm okay. I'm safe. She started to set her phone down, figuring Thea would text her back whenever she woke up.

But Thea's response was immediate. *What? You can't just leave me hanging without details! What's going on?*

You're up?

Hell yeah. Couldn't sleep so I started on my treadmill. Gonna go for another forty-five minutes.

I say this with love, but you're a freak.

Tell me something I don't know. So. Spill. Now.

Hope quickly typed out the details about the video, leaving out all the other stuff. Just that some masked men had broken into her dad's place while she was out, and some weird things had been happening. She alluded that it might be related to a story, but didn't give anything more. She simply wanted her friend to know she was safe.

Thanks for letting me know, I definitely would have worried. And keep me updated. If you need a place to crash, you know I've got you.

Thank you. She paused for a moment, then added, *In case I don't tell you enough, you're a great friend and I'm lucky to have you in my life.*

Thea responded with three big-eyed, tear-filled emojis, then a couple hearts, which made Hope smile.

Just as quickly, her smile died when Berlin cleared her throat pointedly.

Hope looked up at her, felt her stomach tighten at the woman's expression.

"Listen, I just heard from the guys. I don't want you to freak out or anything, but Bradford has been injured."

CHAPTER 31

"I'm fine," Bradford grumbled as Hope laid out the first aid kit.

"I can see that." She tried to keep the tartness out of her tone as she started cleaning his wound.

"I'm sensing the sarcasm."

"No sarcasm. Just worry." She gently cleaned the slice along his upper shoulder. He'd already cleaned it on the way back and done a half-assed job of bandaging it, but she wanted to give it a fresh one with new antiseptic. "You got really lucky." She was trying to keep her emotions in check, but her voice trembled as she spoke. When Berlin had told her he'd been injured, she'd prepared for the worst.

"I did. And thank you," he murmured, lifting his uninjured arm and cupping her cheek with his free hand. "I swear I'm okay and I'm sorry that you worried. Also, because we haven't talked about it... are you still on the pill?"

Realizing what he intended she eyed him cautiously as she set the antiseptic on the bathroom countertop. "I am on the pill. But what...are you doing?"

He was sitting on the countertop in just his pants, and she recognized that expression far too well. And no. Just nooooo. Not happening.

"I'm only trying to show you how fine I really am."

She batted at his hand. "Bradford, I swear to god—"

Grinning, he grasped onto her hip. "I'm not even bleeding anymore."

"You're being ridiculous." But she leaned into his hold anyway as he spread his thighs wider. "But I'm glad you're okay," she whispered, gently holding on to his waist, trailing her fingers over his bare skin. He was here and safe and had escaped mostly unscathed.

"Of course I am." His gaze dropped to her mouth, that familiar hunger in his eyes sending a shiver spiraling through her.

"There is no *of course*. You're not bulletproof." And if that bullet had shifted by even an inch in the wrong direction, he could have lost use of his arm. Or a whole lot worse.

"I can't spend my days worrying about the what-ifs, Hope." He pulled her closer, sliding his arms around her and holding her tight even as he tried to hide a wince. She buried her face against his neck as he said, "And I would really like to get naked in the shower with you right now."

She let out a startled laugh and pulled back to look at him, trying to gauge his expression. "Are you serious right now?"

"I figure if I don't ask..."

"How can I say no to you when you've just been shot—"

"Almost shot."

"Fine, *almost* shot, helping me out. Grazed by a bullet, to be more precise."

"Hope, if you don't want—"

She leaned forward and kissed him because who was she kidding? There was no world where she didn't want to jump him. Especially not after he was doing everything he could to keep her safe, had enlisted his friends to help her, and was the kindest, most gorgeous man she knew.

He just kept showing up, kept showing her exactly what kind of man he was—the kind worth fighting for.

He took over with ease, only wincing a little as he lifted her pajama top up and over her head.

"I'll deal with my clothes—and yours," she added. He might not be bleeding right now, but she didn't want him straining himself at all.

"I mean…I won't argue if you want to do a little strip show." He nipped her bottom lip then leaned back as she shimmied out of her pants and panties.

"That's about as sexy as you're getting right now," she said with a laugh.

Which just made him laugh as he slid off the countertop.

She moved in close, sliding her palm over his covered cock. "You're sure you want this now?"

"If my answer to that question is ever no, put a bullet in me," he groaned as she squeezed him once.

Then he leaned down to capture her mouth with a hungry groan. As he teased his tongue against hers, she quickly unbuttoned his pants and shoved them down his legs before they stumbled toward the shower.

She knew she should probably put a stop to this, but she wasn't walking away from him.

Ever.

Even if the shitty part of her anxiety brain tried to tell her that this was too good to be true, she was just going to have to risk it.

Risk getting hurt and dealing with the fallout if it happened. Because she couldn't protect herself forever. And if she was being honest with herself, she'd been running from him, and herself, for far too long. It was time to stop telling everyone else's story and live her life.

After he started the shower, he pressed her up against the cold tile, making her back arch—and him smile as she basically thrust her breasts at him with her reaction.

Taking over in that way she loved, he cupped one breast, teasing the already tight bud with his thumb and forefinger as he sucked on her other nipple.

Careful not to clutch onto his injured arm or shoulder, she slid her fingers through his hair as he teased her with sharp tugs from his mouth. She hadn't been expecting any of this tonight and the sensation of touching him was never going to get old.

She'd been so damn touch starved for years, trying to lock herself up tight from the world. And now the man she wanted more than her next breath was right here.

Still pressed up against the wall, the water now steaming as it pounded down around them, she wrapped one leg around him, digging her heel into his ass as she tried to urge him closer.

But he stayed in control, sliding his hand down to her hip, holding her in place as he continued teasing a path down her abdomen, then lower until he was kneeling on the tile in front of her.

"Are you sure you're okay to do this?"

He looked up at her, his expression pure fire as he slid one of her legs over his good shoulder. And then she forgot to breathe or think as he began teasing her clit with the perfect amount of pressure.

"Don't hurt yourself," she managed to rasp out.

In response, he sucked on the sensitive bundle of nerves.

At the shock of pure pleasure that punched through her, she arched off the shower wall and felt the rumble of his laugh against her clit.

The reverberation sent another thrill through her, even as he continued teasing her until she couldn't hold on to her control at all.

She'd never been able to truly let go with anyone until him. That need to remain in control, to always have a handle on things, had been a real presence even during sex.

Except with him.

When he slid two fingers inside her, pushing deep, she jolted at the sensation, need coiling tight inside her. He'd always known how to bring her pleasure, to make her feel safe.

"I'm so close," she admitted, the words tearing from her. It should be too soon for her, but she'd almost lost him.

And now he was in front of her, on his knees, teasing her clit. The visual was enough to set her on fire.

She rolled her hips against his teasing strokes, her inner walls tightening faster and faster—until he sucked on her clit and she was lost.

She came with her entire body, the orgasm punching through her as he buried another finger inside her.

"Bradford." His name tore from her as wave after wave of pleasure rolled through her, until she sagged against the tile, her entire body one raw nerve.

With a very satisfied expression, he stood, his thick erection at full alert, and oh, she reached for him, wanting to bring him as much pleasure as he'd brought her.

She gripped him tight as he placed a hand on the tile above her head. Stroking him once, long and hard, she held his gaze. Savored the way his eyes dilated as he sucked in a breath.

She loved touching him, stroking him, making him lose his mind. There was no other power like it in the world, and doing this for the man she loved? It was a turn-on all in itself.

But she didn't want him coming in her hands or on her.

Leaning up, she was glad when he met her halfway, captured her mouth as she continued stroking him with that hard pressure she knew he loved.

She bit his bottom lip as she slowed her strokes. "Are you good if I bend over?" Because she knew he couldn't hold her up against the tile. Not now. They could do that later once he'd healed, but she wanted to feel him inside her.

He groaned, stealing her breath as he claimed her mouth again. "Again, if I ever say no to that…" He gripped her hip with one hand and turned her around.

She arched into the fall of water as he guided himself inside her.

The sensation of being filled by him nearly overwhelmed her senses until she felt the hint of another orgasm.

As if he read her mind, he reached around to her front and began teasing her clit in hard little strokes.

"I know you can come again," he growled, sliding his big palm down her back as he continued thrusting in wild, unsteady strokes.

She clenched around his thick erection, enjoying the way he groaned behind her. She wanted to make him lose control too. But he was right, she could come again, and she desperately wanted to while he was inside her.

"Faster," she demanded, desperate for another release.

As he increased the tempo, it didn't take her long until another orgasm slammed into her, this one harder, more intense.

And he was right behind her, clutching onto her hip in a tight grip she knew would leave a bruise as he found his own release.

When he finally eased out of her, she gasped at the loss of him, but turned around and wrapped herself around him, savoring the skin to skin of their bodies. "I could have lost you." Her voice nearly broke on the last word, the emotions she'd been trying to keep buried popping back up to the surface.

"I know, baby. But you didn't." His tone was soothing as he held her close. "And I'm not going anywhere."

She wasn't sure if there was a double meaning in those words, but she chose to believe there were.

Because she wasn't going anywhere either. He'd have to be the one to leave her. Because she'd gone and fallen in love with her husband.

CHAPTER 32

*How you make others feel about themselves,
says a lot about you.*

"Hey, Mia." Hope answered her phone on the third ring as she hurried out of the bathroom. She'd woken up twenty minutes ago and Bradford had been gone. She knew he wouldn't have left without telling her, but she still wanted eyes on him.

And you know, also her hands and mouth. Especially after what they'd shared a few hours ago in the shower.

She wanted to tell him that she loved him—and she would. But not until this mess was behind her.

Behind *them*.

He deserved all of her, and not when the pressure was on.

"Hey, are you okay?" Worry tinged Mia's voice.

"Um. Yes. Are you okay?"

"Yeah. I mean...I saw that video at your dad's place. Your place, I mean. It's all over social media with a lot of speculation but no real answers."

Oh right, the video. She'd sent it to people she worked with, then basically fallen off the face of the earth once Bradford had gotten back bleeding. As she sat on the bed, she pulled up her email account and winced. She also had a handful of missed phone calls, but not many people had this number outside of her work. And they knew she was somewhere safe.

Chelsea and Kim had called. The sheriff too. Okay, so this thing was definitely making the rounds. *Good.*

"I'm fine. I promise," she said as she pulled up various social media outlets and saw that oh...the video was trending on one of them. And her name was trending on another. *Ooookay.* That made sense that Mia was calling. "I'm somewhere safe," she added, because she wasn't going to get into all the details.

"You're sure? That video was terrifying. Those masked men breaking into your place... Is it... Do you think it has anything to do with my story?" she whispered.

Hope blinked. "What? No! No, no, no. I know what this is about, and while I can't give you any details, I promise it has absolutely nothing to do with you."

"You're absolutely sure?"

"A hundred percent. I have no reason to lie," she added. "Now, how are you doing?"

"No, no, we're going to talk about this. I'm worried about you."

Hope tried to scan through some of the comments, but gave up so she could focus on Mia. "You don't need to worry about me. I've got people in my corner." That knowledge had a ribbon of warmth curling through her.

She really did have people now, and they all had her back. It was a heady, surreal feeling.

"Okay, good. I've been so worried... Also, I think we should release the video."

Hope held her breath for a beat, unsure she'd heard right. "The one you sent me? Of him attacking you?" she added, because she wanted to be crystal clear.

"Yes. I don't know that I'm ready to tell my story yet, but...I want the video out there. He'll be running for reelection in a few months, and screw him. I've already talked to my new boss and they support my decisions. I don't think they care if there's any blowback."

"Okay. I love this, but I'm going to wait a couple days. Is that okay?" Hope wanted to give Mia time to think it through, and she also wanted to wait until the dust settled on her own bullshit. She didn't want anything to distract from Mia's story once she told it—and she didn't want the wider public to think there was a correlation between the governor sexually harassing Mia and the men who'd broken into her home.

"Definitely okay. And thank you...for everything. You've been so patient with me."

"You don't have to thank me for that."

"Well, I am. Because I appreciate it and you."

"You're welcome, then. And I'll give you a heads-up before I post any-thing," she said as the bedroom door opened.

Just like that, she could pull in a full breath without pressure on her chest. Bradford stepped in carrying a mug of what had to be coffee for her. She wanted to tell him not to strain himself, but knew how that would go over.

And she didn't really have a leg to stand on since they'd had sex in the shower not too long ago.

"Thank you. I'll talk to you soon," Mia said.

Once she said her good-byes, Hope set her phone down and smiled at him. "Hey, how are you?"

He rotated his injured arm as he handed her the mug. "Barely feel it."

She stood as she took it, gently kissed him in greeting. "Somehow I doubt that. But thank you for the coffee. So...the video has gone viral, apparently?"

He nodded, his expression neutral as he motioned for her to sit with him on the bed.

Inhaling the rich breakfast blend, she crossed her legs as she sat, enjoying the way he casually laid his hand on her thigh. "So...what's your expression about? Something else happen?"

Bradford shook his head. "No, but we got a lot of intel from the phone we took last night. And from the fingerprints we took."

She nodded slowly. "Are you trying to tell me that you're about to go do something to someone, somewhere, you don't want to give me details on?"

He laughed in surprise, but leaned forward and brushed his lips over hers. The bed depressed slightly with the movement. "Pretty much," he murmured.

"Okay. I mean, I don't want you to go, but at this point I don't want any of this. And we need to finish this thing, see it through." Because it was the only way they'd have a real shot at a life and a future together.

"I expected an argument."

She shook her head as a yawn escaped. Yep, she needed a lot more coffee than this. "You're skilled and prepared and smart. And I know your people have your back."

He gave her a soft smile. "They really do. Ezra will be staying behind because Magnolia hasn't been feeling well. So the house is covered... Have you looked at any of the comments online?"

"Not really. One of my contacts called and was worried about me. She alerted me that the thing took off."

He nodded. "In that same vein, according to Berlin, Killeen's wife saw the video she emailed her, but hasn't said anything to her husband yet. But she *has* been moving some money around. And she and her son are still in New Orleans."

"That's interesting."

"Yep. And Killeen is pissed about that video at your place. He's been on the phone all morning putting out fires with people worried they're not going to get their 'product.' According to Hailey and Berlin he's also trying to figure out if you're actually writing a story on him. He didn't think you were before, but he's fully lost his shit at this point. Though that's mostly over all his destroyed product. He suspects a cartel with a heavy presence in Texas of making the strike against him." Bradford looked very smug at that.

As he should. The strikes against Killeen last night had been damaging.

"He's got a couple meetings set up today and it doesn't sound like he has any plans to go after you. Yet," he added, his expression darkening. "And we're going to stop him before he comes after you again."

"I know you will." She'd been taking care of herself for so long that having someone else in her corner was going to take some getting used to. "Do you have to go now?"

"Yeah." She could hear the regret in his voice.

"I'll be safe here, so go and don't think about me. Just...be safe. Take care of my husband."

He paused for a long moment. "Your husband?" he rasped out.

"That's right."

His jaw clenched tight, but he leaned forward and claimed her mouth in one hard kiss, before he stalked from the room.

She sat there for a long moment, trying to catch her breath, but when her phone buzzed again, she snapped it up. He was going to take care of things for her; she needed to take care of her own business. And that meant returning all the missed calls and emails.

When she saw it was Kim calling, she answered immediately. "Hey, Kim."

"Hey, you're okay!" She sounded out of breath or close to tears.

"I'm fine. More than fine. I take it you saw the video?"

"Oh yeah. The whole town is buzzing about it," she whispered. "I'm currently hiding in the cooler to call you. I think I can guess who broke into your daddy's place, or at least who sent those guys?"

"Your guess is probably the same as mine."

Kim sighed. "That's what I figured."

"What's everyone in town saying?"

"Mostly just wondering what the hell the world is coming to. Everyone's worried about you. I heard the sheriff say he's sending a deputy to your place to check on you. But...I assume you're not there?"

"No, definitely not at home." She read the first post, saw an outraged blurb from one of her favorite colleagues lamenting that a fellow journalist wasn't even safe in her own home.

"Well, good. If you need anything, you let me know."

"Of course. And if you hear anything worth knowing, you better let me know."

"Absolutely... And since we're on that topic, an old friend of Hank's reached out. Nestor Rivera."

"Oh yeah, Mr. Rivera." He was on the list of her dad's friends she'd been planning to talk to. He'd sold his farm and moved to Florida to be closer to his kids and grandkids. "How is he?"

"Good enough, but he wants to meet up with you. He was in New Orleans with his church group for some choir thing and saw the video."

"Jeez, really?"

"It's at thirteen million-plus views and growing. Someone from town had to have told him about it or he just saw it himself. Anyway, he wants to meet with you and had no idea how to reach you."

"So he contacted you?"

Kim sniffed slightly. "Course he did."

"You trust him?"

"More than most. About a decade ago, we had a rough couple years and he helped us out. No strings attached either. Just pitched in and told us to pay him back if we could. Eventually Andrew and I did and I never forgot that kindness. So yeah, I do trust him."

Hope leaned back against the headboard, taking a sip of her coffee. "I actually remember him stopping by the farm occasionally to check on my mom. I think he gave her money sometimes."

"He did," Kim said bluntly. "And Hank thanked him for it later. I think that's why Nestor wants to see you now. He's worried, says he needs to talk to you."

"*Needs* to?"

"Yeah."

"Did he say about what?" Hope asked.

"No, but he seemed really worried."

"Can you send me his number?"

"Of course... Do you want me to tell anyone I talked to you?" Kim asked.

"No. Not yet. I'm still lying low, though I'll probably check in with Chelsea just to let her know I'm okay." She thought about touching base with the sheriff since he'd called a couple times, but hadn't decided yet.

"I won't even tell Andrew," she whispered. "Gotta go."

A few seconds later, her phone alerted her to an incoming text with Nestor's phone number.

She sat on it for a moment, then headed downstairs. Hailey was sitting in the kitchen with her husband Jesse and they looked as if they were having a moment, so Hope started to step back. But Hailey waved her inside when she saw her.

"Come on in. We're just talking."

Her husband's slightly surly expression said otherwise, but then he gave her an easy smile. "I've got some work to get to anyway." He kissed the top of Hailey's head before disappearing, a pastry in hand.

"I didn't mean to interrupt."

"We're good, I swear. Bradford said you'd seen everything online?"

"Sort of, yeah. I started scanning, but it's a lot. And I learned very early in my career not to even search my name. I don't think we need to read what strangers have to say about us."

Hailey snickered. "Isn't that the truth, and something I've learned big-time the last couple years. You hungry? Rowan cooked before everyone left. He made a bunch of mini sausages wrapped in pancakes."

Her mouth watered at the mention of that. "Uh, yeah. I need more caffeine too. So is Berlin with them?"

"Yep. But if you need anything, I'm here too. Despite what that lunatic says, I'm just as good as her. Just...maybe not as crazy."

"Bradford says you're both equally good. And crazy," she added with a laugh.

Hailey snickered. "God, I love him. And I love you two together."

"Thank you."

Hailey narrowed her gaze slightly at her. "Huh. Okay, then. So you kinda look like you've got something on your mind."

"Maybe." She quickly recapped her conversation with Kim, then said, "Obviously I want to be careful about meeting him, but the Nestor I remember was a good man. If he wants to meet, I don't want to miss the opportunity."

Hailey grabbed her laptop from the kitchen table while Hope heated up her breakfast. "I'll do a search on him. Also, send me his cell number, I'll see about tracking him. We'll figure out if this is a trap or not."

***

Hope glanced around the quiet coffee shop, didn't pause on Ezra, who'd arrived twenty minutes ago to get a lay of the place. She knew not to make eye contact with him or act like she knew him. They were a few towns over so she wouldn't be recognized by anyone in King's Creek.

Hailey was in a vehicle out back with her husband waiting so she had plenty of backup.

And...she spotted Nestor. Right where Ezra said he would be. In a back booth, sipping an espresso, a cruller mostly untouched in front of him.

Relief flooded his expression when he saw her and a rush of memories hit her all at once. Jesus, how had she forgotten? He'd come by the farm more than a few times. He, Kim, and a bunch of others had dropped off casseroles at least once a week. And Kim had always given her free pie whenever she'd been in the diner, all the way up until she was eighteen and left town. Something she'd never thought of because she'd been a kid.

"Hope," he said with a shaky smile as she approached, sliding out of the booth. "You look so much like your mother."

"Thank you." She stepped into his open arms, realized she was a little taller than him and felt his tears on her neck when he hugged her.

He wiped at his face once they parted. "I'm so glad that you're okay," he whispered, even though there was no one nearby.

Ezra was near the front and the barista was on his phone behind the countertop near the front as well. And Nestor couldn't know that she had a listening device on her. But he seemed...nervous maybe. Or just shaken, she couldn't tell.

"I saw that video and..." He motioned back to the booth. "Here, sit. And eat the cruller. I've been too worried to eat."

"Mr. Rivera—"

"Oh, sweetheart, call me Nestor," he said with a laugh.

"Okay, Nestor." She found herself smiling, taking in his wrinkled face and sweet smile. He still looked like the same man she'd known as a kid with a few more laugh lines, but the same kind eyes. "I appreciate you being worried about me, but there's obviously something more going on, isn't there?" Otherwise he wouldn't have reached out to Kim to get her contact information.

"Yes." He held on to his espresso cup tightly, the whites of his knuckles showing before he took a deep breath.

She'd learned with her job not to push people, even though that was exactly what she wanted to do right now. But that often stressed people out, made them shut down faster. So she waited. When he didn't say anything, she nudged a little. "Want me to go grab a coffee while you gather your thoughts?"

"No, no. I was just wool-gathering. Your father...he was a complicated man."

"I've been hearing that a lot lately," she said dryly.

Which brought out a startled laugh from Nestor. "I can imagine you have. He was a shitty father and a shitty husband to you and Grace. But he wasn't always like that. And he was a good neighbor. I was glad when he finally kicked his demons." He cleared his throat. "My mama had a problem with alcohol too."

She was silent as he went quiet for another moment, unsure if she should respond.

But then he looked back at her, clear-eyed and worried. "Do you know who broke into your home? The men from the videos?"

"Not the men specifically, but I can guess."

He nodded slightly, then leaned forward. "Does it have to do with one of your stories?"

She shook her head.

"Okay, okay. That's what I figured. Like I said, your father was a com-plicated man. He discovered that one of his neighbors was running drugs… Heroin."

"The Killeens?"

He nodded again, this time more fervently. "Yes, yes. I sold my farm to Edward. I didn't know what he was doing when I sold, I swear to you." He shook his head, frustration clear on his face now. "But he made an offer I couldn't resist. I'm too old for farming, and my family had moved away. I missed my grandkids and… Sorry, I'm rambling, as my daughter likes to say."

Hope gave a faint smile. "Take your time."

"Anyway, your dad, he started investigating and roped a couple of us old-timers into it."

"His AA buddies?"

"Mostly, but he brought me in too. Said he needed people he could trust."

"What about Chelsea Ortega?"

"The lawyer? No. She lost her daughter to drugs on a spring break trip in Destin. Hank said it might be too much for her to get involved. Plus…he might have done some breaking and entering and trespassing. I don't think he wanted to involve her for legal reasons as well. And the short of it is…he gave me some information. A flash drive and pictures mostly."

"Yeah?"

He nodded. "Told me to hold on to it just in case. And then he died. I've been sitting on the drive trying to figure out what to do with it. I have no idea who to talk to about this…and then I saw that viral video. Actually, one of Hank's AA buddies from town sent it to me. Said he was worried about you and wanted me to know what was going on since we'd all been part of his investigation."

She nodded, pretty sure she knew where he was going with this.

Then he slid a small leather bag across the table. "This is for you. You're a journalist, and if I'm being honest, I've got kids and grandkids. I don't know what would happen if I turned this over to the Feds or whoever. I don't want to risk them getting hurt. But hopefully you'll have the right contacts?" He looked so hopeful in that moment that she found herself nodding.

"I do, actually. And after I look at this, I'll figure out what to do from there." She couldn't make any promises until she'd seen exactly what he'd given her.

"Good, good. I... Sometimes I swear I'm being followed. I feel paranoid saying that. But some of the other farmers, the ones who used to work with Hank on all this...they say the same thing."

"His AA friends?"

Nestor nodded, then glanced at his phone, smiled at whatever he saw on the screen. Then he showed her a picture of a smiling, chubby girl who couldn't be more than three smashing bananas all over her face. "This is my heart right here."

She smiled at the clear love in his voice. "I'm glad for you. And I know I never said thank you, but thank you for all you did to help my mom and me."

He shot her a surprised look. "You were a child. You don't need to thank me. It was my duty as your family friend and neighbor to help. More than that, I wanted to. I loved your mother," he said simply.

And she couldn't tell if he meant platonically or more. She definitely wasn't going to ask either because she had way too much to handle right now. Talk about complicated.

"Well thank you anyway. We were lucky to have a neighbor like you."

He reached out and patted her hand gently. "I'm so proud of who you've become. And Grace would have been proud too. In case you ever have any doubts. Now," he said, clearing his throat, "I have to get back on the road or I'll hit traffic back in New Orleans."

Nodding, she slid out of the booth with him and gave him a big hug. After he'd left, she'd planned to head out front but stopped when she saw a text from Ezra.

Someone followed your friend. They planted a tracker on your car. Head out back. Hailey will pick you up.

She texted back a thumbs-up emoji, then casually ordered a drink from the barista. Once she'd paid, she asked, "Where's your bathroom?"

He pointed. "Hallway. Your drink will be ready when you get back."

She nodded, then left, bypassing the bathroom door and stepping out into the bright sunlight. Shielding her eyes, she started to scan the alley, but Hailey was already pulling up to the rear door.

Or Jesse, she realized, was driving, Hailey in the front seat.

Her heart rate kicked up, Hope slid into the back seat without pause. "He was followed?" she asked as she shut the door behind her.

"That's what Ezra said. Got the guy on video too. Said he was subtle about the tracker, but not subtle enough. Ezra's going to tail him, see what happens."

There really was something to be said about working with a team. "What about Nestor?"

"Ezra's going to head out, see if the guy follows Nestor. If someone else does, he'll tail him instead."

Relief slid through her. At least Nestor would be safe—she could only hope that Bradford was safe as well. Seeing how his team worked the last few days, she had no doubt that they all had each other's backs.

CHapter 33

"This isn't what I was expecting." Bradford scanned the pristinely mowed lawn and home from the woods, saw a two-story farmhouse with white paneling on the side and ferns hanging from the front porch. There was a basketball hoop in the driveway and evidence of kids, given the random toys in the front yard.

The place was on seven acres and tucked back from the nearby main road.

"Me neither." Adalyn lowered her binoculars. "But this showed up as a location that White visited at least once a week."

As they remained hidden in the woods, a minivan pulled out of the garage so he raised his binoculars again.

A blonde-haired woman was driving, and even with the tinted windows, he could see at least two kids in the back, maybe a third in the last row.

"That'll be Amberlyn Jones," Rowan said. "According to what Berlin found. Looks enough like her from the file we've got."

"I say we go in now, do a search of the home and shop," Bradford said. "She might just be running errands but we should have half an hour or so at least." The property was far enough out from town that just her driving there would be about fifteen minutes in one direction.

Adalyn looked at her watch, then nodded as she pulled out her jammer. "Rowan and I will take the main house, you and Tiago take the workshop."

Bradford nodded, then he and Tiago made their way across the lush green lawn, past the driveway, the sparkling pool behind the house, and onto what, according to the plans that Berlin had found during her research, was a workshop for the husband, Wesley Jones.

The guy didn't have a link to White that they'd found. But that didn't mean much if Jones was using a burner to talk to White. Still, the guy owned a restaurant and a couple feed stores. He was definitely well off, but Bradford still couldn't see the connection.

And Berlin hadn't found one.

It didn't take long to pick the lock, but he did notice there were three cameras in front of the workshop. "Three seems like overkill, right?" he murmured as he and Tiago stepped inside.

Even though they were jamming the Wi-Fi signal, they still wore masks. Sucked because of the heat, but they weren't going to risk revealing their identities to anyone.

"Yeah, it's interesting all right."

Inside the shop, the two walls on the left and right were lined with neat bins and organized tools. It was big enough to hold a four-wheeler and two worktables. There were a couple rocking chairs in progress and six empty beer bottles scattered around the other empty table.

"This might be where Jones meets with…whoever," he murmured to Tiago as he nodded at the bottles. He could have a poker night or whatever, but White's consistent presence here, according to his phone's logs, had them all curious to know who this Jones guy was.

They moved methodically through the bins, checking each one for weapons or drugs. But it was just normal storage stuff like Christmas decorations and tools.

"Guys, time to get out of there. Someone's turning onto the drive. Truck plate tells me it's Wesley Jones," Berlin said through their comm line. She was back on the main road as lookout.

"Nothing here anyway," Adalyn said.

"We'll be out in a minute," Tiago said, motioning for Bradford to join him at a giant filing cabinet near the back with a heavy-duty padlock on it.

Bradford's heart rate kicked up at the sight. "That's some serious hardware. Can you open it?"

But Tiago was already kneeling in front of it.

"We're going to need a few more minutes," Bradford said. "Might have something."

"He's in the driveway now." Adalyn's voice was tight.

"Got it," Tiago said triumphantly.

"Parking," Adalyn continued.

Bradford moved the door of the shop, ready to knock the guy out if he came this way. It wasn't ideal, but he could knock Jones out so fast he wouldn't even see who'd attacked him or how many people were in his shop.

"Shit," Tiago murmured.

"How're we looking?" Bradford asked.

"He's heading inside the house. Your window is closing. Get the hell out of there now."

Tiago let out a short whistle, motioned him to the back of the workshop.

"We're leaving," Bradford said, even as he jogged over.

Tiago had his phone out and was taking pictures of...

"What the hell?" Bradford pulled out his own phone, snapped away before Adalyn had enough.

"Get out of there now! I can see him in the kitchen window on the phone. His back is to the pool and shop. We don't want him to know anyone was here."

Bradford eased the cabinet door shut and Tiago snapped the deadbolt back in place.

"We're at the door. What's your visual now? We clear?" Bradford asked as he wrapped his hand around the doorknob.

"He's still in the kitchen...but now he's heading out to the pool."

Shit. The pool faced the shop.

"Hold on, I've got this," Berlin said. "Get ready to run."

He wondered what she was going to do, then seconds later the ear-piercing sound of an alarm filled the air, audible even in the insulated workshop.

"He's heading inside. Go now," Adalyn snapped.

They slipped outside and he twisted the bottom lock into place. They didn't have time to relock the top one so this would have to do for now.

Instead of heading the way they'd come, they looped back around to the rear of the shop and raced for the nearby woods. It was going to be a trek returning to the main road from here, but they'd gotten away unscathed.

Only now he had more questions than answers.

***

Bradford had to hide his surprise when Hope greeted him with a hug in front of everyone. She slid right off the high-top stool at the kitchen island and wrapped her arms around him in a tight embrace.

She might not have said the words he needed to hear yet, but she'd called him her husband. And he knew what that meant for her.

Things had shifted and he was never letting his Hope go.

"Berlin texted," she said against his chest. "Said you found something."

"Berlin texted you?"

"That's right." Berlin was right behind him and fist-bumped Hope as she leaned over and grabbed a spanakopita pocket from the big round plate on the island. "Gotta keep my girl in the loop."

He blinked at Berlin's words, but Hope just grinned. And that was when he realized that his friend had not only accepted Hope into their world, but she genuinely liked her. At the end of the day, he didn't need approval from anyone when it came to Hope, but it still mattered that his people—especially Berlin, one of his favorite humans—had not only accepted her, but was welcoming her into the fold.

When Hope turned back to grab a spanakopita for herself, he nudged Berlin and she winked at him. And he swore his heart grew three sizes.

"So, spill," Hope said, sliding one of the spinach and cheese pastries onto a plate in front of him.

His stomach growled, but he wanted to get this out before he ate, so he sat down at the island as the others filtered in and took seats. Tiago was next to him, his expression a grim mirror to Bradford's own.

"Berlin already has the pictures," he started, nodding once at her. "But basically, there was a handbook—"

"Multiple instructional pamphlets," Tiago murmured.

Bradford nodded. "Yeah, exactly. Instructional pamphlets for how to make bombs. The instructions break it down into what's essentially a DIY YouTube instructional. There's a little symbol on the top left of the copies that's been linked to an extremist group. No actual stated political affiliation, but their beliefs are very right-leaning—heavy themes of white supremacy."

"Terrifying shit," Tiago murmured. "There was also a sort of manifesto that read like their bible, I guess. The symbol is on every page of the manifesto as well."

"But we didn't find any actual materials for making bombs or weapons, and no drugs either. We didn't get to do a deep dive, but the place looked clean at first glance. And..." Bradford shrugged. "As far as I know, there's nothing illegal about possessing bomb-making instructionals."

"If they distribute them with the intention of committing a crime, it's a federal offense," Hope murmured.

Bradford wasn't even surprised that she knew that. She'd written multiple stories on extremists with different ideologies.

"While their literature was terrifying...I still don't know how this ties into Killeen." Adalyn shoved her hands into her pockets as she leaned against one of the countertops.

"I don't think it matters at this point," Hope said quietly. Then she looked between Bradford and Tiago. "Were there any specifics in the literature you saw? Any plans?"

He shook his head, even as his gut tightened. Just because there hadn't been anything tangible didn't mean these guys weren't planning something.

"I've called in the Feds." Skye's voice from the doorway made them all turn as she and Axel strode in. "I know how much we can handle, but they've got more people. Hazel is on this, flying in today. She's already mobilized a team—mostly because I already gave her a heads-up that shit was going down here. I think she's bringing in the DEA now too."

Bradford knew it wasn't an oversight that Skye had said Hazel's name in front of Hope.

Then Skye looked at Hope. "I don't actually think I need to say this, but you know you can't write about any of this, right?"

"I know. I might write a story about Killeen later—if he actually gets arrested. But not about this, not about you guys." She slid up next to Bradford, wrapped her arm around his middle. "I would never put any of you in danger. You've all saved my life and it's clear that you're doing really good work. So thank you."

Skye blinked, then grinned. "Okay, then. For right now, we're sitting back and doing nothing. I know that's going to be hard, but the FBI has got this. And we need to let them do their jobs."

"Maybe we could help them a little," Hope murmured, her expression almost feral.

CHAPTER 34

Hope knew she wasn't alone, but it was still nerve-racking sitting at Cross's Diner waiting for the sheriff to arrive. After going over everything with Bradford's people and getting a good night's sleep, she was as ready as she'd ever be for this.

If it worked, it did. And if it didn't...well, then it was a risk she was willing to take.

"Hey, Sheriff," Kim called out when the bell overhead jingled with his arrival. "I'll bring over your usual."

Hope hadn't even seen him drive up, but maybe he'd pulled around back. Or just walked from the station. She'd interviewed hundreds of people over the years. People who made her skin crawl. The sheriff didn't even rank in the top ten of the crappy people she'd faced down. She could do this, she reminded herself.

She couldn't get a read on him as he approached the booth, but he smiled as he slid in across from her. "Glad to see you're okay. You've had everyone in town and beyond talking."

She shrugged, keeping one hand wrapped around her mug to steady her. "It's been a wild few days."

"So what's going on? What was that video all about?"

"Pretty sure you know who was on that video. Or you can at least guess," she said quietly as she gave him a pointed look.

To his credit, he didn't seem all that surprised by her words. He just sighed and leaned back in the booth, but didn't respond.

"I had an interesting conversation with one of my dad's old friends yesterday," she continued when it was clear he wasn't going to say anything. "Told me my dad had been doing a little investigating of Edward Killeen." She paused when Kim strode up, a coffee mug in hand and two pieces of pie.

"Figured you could both use some pie," Kim said with a big smile for both of them.

"Thank you," she murmured, with the sheriff doing the same, but his smile didn't reach his eyes. Once they were alone again, she cut into the blackberry pie with her fork, but didn't take a bite yet. "I've got some really interesting information on Edward Killeen now. The kind of stuff that will land him and anyone on his payroll in jail. As I looked at the videos and photographs—oh yeah, I've got rock-solid evidence about all his drug running," she added as he clenched his jaw. "I kept thinking, why wouldn't Hank talk to someone? Someone like...you. And then I realized that of course he would have gone to you."

His jaw tightened again as he glanced around. "Where's your phone?" he demanded even as he snatched her purse off the side of the table.

She leaned back as he pulled out her recording device. Glaring at her, he turned it off.

Then he held out his palm. "Phone."

Sighing, she lifted it from where she'd been keeping it on her lap.

He took her phone, turned it off, then set both the phone and recorder under an empty pie display on the countertop. If he noticed the strange looks a couple of customers gave him, he didn't let on. Or more likely didn't care.

His expression was dark as he slid back across from her. He leaned forward, his mouth pulled into a tight line. "What the hell do you want?"

"Did you kill my dad?"

He blinked in shock, the kind you can't fake. "What? No. Hell no. And for the record, no one killed Hank. He died of a heart attack."

Yeah, she knew that, she'd just wanted to take him off guard and get a baseline for how honest he would be. "Did he come to you about the Killeens?"

The sheriff's jaw did that clenching thing again. "Jesus, Hope. The town is doing well," he finally snapped. "Businesses are popping up everywhere. People are actually moving here and having their kids here. This is what we needed for growth."

"Drugs are what we needed?" She kept her voice pitched low.

He struggled with her question, she could see it in his eyes. "We've got two factories here now. Legit ones. And everything else that comes with that. Your dad..." He shook his head, looked out at the half-empty parking lot. "He was upset, but he let it go once I explained things to him."

"Explained things?"

"That our town needs the Killeens. I hate what they're doing, but...there's no fighting them. He has too damn many people working for him. They're an army."

"So you just look the other way while he grows his heroin and poisons people?" She let the mask on her rage slip so he could see how angry she was. And it wasn't hard. Because that internal fury was feeding her. This man had been voted in to protect this town, the people in it.

Instead he'd lined his own pockets while some asshole built up an empire on other people's pain.

"It's not like that. He's not some low-level dealer. He doesn't...do anything here. This is a safe town." There was a hint of desperation in his tone, as if he didn't quite believe what he was saying. "Now tell me what kind of evidence you have. We can figure this out. I can keep you safe from him. I promise we can make all this go away."

"I'm keeping myself safe," she shot back. "Now why don't you tell me who broke into my house?"

He leaned back again but didn't respond. Instead he had that same hard look on his face she'd seen before and she knew this conversation was over. "I'll reach out later and we'll talk again once you're thinking more clearly. Because you do not want to go up against someone like him."

She held back a snort of derision as he stood and dropped a twenty on the table.

Before he'd made it to the door, two FBI agents strode out from the back of the diner just as an SUV pulled into the parking lot sideways blocking the front door.

The sheriff looked back at her, his dark eyes flinty, but she just shrugged and took a bite of her pie as one of the agents slapped cuffs on him and began reading him his rights.

She wasn't surprised that he didn't struggle or make a scene—though the rest of the diner was watching with shock as he was marched out the front doors and tucked into the back of the idling SUV.

Once the darkly tinted SUV pulled away, Kim grabbed Hope's cell phone and recorder, then sat across from her. She started to speak, but turned around and shouted, "Everyone eat your food and mind your business!" and everyone did just that. Because Kim was a little terrifying and no one wanted to get on her bad side and risk being banned from the diner. Not with pie this good.

Hope was pretty sure everyone was murmuring about what had just happened, but at least they weren't staring at her and Kim or trying to eavesdrop.

"How's the pie?"

Hope blinked at the unexpected question. "So amazing that it deserves its own Pulitzer. Or a trophy at the very least."

Kim cracked a smile. "Right answer. So...what happens now?"

"I honestly don't know." Last night Hope and Bradford had reached out to Kim to ask her about wiring her diner for a mini-sting operation. Hope hadn't been sure if she'd be into it, but the woman had jumped at the chance to take down the sheriff. "My guess is that he'll cut a deal."

Kim's face scrunched up. "Sneaky bastard." She glanced out in the parking lot. "You're sure you're good to be out in public?"

"Yeah. I mean, as much as I can be sure." The truth was, Bradford and a couple of the others were also waiting for her in at Jeep in the parking lot. And Rowan and Adalyn were stationed at the back of the place.

The Feds had jumped at the chance to get the sheriff incriminating himself because they desperately wanted to flip him, but Bradford hadn't been about to let her out of his sight. Another reason she loved him.

"I think it'll just be a matter of time before..." She shrugged, not wanting to say anything about Killeen even though no one seemed to be paying attention to them.

At this point, enough people had seen the sheriff arrested by the FBI so word would be spreading like wildfire. Which meant she did need to get out of here soon...

Almost as if he read her mind, Bradford texted her. *Time to wrap it up.*

"We'll see what plays out, but no one will know about you letting the Feds plant listening devices. I mean, the sheriff will but I don't think it'll matter." Because he would be cutting a deal, she had no doubt. If he had something to hand over and bring down the bigger fish, he'd probably sell his soul to get out of going to prison.

And she hated that he likely would, but that wasn't her problem anymore. She had to focus on the future—Bradford.

"I'm not worried about that," Kim said, then glanced behind her at the few customers. "Don't get me wrong, I don't trust everyone in here, but I think the Killeen family has a lot more to worry about than me."

Hope snorted in agreement.

Kim continued, "Oh, I heard from Nestor. He's good, heading back home with his church group tomorrow. I'll pass on whatever you say is okay."

"Just tell him thank you again from me. That's it. I appreciate everything he gave me." The videos her father and some of the others in his AA group had taken on Killeen's property had been what the FBI and now DEA needed to start infiltrating Killeen's holdings—of which there were many.

They were going to be untangling a lot of threads in the near future, and while she didn't think she was out of the woods yet, she didn't feel like she was walking around with a bull's-eye on her chest either. Not with the Feds closing in on him. She still wasn't sure what would happen with the frozen bodies but figured that wasn't her problem.

"I will. Oh, I've got two pies packed up to-go, for you and your friends," she said, whispering the last part.

"You are an angel."

By the time Hope said her good-byes and made it to the waiting Jeep with two pies in hand, she was already breathing easier.

"Ooh, what's in the box?" Berlin asked.

"What's in the boooox?" Hope and Bradford said at the same time in maniacal voices before cackling. God, she hadn't laughed like that in a long time and it was all because of him.

Berlin turned around and stared at the two of them. "What the heck was that?"

"It's from a movie before your time," Tiago murmured, throwing the Jeep into reverse.

"We can all watch it," Bradford said.

Berlin looked between the two of them before turning back around. "I think I'm good."

Hope grinned at Bradford, a lightness in her chest she hadn't felt in ages. This man brought out a side of her she'd kept buried for so long, afraid to have too much fun. To just live.

CHAPTER 35

Hope rolled over at the sound of a knock on the bedroom door.

Bradford did the same, but kept a hand on her leg because apparently he needed to be touching her at all times. "Yeah?"

"You guys decent?" Skye asked even as she opened the door.

"Good thing you waited for an answer," Bradford grumbled as he sat up.

Luckily they were dressed—now. After the arrest of Sheriff Crow yesterday, they'd all been lying low at the safe house as the FBI did their job. They'd gotten a few check-ins from Hazel—aka Special Agent Hazel Blake, who went way back with Skye. The woman had been an Air Force Cobra pilot years ago and served with Leighton, another of their founders. Just an all-around badass. Though to look at her, you'd never know.

Skye shrugged, but chin-nodded at Hope. "Hazel is here to talk to us. You up to answering a few questions?"

Hope was off the bed in seconds. "Yeah. I'm good to go."

Bradford wasn't as eager—he'd been enjoying just lying in bed with her after the chaos of the last week. But he grabbed a T-shirt and pulled it on before heading downstairs with her.

Hazel and her partner were waiting in the living room, both wearing dark suits, white undershirts and matching dark pants. They looked uncomfortable sitting on the love seat and both stood when Hope and Bradford entered.

He kept his hand on the small of her back, wanting it clear that she was his. Caveman? He didn't care.

"Ms. Berkley," Hazel said, stepping forward with a tired smile. "I'm Special Agent Hazel Blake and this is my partner, Special Agent Harvey Nelson."

"You can just call us Hazel and Harvey," Nelson murmured, smiling politely at the two of them.

Bradford had seen the guy rip into a suspect once like a feral hyena, metaphorically speaking, so he knew there was more to the soft-spoken agent who normally partnered with Hazel.

"Ah, thank you. And just call me Hope. Please."

"You want to sit?" Hazel asked, looking between the two of them.

The others weren't anywhere to be seen. Even Skye had disappeared once they'd come downstairs so it seemed it was just the four of them.

"Sure." Hope slid her hand into his as they sat on the opposite couch.

The living room of the rental had high beams across the ceiling, and welcoming, comfortable furniture in soothing earth tones.

"So..." Hope squeezed his hand and he scooted closer to her.

"What's the deal? Did you guys arrest Killeen?" Bradford asked. There was no sense in making small talk.

Both Hazel and Harvey pushed out a breath, clearly on the same page.

Hazel nodded. "Both Killeen men, but Patrick is making a deal."

"Weaselly little shit," Harvey muttered.

Hazel shot him a glare and he shrugged.

"Anyway," Hazel continued. "Patrick is making a deal, mostly because his mom has a ton of intel. They're going into WITSEC in exchange for testifying against Edward Killeen."

"Man shouldn't have screwed around on his wife." Harvey shook his head slightly. "He's finding out just how bad he messed up."

Hazel snorted, but lifted a shoulder. "We had a decent case, but she's serving everything up to us on a silver platter because *someone* sent her a video of her husband screwing around."

"So what does that mean for Hope? Is she safe?"

"I'm unofficially advising you that she's not in any danger. From what we've gathered—mostly from former Sheriff Crow and Tara Killeen—Edward didn't want you causing trouble for his boy. But more than that, he was worried your father had given you something. Or that you'd have access to something if you stayed in town long enough," Hazel said. "He thought Hank had hidden something in his house or in his shop and was determined to find it."

"Right now he's fighting for his life," Harvey added. "And he doesn't care about keeping his boy out of trouble since Patrick turned on him. You're as safe as anyone. But my two cents, I'd stay here for another few days at least until the dust settles."

"What about the rest of the sheriff's deputies? Any of them dirty?"

"Two, that we've uncovered. Crow gave them up easy." Hazel shook her head. "They're all turning on each other. It's like a feeding frenzy."

Hope nudged him and gave him a look he understood.

He cleared his throat. "What about Alden Phillips? He followed Hope around for a bit."

"We brought him in. He did a lot of random jobs for Killeen, mostly PI-level stuff but without the actual PI license. From what we can tell he's not linked to the drug side." Hazel lifted a shoulder.

"So...what about Wesley Jones?" Bradford and the others still didn't have a clear image of how he tied into Killeen and the others. And if Hazel was here, he was getting answers about everyone involved in this thing now.

The two agents shared a look, then Harvey stood, murmuring that he had a call to take. Which was clearly a lie, but Bradford understood.

Once he was gone, Hazel looked between the two of them, but her expression was hard as she zeroed in on Hope. "Everything I say stays in this room."

"She's not going to say shit," Bradford snapped, that protective urge swelling up lightning fast.

Hope nudged his leg though and held out a palm to Hazel. "I understand your concern. I'm not here as a journalist. I'm here as Bradford's wife and friend. I would never do anything to expose him or the people he considers family."

Her words found their mark, because Hazel let out a slow breath. "That's what Skye said and I trust her with my life. Just wanted to confirm. So. Jones." She sat back on the love seat, clearly debating how much to tell them. "He's under surveillance. Has been for about six months. That much I can tell you."

"Is he a threat to Hope?"

"Not that we know of, no."

"How is he connected to Killeen?"

"We don't know that he is." She paused again. "Thanks to an anonymous tip, we know that he's been linked to at least one of Killeen's guys. But Killeen had a lot of people working for him. A lot of locals. They helped with growing, transporting, lots of stuff. But there's nothing there that we can find that ties Jones and Killeen together."

"So why is he under surveillance?"

"I can't give specifics. But think...domestic terrorism."

Considering what they'd seen in his workshop, that made sense.

"There's been no mention of you," Hazel continued, looking at Hope.

"He might have been working with some of Killeen's guys. Or more likely, they were or *are* his recruits, for lack of a better word. But we don't suspect him of running drugs. That's not his thing."

Hope nodded, but he could feel the tension buzzing through her. It mirrored his own. "Okay, well, thank you for the update. I really appreciate it," he added.

"Me too. I know you didn't have to come here," Hope said softly.

Hazel gave them a wry smile as she stood. "I kinda did. If anything changes, I'll let you know. But Killeen is in custody and we've bagged everyone involved in his operation—including the men who broke into your home."

"You're sure?"

"Yep. Former Special Forces guys working...I wouldn't say for Killeen exactly. But with him. They're going to be charged with a whole lot worse than him, but that's all I can say about that. The DEA has been on them for a while. They'll go away for life."

Bradford figured that they were the ones responsible for the drug-related massacre in Arkansas but simply nodded and stood with Hazel.

Hope moved with him, and once the agents were gone, she buried her face against his chest as he held her close. "I feel like it's finally over."

Unless she decided to run again.

If she did, he was following this time.

CHAPTER 36

Four days later

"It feels almost surreal to be back here and I don't know why." Hope stepped into her kitchen, Bradford right behind her.

It was Wednesday morning and everything at her family home was quiet. Peaceful.

"Because you've been through a lot the last couple weeks." He moved in behind her, wrapped his arms around her in a comforting hug.

She loved when he held her like this, as if he treasured her. She leaned back into him, savoring the protectiveness of his embrace. "You have too," she murmured. "I'm going to miss your friends," she added.

"Eh. I'm glad they headed back to New Orleans." His tone was dry. "I want some alone time with you."

Which just made her laugh. "Your friends are amazing." And they'd very much accepted her, which was the best feeling in the world. Hailey and her husband had been the first to leave three days ago. Apparently he had some merger to deal with and they were the only ones headed back to the East Coast.

Then Ezra and Magnolia had left so she could get back home to "do nothing but rest" according to him. And finally this morning the others had trickled out.

Now... "Okay fine, I'm glad it's just the two of us here. How long can you stay with me?" she asked as she turned in his arms so she could face him. They hadn't talked about the future and she was ready to tackle it.

He looked down at her, his expression hard to read. "I already told you as long as it takes."

She wanted to ask exactly what that meant, but the words stuck in her throat. She loved this man, knew it to her bones. But saying the words, actually asking him if they were...well, *what* they were and what the future might look like for them, was... The words were sticking in her throat.

Because she cared too much.

"Okay," she whispered, leaning up on tiptoe to brush her lips against his. That seemed like a safe enough response.

He immediately deepened the kiss, taking her mouth in a hungry claiming she felt to her core. As she started to wrap her legs around him, he pulled back slightly, a half grin on his face. "Before we do this, I'm going to take our bags upstairs. Then we're going to eat, and *then* we're going to talk about our future."

Their future. Tingles settled in her abdomen at the way he said *our future*. It was like he was in her head. "I can help."

"Nope." He kissed her forehead then stepped back. "But you can pull out one of those casseroles from the freezer. We can pop it in the oven for lunch."

"I will." But as he headed up the stairs, she stepped outside to grab something she'd been meaning to show him.

And now seemed like the best time to do it. She might be good with words on paper, but actually telling someone how she felt?

She wasn't sure who'd brought her vehicle back home, but she was glad for it as she popped the trunk. Feeling almost embarrassed, she pulled out the first aid kit and withdrew the thing she'd been traveling with since the morning after that fateful night in Vegas.

Instead of telling him, she was going to show Bradford exactly what he meant to her.

"Hands where I can see them."

A menacing voice from behind made her jump and hold her hands in the air on instinct.

"Back away from your trunk and come with me. Or I put a bullet in that pretty face of yours."

CHAPTER 37

"Hope?" Bradford frowned as he stepped back inside the mudroom from the garage.

She wasn't anywhere downstairs and a prickle of panic had settled at the base of his spine. Had she... left again? No. His brain rejected it even though that fear tingled at the back of his head. Moving fast, he hurried outside. Her car was here. So was his truck.

But her trunk was open.

Withdrawing his pistol, he scanned the surrounding area as he moved toward the back of her car.

A shattered picture frame was on the ground... It was of them on their wedding night in Vegas. She was wearing heart-shaped neon pink sunglasses that matched her bright pink cocktail dress, and a sparkly white veil. He had his arms around her as she threw her head back laughing at something dirty he'd just whispered to her. Whoever the photographer had been at that chapel, they'd captured the greatest moment of his life. The happiness on both their faces was crystal clear.

And now she was gone. No way it was of her own accord.

Everything funneled out around him as he sheathed his weapon and palmed his key fob. The second he started his car, he called Berlin.

"I think someone took Hope. Track her now," he growled out.

"Shit... Okay... Working on it... Her cell phone tracker is static at her house but the tracker in her watch is in motion."

"Send a mirror to my nav system—" Even before the words were out, a map popped up on his dash showing him a little dot moving toward town.

Heart racing, he gunned it, tearing down the driveway, dust kicking up as he raced for the main road. He knew Berlin had questions, but was grateful she wasn't asking any of them. Because he didn't have any answers other than the woman he loved was missing.

The only thing he could hear anyway was his own blood rushing in his ears as he sped down the road. If someone tried to stop him... Just let them try.

"It looks like she's headed straight downtown...to the courthouse," Berlin murmured. "Her tracker is moving at a fast clip. I'm hacking into nearby security cameras."

He heard her words but couldn't respond, couldn't do anything but drive toward that blinking red dot. To his Hope.

To his entire world.

He couldn't imagine a future without her in it. Wouldn't.

"You still with me?" Berlin asked softly.

"Yeah," he rasped out. "I'm almost there."

"Good, good." He could hear the faint clack of her keyboard in the background, and it centered him. Hope had people looking out for her—the best people. His people. "There's only one vehicle she could be in... Oh shit. It's a sheriff's department vehicle."

Ice slicked down his spine. "Do you have eyes on her?"

"No, but looking at the camera feed right outside the courthouse, she's gotta be in the back of that SUV. I don't have a good shot of the guy. He's wearing a hat and sunglasses. Okay, he's pulling into the parking garage."

"I'm on Main Street."

Berlin sucked in a breath. "Don't panic. The tracker went offline. But she's in a parking garage."

He gunned the engine, ready to drive right over a median, but spotted two sheriff deputies parked across the street.

And while he wanted to tell them to go ahead and try him, if he got stopped it would only slow him down and take longer to get to Hope if he had to disable them.

So he slowed to just above the speed limit. "I'm turning into the parking garage now." He felt hollow as he managed to rasp out the words.

"She's back!" The relief in Berlin's voice was so palpable he felt it over the phone line. "Sweet dancing pandas, she's back," she whispered. "The tracker is moving. She's on an elevator."

Stark relief punctured his chest and he managed to drag in a breath. "Where's she at now? Can you see the cameras inside?"

"Hold on, pulling up the schematics of the building. It's a new one thankfully... Okay. You need to park, ride the elevator from the garage to the first floor, go through security, then you'll take the interior elevators to the third floor. Keep your comms in. I'll guide you. And you won't be able to take a pistol."

"Yeah, I know." He didn't care. He briefly wondered why this guy was taking her to the courthouse but it didn't even matter.

"Or a knife," she whispered.

"Jesus Berlin, I know. And...thank you."

"We got you. We're already headed back."

"Thank you." It wouldn't matter when they got here, that much he knew. They'd left hours ago and Hope didn't have that much time. She only had him.

And he wasn't going to fail her.

"Adalyn's contacted Hazel so she's en route too."

He wasn't sure if that was necessary but he didn't care. Someone had taken Hope for a reason. Though the reason didn't even matter. Just saving her mattered.

"I'm in!" Berlin shouted again right as he parked.

Though he hated to leave his weapons behind, there was no other choice. "I'm making my way to the elevators."

"Yeah…" The rest of her response was garbled as he slammed open the door to the stairs. There were three people waiting at the elevators and he wasn't wasting time.

He barely remembered the sprint, but he made it to the first floor and managed to drag in a breath and try to calm the chaos of his mind as he opened the door into the lobby.

There were three metal detectors and three old men wearing sheriff's uniforms all talking and laughing with each other.

Get it together, he ordered himself. Normally he was good with people, but he was keyed-up and knew that the energy rolling off him was too much. If he didn't get himself under control, they might pick up on his murderous vibe.

"Ask where Judge Collins's floor is. She's traffic court and it's the most common place for people to go. Say you're going there for a speeding ticket. She's in session right now," Berlin said. "And try to relax."

Thankful she was in his ear, he did exactly as she said and somehow managed to keep his expression neutral—or at least not look like a killer ready to go on a rampage—as he asked about the judge's floor.

"What do you see on the cameras?" he demanded once he was on the elevator, heading up to the third floor.

"She's with a man in a sheriff's uniform. She...looks scared, but she's alive. They're heading down one of the corridors. I'm sending you a map to navigate on your phone. Okay...they're stepping into courtroom 3-H. From the schedule it doesn't look like there's anyone in there today. I'm running his face through facial recognition now," she added.

"Send me a feed to the cameras."

"I can't. There's no feed that I can find in the courtrooms. Any of them."

Shit. So he was going in blind. "What do the third-floor corridors look like? Any guards up there?"

"Ah, yeah. Two on the south end and one on the east. There could be more in the courtrooms."

"What's the lone guy doing?" he asked.

"Talking on his phone, staring out at the parking lot. Seems like he's on break."

Okay, he could work with that. "What kind of weapons can you see on him?"

"Standard-looking pistol and Taser. Might have more, but those are visible on his belt."

"Thanks. Drop me his location and be my eyes. Can you kill security in that hallway for a couple minutes?"

She cursed, but said, "Fine."

The man was still at the end of the hallway as Bradford rounded the corner. He slowed himself so he didn't look like a bull racing at the security guy. Then he held his phone to his ear and pretended to talk to someone.

"I'm on the third floor. Yeah...I'm not sure. All the hallways look the same. No, babe, I swear I don't see you." He could see the security guy out of the corner of his eye look over, but then dismiss him as he went back to his own conversation.

Which sounded rife with drama.

Bradford tuned it and everything else out as he made his move. He struck without warning, hitting the guy in the temple enough to stun him. Shocked, the man sprawled into the glass windows with a rattling thud.

Bradford moved in fast, pinning the guy in place as he wrapped his forearm around the guy's neck. He hated hurting someone like this, but the only thing that mattered was getting to Hope. It didn't take long until the man fell limp in his arms.

"Two guards will be on you in three minutes. Drag him into the nearby bathroom," Berlin said.

After gagging him and tying him up, he secured him to the toilet in the handicap stall. Then he locked the door and crawled out underneath.

It wouldn't be a deterrent for long, but it gave him enough time to get away with two weapons.

"She's on the move." Berlin's voice sounded urgent. "I'm not sure where she is...the layout isn't making any sense. Oh shit, I think the guy is taking her to a judge's chamber. They're behind all the courtrooms."

He nodded politely as he passed the two guards, let out a breath when they didn't pay him any attention.

"You're coming up on the courtroom she originally walked into. There's got to be exit doors somewhere near the judge's bench, but I can't see anything."

"I've got this."

He had no other choice. Hope was depending on him.

CHAPTER 38

"Sit." The sheriff's deputy, whose name tag read *L. Manning*, nodded at the chair in front of a judge's desk.

He didn't pull out his pistol—he didn't have to.

Because once they'd stepped into that courtroom, he'd strapped a small vest rigged with explosives over her chest, then given her a purple and yellow LSU sweatshirt to put on over it. And he was holding the trigger in his hand.

She wouldn't have come with him if she'd known about the bomb, she'd have taken her chances. Now it was too late and she had to get out of this.

"Why are you doing this?" she asked, keeping her voice pitched low. She'd tried talking to him before, but he'd put her in the trunk of his cruiser. And then once he'd taken her out in what turned out to be a parking garage, he'd told her to shut her mouth or he'd put a bullet in her and anyone she tried to ask for help.

Not that it had mattered. They'd passed by exactly two people on the way up to this floor. He'd bypassed security, using his badge to take an elevator that must be reserved for law enforcement and judges.

When he didn't respond, she tried again. "Is this about Killeen? Or Sheriff Crow? Some kind of revenge?"

He glanced over at her, and that was when she saw the rage, the hate.

"Are you with the men who broke into my family's house?" she whispered.

"I had nothing to do with that," he finally snapped. "There's been corruption in this town for years and I never understood why so many people kept getting let off. But now I know—the corruption went all the way to the top."

"I *know*. I helped reveal that corruption." She wanted to humanize herself, get on this guy's good side. He had a wild look in his eyes that told her it likely wouldn't matter, but she still had to try. She wasn't going to go down without a fight.

He frowned at her again as if she was stupid. "That's why you're here."

"It is?"

"Your father was part of it. Part of this whole corrupt machine," he snarled.

"Hank was?"

His eyes seemed to glaze over for a moment, his knuckles going white as he clutched onto the back of one of the judge's chairs. "My sister...sweet Georgia."

"Georgia was your sister's name?" she asked softly, trying to get something out of him.

Jaw tight, he nodded. "She was killed by a drunk driver. Sheriff said the Breathalyzer came back negative. And your father," he snarled again, "testified that Quenton had been sober, had just left one of those meetings. But I know they all covered it up. Including the judge. I hadn't been sure before, but after everything that just happened..." He was vibrating with rage now, his dark eyes filled with a manic sort of look she'd seen in zealots before. "You're going to help me expose the rest of the corruption in King's Creek."

"How are we going to do that?" She used her soothing journalist's voice and held his eye contact. She didn't think he could be reasoned with, but she still had to try.

"My…we know what you did to help trap the sheriff, but it's not enough. Not enough to pay for what your father did. For what everyone else did."

Okay, who the hell was this *we*?

"The Feds don't know everything," he continued.

"What is it they don't know?"

"Steve had multiple judges in his pocket."

"The sheriff?" she asked, wanting to clarify, and also just keep him talking. If he was talking, he wasn't letting that switch go.

"Yeah, who else?" he snarled.

She nodded gently, wondering if Bradford had realized that she'd been taken yet. If anyone could find her, it was him and his people. "I just wanted to make sure that's who you meant. He's been arrested. I know that he's giving up the names of everyone involved in their criminal organization."

"You actually believe that?"

She did, but wasn't going to tell him that. Steve Crow was a self-serving coward who'd rolled over on everyone so he could get into WITSEC. He wouldn't break that contract and risk going to prison. He'd die there and knew it. "Why are we in…Judge Yardley's chambers?" She read the plaque on the table.

"The *Honorable* Penny Yardley let my daughter's killer go free. And your father and Steve helped her do it." He hit himself in the head once, as if trying to make himself focus, and she forgot to breathe as she waited for the vest to go off.

When nothing happened, she quietly breathed out. Though she wanted to ask more questions, something told her that the time for that was over.

"You're going to question her, make her admit what she did. How dirty she is," he snarled even as he looked at his watch again. Excitement rolled off him now and she knew the judge must be taking a scheduled break from court if his reaction was any indication. Her time was almost up.

"Okay. Do you have a list of questions I should ask?"

Nodding, he pulled out a folded-up paper from his back pocket. As he stepped forward, she thought she saw the door handle behind him move.

"Are we going to be recording this, like in an interview?"

"Yes, yes. I want all her crimes recorded. Once she's admitted to what she did, then it'll all be over."

Oh, hell. By all over, she had no doubt that he meant he'd blow them all up. "What's this little symbol?" she asked, even though she knew what it was. On the top of his neatly typed list of questions (which weren't real questions at all, but accusations), was the same symbol on the manifesto and bomb instructions that Bradford had found in Wesley Jones's workshop.

"It's not important."

Okay, the door handle had definitely moved. "This is kind of smudged, can you tell me what this says?"

He stepped forward, his boots thudding over the hardwood floors as Bradford slipped in behind him.

Her heart stopped, the world coming down to a pinpoint of this moment in time.

It took everything in her not to react or to look at him.

"Tell me why I should even question her." She changed tactics as she dropped the piece of paper. "Especially since you've strapped a bomb to me." She needed Bradford to know exactly what was going on, what they were up against. "You're just going to kill me when this is all over."

"I'm not. I just want her to tell the truth! She owes me that much. But I swear I'll let you go once she does. I know you're not your father."

He leaned down to pick up the fallen paper and Bradford moved in behind him like a wraith, blade up.

He must have made a sound because Manning turned at the last second, eyes wide. "What—"

Bradford slashed out, slicing across the man's carotid in a savage, killing move.

Blood arced over her and the desk in a warm wash of liquid.

A short scream escaped as she dove forward, reaching for his hand. "Dead man's switch!" she shouted as she wrapped her hands around Manning's own.

Bradford grabbed onto her hands as they all fell to the floor. "I've got you!"

Tears streamed down her face as she waited for the pain, for the explosion...but they'd done it. Oh god, they'd stopped him. She was holding on to the man's trigger finger and Bradford had his own hands wrapped tight around hers.

She let out a sob of relief. They were alive.

"What the hell is going on in here—"

"This man brought a bomb in here," Bradford snarled at the wide-eyed, white-haired woman in dark judge's robes.

Judge Yardley.

"It's on a dead man's switch. Evacuate the building. Now!" he continued.

She still stood there, staring at the three of them.

"Judge." Hope's voice was calmer. "This officer strapped a bomb to my chest. It's underneath this hoodie. He says you let his sister's killer go free, that you covered up the crime."

She stared down at the body. "No, no, no. It was a tragic car accident—"

"That doesn't matter. I'm just letting you know so you understand that this is real. You need to leave and make sure the building is evacuated. Can you do that? We need everyone out of here now."

"Yes, yes…" She hurried from the room, the clicks of her heels fading as she raced away.

"Feds are on their way," Bradford said, still holding on to her.

"Really?" Relief slammed through her.

"Yep. Berlin is in my ear. She's on it. They've got an office an hour away and left in a helicopter not too long ago. They'll be here soon."

Tears pricked at her eyes but she blinked them away. Now was not the time to start crying. Not when a dead man was on the floor between them as they held on for dear life.

"I love you," she blurted. "In case…in case things don't work out here. I just want to tell you that. I knew I loved you when I ran out of that hotel room. It's actually part of why I ran. I don't know how to love or be loved, but I want to learn. I want…you. I want a future with you. I want our marriage to be real, not just something on paper. I want to live in a house or a condo or a van with you. You are my home. I want to wake up to your gorgeous face every morning. I just want you, Bradford."

"You've got me."

"That's it?" He just…*accepted* her?

"You've always had me, Hope. I love you."

And for him, it was as simple as that. Maybe it could be as simple as that for her too. She probably needed therapy to deal with all her childhood trauma, but…yeah, it *was* as simple as that.

"We're going to make this work," she whispered.

"I know." His voice was a lot more confident than hers. "And Berlin says we're getting married again in front of everyone. And that she's going to be one of your bridesmaids."

"Pretty sure I'd give her a kidney if she asked at this point."

"She says she approves. And for the record, I really want to kiss you right now," he whispered.

"This is a weird conversation to be having over a dead body." And with a bomb strapped to her.

"I'm trying to distract you."

"Well it's working... You hear that?" The *whop-whop-whop* of the helicopter.

Relief flooded his expression and he nodded.

They really were going to be okay.

EPILOGUE

Sometimes the right place is a person.

Three months later

"I feel a little ridiculous," Hope admitted as Fleur did the finishing touches on her eye makeup. Over the last couple months since she'd moved to New Orleans, they'd become close. Mostly because Hope had allowed herself to let people in. It was a process, but she liked this new version of herself.

She found that trusting people wasn't the worst thing—and that not everyone was going to let her down. She still hadn't read the letter that her dad had left for her but would someday. Probably. *Seriously, baby steps.*

"What? Why? You look so gorgeous I want to cry. That makeup." Fleur did the chef's kiss with her fingers and grinned.

"It's not that. I mean…Bradford and I got married in Vegas." And she felt like they were making a big deal out of something they'd already done. And fine, she also hated being the center of attention. There was a reason she was a writer. Introverts gonna introvert.

Skye, who was stretched out on one of the chaise longues in an elegant purple and black jacquard suit that somehow looked stunning instead of ridiculous, shook her head. "You're doing this to celebrate with your friends. Take it from someone who fought against having people in my life—you're in this now, sis. This is your family, and we want to celebrate you and Bradford. Accept it and your life will be easier. Because before you know it, you'll be in a book club and having people stop by your place at all hours simply because they love you. There are worse things. Trust me."

"Okay, now I'm gonna cry for real." Hope wiped at the few tears that pricked her eyes.

"Jesus don't cry in front of Skye," Adalyn muttered as she shoved Skye's feet off the end of the chaise and sat next to her. "She gets all panicky."

Skye snorted, but didn't deny it.

"Okay, it's almost time." Violet, a friend of Bradford's and their unofficial wedding planner, gently clapped her hands together. "And you look so beautiful I want to cry."

Hope turned away from the mirror and grinned at the other woman. Her dark blonde hair was up in a fancy twist and she was so elegant in her satin purple suit that she looked like she'd just stepped off a runway. "I bet you say that to all the brides."

"I do, but I mean it this time." She held out her hands and motioned for Hope to stand. "Now spin. I want to see everything."

"It's not like it matters," Thea murmured. "That man doesn't care if she walks down the aisle in nothing—he'd probably prefer it."

Hope giggled as she stood. Her friend wasn't wrong. But she stood and did a twirl anyway because she loved this dress and wanted to show it off. Unlike the wild pink cocktail dress she'd worn at her Vegas wedding, she'd chosen an eggplant-colored A-line tea-length dress with tied shoulder straps that showed off enough cleavage that she knew her man was going to be fighting not to toss her over his shoulder and get out of here.

Her bridal party was way bigger than she ever could have imagined, and they'd all decided to wear suits instead of dresses. Before diving into life in New Orleans with Bradford, she would have only had Thea stand up with her, but her circle had grown. And since all his friends were in his party, she'd asked their significant others who had become her friends too.

"You're perfect." Magnolia, who was breastfeeding on another chaise smiled at her. "Just perfect. He's going to be speechless when he sees you."

Her throat tightened and all she could do was nod. Luckily Thea was right there next to her, wrapping an arm around her. "You've got this, girl. Then we're all going to party like it's 1999."

She snickered. "God, you're such a nerd."

"You love me."

"I do." Heart in her throat, she headed out of the little waiting room with the others, glad that someone was there to scoop up Magnolia's sweet baby as they all exited.

She and Bradford had chosen an outdoor wedding at one of their favorite restaurants. The courtyard was all brick with a gorgeous fountain where they would say their vows in front of all their friends and chosen family, and then afterward there would be dancing, drinks and general merriment inside and outside. Luckily the weather was gorgeous and the exterior Edison-style lighting gave everything a fairy-tale feel.

Not something she'd had a lot of in her life so she was embracing it now.

As she and the others got set up for the walk down the aisle, all she could think of was Bradford. And by the time it was finally her turn, she couldn't even hear the music playing, couldn't see anyone except the man waiting for her by the perfectly lit fountain.

He had on a dark tux with a bow tie that matched her dress, and a hungry look on his gorgeous face as he watched her walk toward him.

It didn't matter that they were already married. Skye had been right—this mattered too because it was in front of the people who loved them.

Their vows were a blur and so was their first dance, though she leaned into him as Ella Fitzgerald crooned "Love is Here to Stay." Finally, after the cake was cut, she swore the world around them seemed to click back into place and she was aware of everyone else once again. Because for a while, it had just been the two of them.

"This cake is so good I'm thinking about cutting off a couple slices and sneaking them out," Berlin said before she shoved another bite in her mouth.

"I got you covered, babe," Chance said with a nod.

Hope leaned into Bradford, enjoying soaking up all of him as he wrapped his arm around her shoulders. "Take as much cake as you want."

"No way," Bradford said. "We're making good use of all that buttercream frosting later."

Chance's eyes widened slightly. "I can't actually tell if you're joking."

Berlin just cackled and slipped her arm through her husband's. "Come on. Let's go get another piece before this perv gets to the cake."

"I can't tell if you're joking either," Hope murmured.

"I was. At first." Bradford leaned down and brushed his lips over hers as they gently swayed to another old-school Frank Sinatra song. This one was "That Old Black Magic."

"I mean, I won't say no to eating buttercream off you." She kept her voice pitched low since they were standing in front of the bride and groom's table as people stopped to talk to them. It was a magical New Orleans night, with street noise still audible from nearby. She loved the life of the city and everything about it.

"I say we get out of here now," he whispered as Tiago and Fleur approached with twin smiles.

"No way, man, I recognize that look. And you've got some more dancing to do." Tiago pulled Bradford then Hope into a bear hug that made her laugh.

Fleur just shook her head, but was smiling. "He's not kidding about the dancing," she murmured as Bradford and Tiago stepped aside to talk in quiet tones.

"I know. I heard them talking about some kind of dance-off before. For the record, Bradford will destroy everyone with his moves," she added.

Her husband looked over midsentence and grinned. "Yeah, that's what I'm talking about."

She winked at him, then turned back to Fleur. "It seems like everything has gone smoothly. Am I needed anywhere? I feel like I should be doing more."

"Girl, you are right where you should be. You're enjoying yourself with your husband. That's it. And I see some of your friends coming this way," she whispered, side-stepping to join Tiago and Bradford.

Hope smiled as Chelsea, Kim and her husband, Andrew, headed over. She threw her arms around Chelsea first, then Kim, and then got a gentle pat on the back from Andrew. "I'm so happy you guys made it. It's really nice to see some faces from back home."

"Are you kidding? We're so excited to be here," Chelsea said.

Kim nodded in agreement. "Especially at the wedding of someone so famous."

She snort-laughed. "I don't think going viral for fifteen minutes counts as famous."

Kim shrugged. "People are still talking about you back home."

"You and Bradford did stop the courthouse and Judge Yardley from blowing up," Chelsea added. "And then that article you wrote a month later." She let out a low whistle. "Famous or not, we're all really proud to know you."

"Your mama would have been really proud," Andrew said, surprising her.

He'd always been quiet, and his kind words made her smile. "Thank you."

"Hey you guys." Bradford swooped in and wrapped his arm around her. "Do you all mind if I steal my wife for a couple minutes?" he asked as he shook Andrew's hand, making the older man grin.

"Nah, go sneak off while you can."

Hope laughed lightly. "We're not sneaking anywhere," she called out as he dragged her toward the dance floor. Then she looked at Bradford. "We're not leaving yet."

"I know. I just thought maybe you needed saving. I heard them talking about the article."

"I'm good, promise. I don't mind talking about it with them." Mia had stuck to her decision and asked Hope to write the article accusing the governor of Mississippi of sexually harassing and then assaulting her. And once that had happened, other women had come forward until it had snowballed into a resignation and very big scandal. "I got a text from Mia this morning. She was sorry to miss the wedding, but had some big mountain trek thing. I'm just glad she's living her life now."

"Me too," he murmured, pulling her into his arms. "And I'm glad that we are living our lives now. Even if we are surrounded by weirdos."

"Pretty sure we fit right in." She glanced around the dance floor to see Cash and Reese, two people relatively new to her circle, wrapped up in each other's arms.

Same with Adalyn and Rowan. They were dancing with each other as if no one else existed.

Skye and her husband Colt were off to the side of the dance floor, both eating a ridiculous amount of appetizers, and they looked positively blissful.

Mari and Colin were having a heated discussion with Bear and Valentine. And if she had to guess, it was about whether the house Bear was renovating was haunted or not since that was a recurring theme with the four of them.

Ezra was sitting on one of the couch settees holding his new baby, with Magnolia resting her head on his shoulder.

Thea was talking to one of Violet's friends, while Violet was running around directing the waitstaff.

"Hey, you guys." Hailey and her husband moved closer to them on the dance floor. "I heard something about a dance-off later. I want in."

Jesse just groaned slightly, but paused as Easton—also new to Hope's circle, and Bradford's too—danced up to them with his new, adorable boyfriend whose name she couldn't remember to save her life. She'd find out later though.

"If Hailey's in, I'm definitely in. At least I know there's one person I can beat," Easton said with a sniff.

"Hey!"

As the four of them started talking about who was the better dancer (really, it was just Easton and Hailey arguing while the other two watched), Bradford slowly, subtly moved her off the dance floor.

"I've got a surprise for you."

"If the surprise is you taking off your pants—"

Laughing, he crushed his mouth to hers before he dragged her inside the restaurant and passed more laughing and dancing people. This really was a wild party, she realized. There were certainly more people than she'd expected.

The last few months had been a lot, especially with what happened at the courthouse. And that was after the video of those guys breaking into her house had already gone viral. Her name had already been trending, and from there things went absolutely banana crackers.

Edward Killeen had been killed while awaiting trial. She had no idea who'd been behind it, but there didn't seem to be a threat against her or Bradford so it wasn't keeping her up at night. As far as she knew, the former sheriff and Patrick and Tara Killeen were still in WITSEC. They'd testified against more than just Edward Killeen, and a lot of men were in prison for trafficking drugs, people, and murder. So. Much. Murder. Even Alden Phillips had testified against Edward Killeen as long as the Feds relocated him and his grandmother.

The terrorist group that had been run by Wesley Jones had been mostly disbanded—as far as she knew. Jones had used Leo Manning's rage at his sister's death to fuel his own agenda by fanning the already hot flames of Manning's anger at the town's corruption. Jones had wanted the courthouse to blow up—with Manning in it. He'd never thought the other man would get out alive, and he'd wanted Manning's death to add kindling to his growing cause of nuts who wanted to tear down the government.

But Jones was now in custody and the Feds had neutralized his group for the most part—mainly because Jones's wife Amberlyn had turned on him when she thought she'd be separated from her kids. That was all it had taken.

And right now, Hope didn't care about any of that.

She was so excited to be with her husband and friends on their second wedding day as he dragged her into... "Why are we in a walk-in fridge?"

"Because..." He held out a chilled glass to her before he popped a very expensive bottle of champagne, poured for both of them. Then he opened a little box to reveal...

"Sheer pira?" The words literally meant sweet milk in Dari, and it was a sweet fudge flavored with pistachios, cardamom and rose water. It had been a favorite of hers when they'd first met.

"I remember how much you loved these milk fudge things," he murmured, handing her a square of the delicate treat. "And I also fell in love with you the first time you bit into one of these and moaned as if you were having an orgasm."

She gasped at his description. "You can't be serious."

"Oh, I am. And I found a place off Conti Street that makes them." He held up his own square treat along with his champagne. "To my wife, my life, my hope for a future. I love you, Hope."

She swallowed hard and held up her own glass. "To the only man I've ever loved. To my husband and our future."

The slow, wicked smile he gave her had her toes curling in her heels. Feeling buzzed on him more than the champagne, she leaned in to kiss him after they'd finished their treats and found herself pinned up against one of the food racks, and thought...maybe they could sneak away early after all.

ACKNOWLEDGMENTS

It's that time again! I'm so grateful to my mom for all her help over the last year, which has enabled me to focus on writing. For Kaylea Cross, critique partner extraordinaire, thank you for all the things. I'm so grateful for our friendship. For Jaycee, thank you for another fabulous cover! I love all of them. To Julia, I'm so grateful to work with you as an editor. Tammy, thank you for proofreading, and Sarah, thank you for everything you do behind the scenes. To Piper and Jack, my silly writer pups, thank you for keeping me company day in and day out. Last but definitely not least, for my readers, thank you for reading this series! It's because of you that it's still going.

Dear Readers

Thank you for reading the latest Redemption Harbor Security series book! If you'd like to stay in touch and be the first to learn about new releases you can find me on social media and:

Check out my website for book news:
   https://www.katiereus.com

Also, please consider leaving a review at one of your favorite online retailers. It's a great way to help other readers discover new books and I appreciate all reviews.

Happy reading,
Katie

ABOUT THE AUTHOR

Katie Reus is the *USA Today* bestselling author of the Ancients Rising series, the Endgame trilogy and the Redemption Harbor Series. She fell in love with reading at a young age thanks to weekly trips to the library. However, she didn't always know she wanted to be a writer. After changing majors too many times, she finally graduated with a degree in psychology. Not long after that she discovered a new love—writing.

She now spends her days writing paranormal romance and romantic suspense. In addition to writing, she's also obsessed with her dogs, hiking, quilting, and all things aviation.

COMPLETE BOOKLIST

Ancients Rising

Ancient Protector

Ancient Enemy

Ancient Enforcer

Ancient Vendetta

Ancient Retribution

Ancient Vengeance

Ancient Sentinel

Ancient Warrior

Ancient Guardian

Ancient Warlord

Darkness Series

Darkness Awakened

Taste of Darkness

Beyond the Darkness

Hunted by Darkness

Into the Darkness

Saved by Darkness

Guardian of Darkness

Sentinel of Darkness

A Very Dragon Christmas

Darkness Rising

Deadly Ops Series

Targeted

Bound to Danger

Chasing Danger

Shattered Duty

Edge of Danger

A Covert Affair

Endgame Trilogy

Bishop's Knight

Bishop's Queen

Bishop's Endgame

"Falling For" novellas

Falling for Nola

Falling for Valentine

Falling for Violet

Holiday With a Hitman Series

How the Hitman Stole Christmas

A Very Merry Hitman

All I Want for Christmas is a Hitman

MacArthur Family Series

Falling for Irish

Unintended Target

Saving Sienna

Moon Shifter Series

Alpha Instinct

Lover's Instinct

Primal Possession

Mating Instinct

His Untamed Desire

Avenger's Heat

Hunter Reborn

Protective Instinct

Dark Protector

A Mate for Christmas

O'Connor Family Series

Merry Christmas, Baby

Tease Me, Baby

It's Me Again, Baby

Mistletoe Me, Baby

Red Stone Security Series®

No One to Trust

Danger Next Door

Fatal Deception

Miami, Mistletoe & Murder

His to Protect

Breaking Her Rules

Protecting His Witness

Sinful Seduction

Under His Protection

Deadly Fallout

Sworn to Protect

Secret Obsession

Love Thy Enemy

Dangerous Protector

Lethal Game

Secret Enemy

Saving Danger

Guarding Her

Deadly Protector

Danger Rising

Protecting Rebel

Redemption Harbor® Series

Resurrection

Savage Rising

Dangerous Witness

Innocent Target

Hunting Danger

Covert Games

Chasing Vengeance

Redemption Harbor® Security

Fighting for Hailey

Fighting for Reese

Fighting for Adalyn
Fighting for Magnolia
Fighting for Berlin
Fighting for Mari
Fighting for Hope

Sin City Series (the Serafina)
First Surrender
Sensual Surrender
Sweetest Surrender
Dangerous Surrender
Deadly Surrender

Verona Bay Series
Dark Memento
Deadly Past
Silent Protector

Linked books
Retribution
Tempting Danger

Non-series Romantic Suspense
Running From the Past
Dangerous Secrets
Killer Secrets
Deadly Obsession
Danger in Paradise
His Secret Past

The Trouble with Rylee
Tempted by Her Neighbor

Paranormal Romance
Destined Mate
Protector's Mate
A Jaguar's Kiss
Tempting the Jaguar
Enemy Mine
Heart of the Jaguar